SCORPION
TRACKER BOOK 3

DEVEN KANE

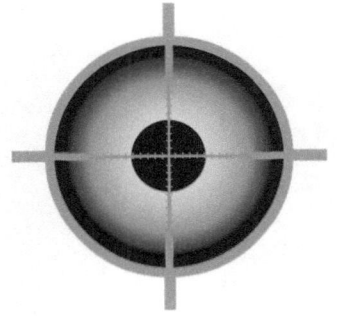

SCORPION

TRACKER BOOK 3

RAGe Real Author Guaranteed edition. 100% human.

Author photo by Wendy McAlpine

ISBN-13: 978-1-989509-01-2

BISAC: Sci-fi & Fantasy | Dystopian

Books by Deven Kane

Tracker Trilogy

    Tracker

    Dissident

    Scorpion

Darkwood: Some Thing Lurks Below

Treehawke Saga

    Treehawke

    Grave Dagger

nemesis [**nem**-*uh*-sis]

noun

1. A long-standing rival; an archenemy.
2. An opponent that is very difficult to defeat.

ONE ◉

A GUST OF COOL WIND rustled the leaves under Amos Morgan's feet, a subtle reminder of the impending change of season. Towering evergreens, like sentinels on patrol kept watch over the rocky hillside. Silence cloaked the idyllic scene, broken at sporadic intervals by an occasional birdcall.

Amos stood over his brother's unmarked grave, hands shoved into his pockets. He was peripherally aware of the wind, the creaking of needle-laden pines, and the infrequent cry of birds. Sunlight filtered through the branches overhead, spilling in uneven patterns across his shoulders. He took a deep breath of cool autumn air—inhale, exhale, inhale, exhale—a steady rhythm that should have had a calming effect.

Peace proved elusive. Tension radiated in its place, revealing itself in his clenched fists, the tingling alarm knotted between his shoulder blades, and an accompanying headache.

I hate this place. The hollow sensation in his gut threatened to overwhelm him. *It's like a dark magnet, dragging me to return.*

Amos glanced over his shoulder, up the steep incline, to the cave. His personal bunker in the wilderness. Moss-covered stones framed the low entrance, overshadowed by tough pine trees above, growing tall and driving roots into cracks and crevices.

Dried leaves and pine needles from countless seasons carpeted the ground. Dozens of similar outcroppings littered the forested hillside, each a minor variation on the others.

His cave was unique.

Amos squared his shoulders, turned his back on the grave, and faced the shadowy cave entrance. The last place he'd seen his brother alive. He steeled himself against resurgent guilt.

Fourteen years ago, he'd left Trey here—seriously wounded after a Hoarder shot him—in order to seek help. And because Amos, twelve years old at the time, was afraid the Hoarders might discover their hiding place.

During his absence, Hoarders found the cave and ended Trey's life. Amos returned, with the promised help, to find his brother's lifeless body a few yards outside the cave.

Amos the coward goes on living, and we buried what was left of Trey in an unmarked grave.

The blame wasn't his. Amos understood that, intellectually. The real killers, who pursued the teenaged brothers, shooting at them for sport—as if they were wild animals—were the so-called "Citizens of the Enclave." Hoarders...

Amos lurched into motion, forcing himself to climb the steep hillside. He hadn't come back to grieve his brother's death, or reminisce about hiding his Implant in the underground burrow. He crouched, peering inside the cave.

It always comes back to the Hoarders.

Hoarders murdered Trey. Hoarders deployed Trackers to hunt down and kill anyone unlucky enough to have an Implant. Like Amos and Aubrey.

He squeezed his eyes shut, as if the simple action was sufficient to hold his memories at bay. He'd like nothing more than to forget they'd met that trio of Hoarders yesterday.

Hoarders that Mateo insisted they partner with against the alien Givers. Hoarders who freely, proudly, admitted to inventing the cursed Implants.

And their leader, Darcy, taunting Aubrey, insinuating he was responsible for her Implant.

And mine, too? He couldn't fathom how Mateo—let alone Colonel Scott—could expect them to work with *any* Hoarder. Especially Darcy Peterson.

Amos crawled into the cave, rolling over on his back to stare at the stone overhead.

Returning here is—let's face it—pretty dysfunctional. His lips curved into a wry smile. Doc Simon would probably send him to a therapist, if their Hub network had access to one. *This cave is where it all started for me. I need space to think.*

He was stalling, and he knew it. Yes, meeting the Hoarders had triggered memories of Trey's murder and his own Implant. Just recalling the hellish meeting wiped the smile from Amos's face.

He was tempted to ignore it, refuse to confront the trauma, but he'd sought refuge in the cave for that very reason.

Yes, to sort things out. But even more, to solve a life-and-death riddle—an ambush by an entire squadron of Trackers.

Someone had betrayed their location. But who?

TWO ◎

MUSTER CHATEAU WAS damp and cold. Aubrey Carter wrapped a threadbare blanket around her shoulders. She sat on the concrete floor, cross-legged, leaning against a cinderblock wall.

She massaged her scarred hand, shivering from a chill she couldn't seem to shake. Her hand ached. Megan's physical enhancements didn't function as originally designed, but she retained a punishing remnant of her Tracker grip.

I'm lucky she didn't break my hand.

"Here, eat this. You need to keep your strength up." Don's gruff voice interrupted her musing. He dropped a handful of dried trail rations into her outstretched palm. Salted meat and some kind of leathery fruit. "It's Sheila's gourmet best. I'll send her chef's compliments on your behalf."

Aubrey smiled and gratefully accepted the rations. *His jokes aren't as funny as he thinks they are, but I love that he tries to keep our morale up.*

"Go easy, though." Jane ran a hand through her dark hair in a futile attempt to loosen the tangled knots. "Those rations won't last much longer. When we stocked the Chateau, we never expected to stay more than one night."

Megan sat to Aubrey's right, chewing mechanically on a chunk of fruit. Her facial expression was hard to decipher, partially obscured by an eyepatch over her ruined eye socket. She continued to be an enigma. A former Tracker, who once pursued Aubrey with murderous intent and, in a twist of fate no one could have predicted, was now part of Eastside Hub.

That Hoarder kid—the blond one—recognized her. Aubrey recalled his look of shock and disbelief. *Good news or bad? Whose side is Megan on?*

Jane's acerbic voice cut her paranoid musings short. "Let me look at your arm, Don. You're soaking through the bandages again. We need to get the bleeding under control."

For once, Don didn't argue. He upended his metal rod, his most recently-acquired weapon of choice. The rod was six feet in length, well over Aubrey's height, and raised a faint echo as he set it down. He seated himself next to Aubrey, his massive bulk dwarfing her.

They'd lingered in the Chateau for a night and a day already. Wisdom dictated they bide their time before returning to Eastside. No one balked when Don insisted on caution. They had no way of knowing if their Hub had been compromised. Not after the Tracker ambush.

"We make for the Eastside tonight," Don said as Jane loosened his blood-stained bandages. Doc Simon needed to treat the gash on his forearm, soon. "I don't think anyone followed us—or any *thing*—but we're not taking any chances. Let's hope Eastside's still secure."

"Deja vu all over again," Jane replied wryly as she bandaged his arm. "Trackers ambushed the Mission last spring, t00. They didn't find the subbasement, but they were closer than they knew. Too close."

"True enough," Don replied, exaggerating his drawl. "But I don't want to lose another night's sleep in this stink-hole."

"Thanks a lot, Don." Aubrey laughed, wrinkling her nose. "I forgot about the smell until you reminded me." Her humor faded. "Garr warned Uncle John to shut Eastside down for a few days." She hoped the Mission's manager had responded in time. "If Trackers are scouting the area, there shouldn't be anything to give Eastside away."

Don winced as Jane tightened the fresh bandage with a deft tug. "Plan for the worst and assume nothing. Megan, can you can tell if other Trackers are nearby?"

Megan shook her head, still chewing. She swallowed with difficulty before replying.

"No more voices," she said in her halting way, tapping two fingers against the side of her head. "No more Givers." She ducked her head and resumed eating.

Conversation over.

Aubrey studied her covertly, unsure of her own feelings. A few months ago, Megan had been just another nameless Tracker, obsessed with killing a young boy for his Implant. At their first encounter, Aubrey was sure she was about to die, along with the boy. She jammed an electric prod into Megan's scanning eye in a final, desperate act of self-defense.

The energy surge flattened Megan like a bolt of lightning, and Garr insisted they bring the crippled Tracker back to Eastside. Doc's diagnosis was dire at the time: she predicted Megan's wounds would prove fatal within a matter of days.

But she survived and, through her, they learned of the real power behind the Hoarders—alien beings who called themselves

"Givers." In an unanticipated reversal, the damage caused by the prod triggered Megan's halting and incomplete journey toward recovering her humanity.

Once a mindless killing machine, now an ally. Sort of. Aubrey massaged her scarred forearm, concealed under her blanket. *I don't regret what I did. Because self-defense ... and protecting the boy.*

"That'll have to do for now." Jane twisted an improvised sling over Don's shoulder to support his injured arm. "You need Doc Simon's tender care. We're good to go, whenever you want to give the word."

"The word, my friend, is given," he replied with a facetious grin. "You know, I've always wanted to say that. Why should Garr have all the fun?"

Jane scoffed and handed him the metal rod. "Garr *never* said anything like that, even when he was still the colonel." She paused, her eyes haunted. "I lost sight of everyone after the attack. Do you think they managed to get away? We can't be the only survivors."

"We're not." Don exuded carefree confidence. "Amos will go to ground and lay low. Once we confirm Eastside's secure, I know exactly where to find him."

"What about Garr?" Aubrey got to her feet, pulling the blanket tighter. "Everything happened so fast, I couldn't see what happened to him."

Don chuckled, his baritone voice reassuringly warm in the chilly room. "He had Sheila by his side, and she's a force to be reckoned with. They'll have each other's back." He paused, suddenly pensive. "I hate to admit it, but Mateo deserves a bit of credit. He's a slippery fish, but he used his Tracker-ness *against* the other red-eyes, not for them."

"Trackers—for us?" Megan's tortured voice caught Aubrey by surprise. "Or for them?" The eye patch and surrounding scar tissue made her expression difficult to read, but Megan's surviving eye held a pleading look. Aubrey couldn't tell if she was asking a question or trying to warn them.

Don broke the silence, flexing his hand around the metal rod. "Were we the targets, or the Hoarders? Excellent question, Megan."

"And who gave our position away?" Jane got to her feet, dusting her hands on her pants. "That's what I want to know."

THREE ◉

CONNOR USUALLY FOUND the bright lights of Cascadia comforting, but they offered no solace tonight. He heard a musical kaleidoscope in the distance, radiating from an assortment of venues and concert halls, beckoning to potential patrons and ticket-holders with the promise of an evening's entertainment and distraction.

Connor enjoyed a commanding view from the twentieth-floor balcony of the villa he shared with Darcy Peterson, his foster father. Here, in the Enclave's historic Oceanview, he normally found a sense of security and peace, a welcome respite from their secret war against the alien Givers.

Peace was decidedly absent tonight. The events of the past few days all but guaranteed it. Connor's hands shook as memories paraded through his mind, a laundry list of disaster. The implausible meeting arranged by Mateo and his band of so-called "Runners." Darcy's near-execution by a deranged savage—the girl with the disfigured arm. The sneak attack by a squadron of Trackers.

All eclipsed by a bombshell revelation...

Connor's gaze fastened on the locket and chain he held. He turned his back on the brightly-lit commercial district and leaned against the balcony rail, opening the locket for the umpteenth time to stare in disbelief at the image inside.

His sister, Megan Sinclair.

Five years ago, the Cascadia Enclave Peace Wardens had informed Connor, after a painstaking investigation, that his parents and sister had been murdered by savages while on a family hunting trip. Cascadia's Infomedia outlets responded to the shocking news by stoking a prolonged and incendiary debate via nonstop public commentary.

The tragedy became the rallying point for a draconian overhaul of border security. Citizens of the Enclave, shocked and justifiably outraged by the savages' barbarism, voted unanimously to adopt the Council's proposed crackdown.

The Sinclair family legacy. Until yesterday.

Despite her disfiguring scars, and the patch covering one eye, Connor recognized her. The image inside his locket confirmed it. His sister was alive...and held hostage by Mateo and his pack of savages.

"Connor? Did you hear what I said?"

Darcy's voice was sharper than usual. Connor, startled by his stealthy approach, clutched the locket in his fist, panicked by the prospect of dropping it off the balcony. He pivoted to face his foster father, his expression harder than he realized.

Darcy's mouth was open, about to issue orders. He caught sight of the silver chain dangling between Connor's fingers, and his lips tightened against his teeth. He stood motionless for several moments before speaking again.

"I've called for Tony," he said in a neutral tone of voice,

but his eyes blazed, hot and feverish. "We have a great deal of work ahead of us, and very little time in which to do it. I need you to—"

"Megan's alive," Connor interrupted, his voice low and grating. "The savages are holding her hostage."

Darcy closed his mouth. His expression was opaque, unreadable. "Yes," he said at last. "It appears so."

"That's it?" Connor's fist tightened on the locket.

Darcy placed a hand on his shoulder. Connor stiffened, unsure how to respond. Physical contact with Darcy was usually shrouded with an aura of menace. "I'm as shocked as you are, Connor. The Peace Warden's report said there were no survivors. There was so little left of the bodies—you know how the savages are. No one could have known she was still alive."

"They *tortured* her, Darcy," Connor said harshly. "You saw what they did to her. She didn't even recognize me …" His voice broke and his eyes burned with unshed tears.

"They'll be punished, Connor, I swear to you." Darcy's grip turned into a claw, matching the ice in his eyes. "I can't imagine how traumatic it must have been for Megan, forced to watch the savages butcher your parents. It might have been more merciful if they'd killed her, as well. Holding her hostage all these years, abusing her to the point where she does their bidding …" He paused for a heartbeat. "Or Mateo's."

Connor stared, stunned.

Darcy dropped his grip. "The savages we met last night, every last one of them, will be converted into drones—weapons against the aliens. Or we'll program them to target the collaborators on the Council." His eyes blazed with the fervor of his cause. And revenge. "If any of the savages survive, it won't be for long. Once Cascadia is under human-only control again, we won't need them. One way or another, the savages will atone for their brutality."

"It's all they're good for, anyway." Connor wiped his eyes with an impatient hand, a cold hatred settling into his chest. "They're animals, nothing more." He paused, eyeing his foster father. "And Mateo—what happens to him?"

Darcy smiled, an expression Connor found more chilling than his fits of rage. "Mateo Reyes is *mine*. Once we've dealt with the Givers, I'll teach that Judas Tracker some respect. It'll be the last lesson he learns."

The doorbell chimed. Connor followed Darcy into their gathering room. The door opened to admit Tony, their chauffeur and most recent recruit. He halted just inside the door, fiddling with his cap as if unsure of his welcome.

"I waited in the parkade." Tony spread his hands in a helpless, aimless gesture. "Cargo's loaded, thirty minutes ago—"

"No matter," Darcy said, cutting him off with a preemptive gesture. Tony was a decent chauffeur, but not the quickest thinker. Connor found him increasingly abrasive. "We were having a father-son conversation, but now that you're ready, we should be on our way."

Their trek down the hallway was executed in absolute silence, as was the elevator descent to the parking garage. The Cascadia Security Monitoring Division, always vigilant against a possible incursion by savages, had been recently granted expanded powers by the ruling Council.

Connor had trouble curtailing his cynicism over the collaborators' blatant power grab.

Under the pretext of "internal security," the Givers and their human stooges had fast-tracked an increase of surveillance inside the Enclave. Darcy and his followers were too savvy to let casual words slip in an elevator—an obvious surveillance trap. Once inside their vehicle, engine running and windows closed, they dared to speak freely. Even so, they kept their voices low. Darcy leaned an elbow on the doorframe, cupping his chin on his hand to shield his face from exterior cameras.

"Clinic is prepped and ready," Tony mumbled into his collar, his words difficult to decipher. "Medical team standing by."

Connor edged forward in his traditional spot, the rear seat, directly behind his foster father. He would never presume to sit up front. "I'm trying to wrap my head around that Tracker ambush last night. How did they know where to find us?"

"Mateo Reyes," Darcy replied instantly, no hint of doubt in his voice. "It's impossible to pinpoint where his loyalties lie —always has been. I've long suspected he was playing one side against the other. It was only *after* the ambush that I deciphered the game he's playing." He paused, clearly enjoying the drama, holding his listeners in spellbound thrall.

Tony spoke first, his husky voice betraying the struggle between wariness and reckless curiosity. "Game? What kind of game are you talking about?"

Darcy rewarded him with an icy silence. Connor knew, without asking, that the chauffeur's over-eager query stole some of Darcy's thunder. Darcy tolerated nothing that cheated him from a moment of triumphant revelation.

They cleared the exit ramp and entered the express lanes on the traffic level before he spoke again.

"Mateo serves the Givers," he said with a knowing smile. "His plan was to lure us all, savages *and* Citizens, to the same location. A Tracker squadron could then easily slaughter us in a single, surgical strike. *Outside* the Enclave. The average Citizen would never hear a word about it."

Connor felt his blood boil at Mateo's treachery, but he kept his mouth shut. Speaking out of turn was Tony's domain.

Darcy leaned back in his leather chair. "Mateo's playing the Judas card on both sides of the fence. He's the ultimate collaborator, even lower than his kin on the Council." He turned to catch Connor's eye. "That's why, when the time comes, I'll deal with him. I want to see the look on his smug Tracker face when he realizes he didn't fool me. And then he'll die."

"And them?" Tony jerked a thumb over his shoulder, his attention riveted on the road. "What if they survive, or figure out what you've done to them?"

Now you've done it. Connor smirked. *Never, ever second-guess Darcy's strategy.*

"They won't, on either count," Darcy replied, his voice as frosty as the glare he threw at his chauffeur. The ensuing silence was more threatening than anything else he might have added. Tony caught on, and focused on driving.

Connor glanced into the cargo area behind him, reaching over the back of the seat to peel back a corner of the tarp. A pair of bodies lay side by side, breathing shallowly, tranquilized. Two of the so-called Runners, en route to Darcy's off-the-books clinic, and Implant surgery.

Connor studied their faces. The savages' leader, the one introduced by Mateo as Garr. And a woman, late-twenties, tall, athletic, long dark hair. He couldn't recall her name.

It didn't matter. Before night's end, they'd simply be drones DR-57 and DR-58.

For the good of the Enclave.

FOUR ◉

THE TEMPERATURE DROPPED after sunset, and the coolness in the cave gave way to a numbing cold. Amos burrowed deeper into his jacket. The last time he'd sought the cave as a refuge—to hide his Implant—he'd been equally ill-prepared.

But the weather was warmer back then. He shifted position, seeking some semblance of comfort on the uneven stone.

You're here to relive what 'failure' tastes like. His inner voice jumped at the opportunity. *This cave's a monument to everyone who died because of you and your Implant. Would Stephen still be alive if he hadn't come looking for you? How about O'Reilly and Quinn at Blackcreek—how many people have you buried?*

Amos gritted his teeth, refusing to be baited into another pointless inner dialogue. *I need a clear head. Wallowing in the past won't help.*

He rolled onto his side, pillowing his head on his arm.

The forest outside was silent, backlit by the full moon's silvery light. Towering pines stood as dark sentinels, their coarse bark thrown into ghostly relief, like veins running up and down their trunks. Here and there, stars peeked between the trees. The breeze had subsided, with only an occasional gust to stir the branches. Everything was peaceful and calm, but he couldn't sleep.

The cold was only part of the reason. His dreams—or the threat of them—fought against his need for sleep, as if waging war against his exhausted body. The Story lurked just beneath the surface of his waking mind, eager for another chance to lash him with painful memories.

His ears picked up on every sound—a creaking branch, the soft hoot of an owl somewhere nearby, the sighing breeze as it rose and fell in its own subtle way. The stream he'd crossed earlier was too distant to hear, but he could imagine the comforting symphony of rushing water without difficulty.

Would he be able to hear the sounds of pursuit? Trackers were as notorious for their stealth as for their persistence.

His fingers traced the scar where his Implant used to be. *Without my Implant, there's nothing for a Tracker to scan. I'm untraceable.*

He didn't need to hear Gabriel, his nagging inner voice, to admit that the cave—while preferable to sleeping out in the open—was an ill-advised refuge, with only one way in or out.

Amos took a deep breath, pulling his jacket tighter. He was exhausted, but he flinched from the thought of sleep and what his dreams might bring. He stared past the pines, seeing and yet not seeing stars in the cloudless sky.

In the end, exhaustion won out, and he fell into a fitful sleep. His dreams, as always, were quick to pounce.

But not the Story. Not this time.

* * *

A SOLITARY FIGURE MOVED between the trees with unswerving

confidence. The brightness of the full moon was irrelevant. A non-factor. It's visual enhancements provided more than enough clarity for it to navigate the uneven terrain. The Givers were as wise as they were generous.

The Tracker stood by the banks of a stream, the dark and tumultuous water presenting a natural barrier to its journey. The frigid liquid was not a serious impediment. Its physical enhancements were designed to deal with much worse.

No, the only concern was the possibility of losing the scent of its prey. To cross the rushing stream at the wrong location would be an unforgivable miscalculation. The Givers were generous but they were not to be denied.

The Tracker balanced atop a large boulder at water's edge, straining to listen above the rapids. It scanned back and forth, up and down, side to side to side. Negligence would go neither unnoticed, nor unpunished.

The turbulent water failed to reflect its features, the only exception a muted red glow encircling its left eye. The burning sensation under its skin was disturbing, but its mental processor rejected the human reaction of alarm. Nothing could interfere with the Quest. Nothing could be *permitted* to interfere.

Fear was encapsulated, buried deep within. Fear was not a factor. A sensation it would have once named *confidence* buoyed it, the certainty of its Quest shoving all other emotions aside. This unit would succeed.

The Tracker caught the scent again. It scrambled over a series of boulders and crossed the stream. Within moments, it stood on the opposite bank, the liquid barrier now behind it, purged from active memory.

The scent was stronger. The Harvest was at hand.

The Givers would be pleased.

FIVE ◉

THE SCENE WAS ETCHED into Amos's memory—seared, like a branding iron. His dreams summoned the emotions and chaos in stark, vivid detail. He felt powerless, as if he'd been seized in a tornado's ruthless grip, whirling helplessly in its vortex.

The tornado deposited him in the deserted mechanical shop, one night earlier. Twin lanterns held the darkness inside the austere shop at bay, benign spotlights illuminating the improbable meeting between Hoarders and Runners.

The vortex spun him past the gathering, orchestrated by the enigmatic Mateo, in his attempt to forge an alliance between the mutually-suspicious groups.

The images swirled, at one moment racing past in a dizzying blur, and then slowing to a crawl, as if to focus in excruciating detail on some particular element. There was no need for his imagination to fabricate additional nuances. The unadorned memory was terrifying all on its own.

Amos recalled the sinking feeling in his gut when he first laid eyes on the waiting Hoarders. None of them were armed, but the menace emanating from the trio was so thick he could almost smell it. Especially the one in the middle—Darcy, leader of the Hoarders.

Amos's viewpoint shifted, allowing him to observe the ragtag group of Runners flanking him. He read the loathing and revulsion on Aubrey's face as she confronted her worst nightmare—the Hoarder who created the Implants.

His dream perspective rotated, and he faced the Hoarders again, standing shoulder to shoulder with his fellow Runners. Fury erupted inside him as Darcy mocked and taunted them.

In slow motion, he saw Aubrey lunge forward. She raised the gun she'd smuggled into the meeting, intent on shooting Darcy. The Glock, dancing lantern light reflected on its metallic gray surface, became the focal point of his dream.

He watched, fascinated, as Aubrey's finger tightened on the trigger. The final sequence to wreak vengeance on the smirking Hoarder.

Do it. His unvoiced plea reverberated in his brain, echoing Jane's verbal challenge. In vivid detail, he watched the muscles in Aubrey's hand shift as she prepared to fire.

The mental vortex spun him around, and he faced his fellow Runners again. The door behind them burst open. Megan rushed into the mechanical shop and disarmed Aubrey. Followed by Mateo's amplified words, echoing in his memory. He wanted to clamp his hands over his ears to muffle the sound.

"This alliance must survive."

Then Amos was back in his own body, observing the shock on the Hoarders' faces as they *recognized Megan.* Darcy retreated a few steps, but the young kid moved forward, reaching out a shaky hand to her.

Megan gazed blankly at the young Hoarder. He called her

by name. She cocked her head to one side, in an odd imitation of Mateo, studying him with clinical detachment.

The first explosion caught everyone off-guard. The Hoarders froze, eyes riveted on the door behind Amos. He whirled, the action taking far too long in his tortured memory.

The door hung askew, and the masonry around the doorframe crumbled as he watched. The brickwork gave way, and the twisted door toppled into the mechanical shop, scorched and blackened.

Just outside, a Tracker advanced with unmistakable menace. The smell of charred flesh stung Amos's nostrils, wafting inside the shop from what was left of the first Tracker … self-detonated in the doorway.

Part of his mind wondered about that as he flung himself away from the smoking doorway. *Trackers aren't suicide bombers. The Givers decide if and when.*

The obvious answer followed as he rolled across the concrete floor. *Unless the Givers have a new strategy.*

* * *

A CLICK SOUNDED in the Tracker's mental processor, signaling a download of new data. It paused for two point five seconds as it absorbed the input.

Analyze. Adapt. Enact.

The Tracker's speed increased despite the steep incline. Completion of the Quest was at hand. Failure was not an option.

This unit would succeed.

SIX ◉

GLASS SHATTERED in the opposite corner of the mechanical shop. Amos twisted around, still on the floor, to spot another Tracker pulling itself through a window in the back wall. It managed to squeeze halfway through when it froze, a look of shock and terror distorting its face.

The Tracker exploded, showering the interior of the shop with a gruesome spread of concrete, entrails, and blood.

A number of Trackers converged on the ruined doorway. Amos was dimly aware of Mateo leaping into the fray, driving the fanatical killers back into the street.

The Hoarders retreated to the far corner of the shop. Darcy shielded himself behind the blond kid. Amos felt a burst of contempt.

Poor little Hoarders. Cowering in the corner won't save you.

"Over here!" Don's shout drew their attention to the rear of the shop, where the side window had been reduced to a gaping hole. The smoky haze cleared in time to see him intercept a third Tracker as it scrabbled over the debris.

Don seized a metal rod from the floor and, using it as a battering ram, drove it into the Tracker's midsection. The impact was oddly quiet, but the force of Don's blow catapulted the Tracker into an alley outside the shop.

The big man followed it through the ragged hole, aiming more blows at the creature, now out of sight. Amos understood his urgency. The Givers' link to communicate with Trackers—and detonate them—required quick action to short-circuit.

Mateo forced his way into the street, leaving the broken bodies of several Trackers in his wake. Megan caught Aubrey's hand—the same hand holding a Glock on Darcy moments before—and bolted through the charred doorway, trailing Mateo.

Amos's ears rang from the deafening roar of explosions in the confined space. He felt someone's presence beside him, and Jane shoved him toward the crude opening left by the second Tracker. Amos held his breath against the clinging smoke as they stumbled over the debris and made a hasty exit.

Amos glanced over his shoulder as he cleared the building. He saw Garr herding the Hoarders to safety, a dazed-looking Sheila stumbling over to aid him.

Garr's a better man than me. I'd have left them for the Trackers. Amos felt a pang of guilt. *The colonel's doing the right thing. We need this alliance.*

He heard the clamor of combat behind him and pivoted. Don lashed out with his improvised weapon at another Tracker. Blood streaked his left arm, soaking his torn shirtsleeve. Jane closed in, unarmed and vulnerable, attempting to distract the Tracker by offering herself as a second target.

Amos grabbed the only weapon he could find—a chunk of concrete dislodged by one of the explosions—and rushed forward, heaving it at the Tracker's head. The creature's reflexes were better than he'd assumed. It ducked to one side and the projectile shot harmlessly past.

The brief distraction was all Don needed. He gripped the rod with both hands and swung at the Tracker's head, catching it off-balance. The Tracker hit the ground with a heavy thud, and Don wasted no time in deactivating it.

"There's more." Jane's voice sounded muffled. Amos followed her pointing finger. Circles of red light betrayed the figures stalking toward them out of the dust and smoke.

Don stood over the deactivated Tracker. He was a wild sight —bloodied, sweaty, chest heaving from exertion. He twisted, looking over his shoulder at Amos and Jane. And beyond, to the approaching Trackers.

How many did the Givers send?

"Split up. Get out of here," Don said hoarsely, every bit as commanding as Colonel Scott. "You know the routine."

Another explosion sounded around the corner. *Are they trying to bring down the building?* Amos spun away from the approaching Trackers, scrambling to what was left of the original door. The corner of the building collapsed, burying what was left of the Trackers felled by Mateo. He saw no sign of Garr, Sheila, or even the Hoarders. He pivoted in a rapid circle, mindful that Trackers were closing in.

He broke into a run, avoiding the streets in favor of back alleys in the Mission district. Under normal conditions, he'd take more care in disguising his back trail, but time dictated otherwise. He settled for putting as much distance between himself and the bombed-out shop as possible.

He sprinted until he couldn't, stumbled, and almost lost his footing on the uneven sidewalk. His shoulder connected against a brick wall with bruising force, wringing an involuntary gasp from his lungs. He regained his balance and leaned against the wall, hands on his knees, catching his breath.

The full moon painted the Old City's deserted streets with an eerie phosphorescence. Amos held his breath, straining to hear over his pounding heart. Nothing. If Trackers were closing in, they were in stealth mode.

He exhaled slowly and stepped out of the alley, scanning his back trail. The Old City betrayed none of its secrets. The only witnesses to his headlong flight were empty buildings and rusting hulks of long-abandoned cars.

In the distance—nine or ten blocks, he guessed—a tendril of smoke snaked its way skyward. The site of the Tracker ambush. He heard no new explosions, saw no red-ringed scanning eyes. A false peace, at best.

Amos positioned himself in the middle of the street, his stance that of a gunslinger—hands on hips, head held high. He'd have to trust that the other Runners had found refuge, somewhere in the Old City's porous underground.

Hidden in plain sight.

A chill breeze—a subtle harbinger of winter's relentless advance—swept over the street, driving dust and grit into his face. He welcomed the abrasive scouring. It kept him sharp, alert.

I need to lay low for a couple of days, clear my head.

Instinct drove his decision more than logic, but Amos wasted no time second-guessing himself. Satisfied he hadn't been followed, he began the long hike out of the Old City.

SEVEN ◎

AMOS WOKE with a start, every sense on instant, nail-biting alert. The darkness was absolute outside of the cave, the profound silence eerie. Something had interrupted his sleep. Something more disturbing than memories of the Tracker ambush.

He stretched his arms and legs, feeling the protest in his aching limbs. The stony surface and cold temperature were no help to his stiff body, but his mind was crystal clear. He crept to the mouth of the cave and poked his head out to survey his surroundings.

The wind gusted and the jack pines and Douglas firs creaked in response. Amos panned back and forth. Once, twice. He was on his third pass when he spotted a darker-than-dark silhouette advancing on his position.

The anonymous figure was taking their time, closing in with cagey stealth. Amos squinted, willing the tree branches to part and allow more moonlight to shine through.

There was no warning.

A circle of red light flared to blazing intensity, and his stalker recklessly abandoned any attempt at concealment. Amos's heart skipped a beat before catching up to the adrenaline racing in his veins.

How did it trail me? My Implant's been gone for months.

A shadow passed between Amos and the half-hidden moon. Startled, he looked above the skulking Tracker, in time to see a dark shape drop like a stone.

There was no time to react. The falling shadow flattened the Tracker. An arm raised, clutching a round object, and struck with vicious intent, twice. The Tracker lay where it had fallen, limp and unmoving.

The shadow rose to its feet, hands held out, palm up. A round object fell, landing on the ground with a solid thud. The figure crouched, raising empty hands up and away from their body. A voice carried to him, hardly above a whisper. "Good welcome, Amos. I trust you slept well?"

"Mateo?" Amos crawled out of the cave, hampered by his cold-stiffened limbs. Taking a cue from his visitor, he kept his voice down. "I guess I should start by saying 'thanks,' but—" he gestured at the body at Mateo's feet, "—how'd you know where to find me?"

Mateo hastened to join him, signaling he should stay low. They crouched in front of the cave.

"I followed you after the attack," he said, his voice a husky whisper. "But I seem to have made a tactical error after yesterday's unfortunate incident."

"Unfortunate incident?" Amos replied mildly, raising an eyebrow. "That's what you call a multi-Tracker ambush?"

Mateo cocked his head to one side, his odd expression accented by the moonlight. "This Tracker wasn't after you. And for that, I must apologize." He gestured at the lifeless form a few yards away. "It was hunting *me*, and by trailing you, I've exposed you to the same threat."

He straightened, the red light under his skin coming to life. He pivoted in a slow circle, surveying their surroundings. Once he completed his scan, the red glow faded into obscurity.

"We're alone for the moment," he said, but Amos detected an unfamiliar hint of anxiety in his voice. "I'm afraid my error may have complicated matters. The Givers are now aware that I continue to exist. They'll want to correct that."

"If the Hoarders don't get you first," Amos replied. "I got the impression Darcy doesn't consider you a friend."

Mateo lifted his head a fraction. "Only together can you hope to defeat the Givers." A puzzled frown creased his face. "The alliance must survive."

Amos shrugged. The tension between his shoulder blades morphed into a headache. "So you keep telling us." He gestured to the dead Tracker. "Well, if they're hunting both of us, where to next?"

Mateo straightened. "Cascadia Enclave, of course."

Amos shook his head, wincing at the sharp pain in his neck. "Somehow, I knew you were going to say that."

EIGHT ◉

"HERE, THIS SHOULD help warm you up." Doc Simon distributed steaming bowls of stew around the table. A mouth-watering aroma filled the mess hall, twice as enticing after two days of dried trail rations. Aubrey couldn't remember when she'd felt so hollow inside.

And cold. She repressed another shiver. *I can't seem to get the chill out of my bones.*

Don eased himself into a chair, sitting opposite her at the scuffed table. He looked exhausted. They all did. Everyone needed a good, hot meal and a decent night's sleep.

Aubrey was relieved to see a fresh bandage on his injured arm. The clean strips of cloth were a welcome contrast to the rust-colored rags from Muster Estates.

Jane sat beside him, hands cupped around her bowl, savoring the warmth. She'd managed to find time to brush out her tangled locks, and with her hair gathered in a loose ponytail, she appeared more like her usual acerbic self.

Megan took a seat next to Aubrey, but the dynamic wasn't

the same. Aubrey felt a solidarity, a kinship with the other Runners gathered around the table, despite the unusual events that brought them together. She felt at home, like she'd found a family of sorts.

Even Snake Lady's part of the clan. A smile flitted across Aubrey's face. *A cranky cousin or something.*

Megan was different. She sat as close to Aubrey as Jane did beside Don, but Aubrey felt an enormous gulf between them. The former Tracker remained something of a blank canvas. She continued to recover more and more of her humanity, but possessed a semi-alien quality that was hard to ignore.

Aubrey stole a glance at her. Megan chewed in a methodical way, and Aubrey couldn't tell if she noticed or appreciated the taste of the warm stew.

"How's the arm, Don?" Doc Simon stood at one end of the table, arms crossed and a concerned look on her face.

Don exhaled a slow breath without looking up. "Infinitely better, now that you're done poking and prodding at it," he said in his gruff but good-natured way. He met Doc's gaze, giving her a teasing smile. "I know, I know—you want to make sure the wound is clean. But ..." He shook his head for dramatic effect, and winced. "Oh yeah, my head hurts, too. I guess that's not surprising after sleeping on cold, hard concrete. I guess my arm overshadowed the stiff neck."

"Dehydration," Doc replied in a no-nonsense, professional tone. "You need to replenish your fluid levels. That goes for all of you, by the way. You've been through a nasty couple of days. You need sleep, but you also need to rehydrate."

She uncrossed her arms and tucked her hands into her pockets, a far-away look on her face.

Aubrey felt a sudden flash of empathy. *Doc was here, alone, the whole time we were on the run. With no way of knowing if we were dead or alive.*

Jane lifted her bowl and drank the last drops of broth. She set the bowl on the table and leaned back in her chair, looking refreshed and energized.

"We need to find the rest of the team," she said, brushing a stray strand of hair away from her face. "It's been two days since the attack. I can't sit around here, wasting time. I'm going to restock my pack, grab a quick nap, and be on my way. Don, are you with me, big guy?"

Don didn't respond immediately, chewing with a thoughtful look on his face. "Everyone took off in different directions." He tapped his spoon lightly on the rim of the bowl. "I'm not trying to be difficult, Jane, but do you have *any idea* where to look? The last I saw of the colonel, he was leading the Hoarders out of harm's way. If I know Garr, he'll make sure they're safe and sound in Hoarderville. If he took a tunnel route, we'd have probably crossed paths at Muster Estates."

"Not necessarily," Jane replied, refusing to back down. She exuded nervous energy. "There's more than one sewer route."

"Have you all gone deaf, or am I invisible?" Doc leaned over the table, glaring back and forth between them. "What part of 'recover' do you not understand? The human body can only take so much stress before it shuts down to protect itself."

"Garr left with the *Hoarders*, Doc," Jane replied, undaunted by her outburst. "We haven't seen or heard from him since. Doesn't that worry you?"

"Sheila was with him," Aubrey said, her confidence dwindling after Jane's reminder. *Garr and Sheila, stuck with Darcy and the rest of the Hoarders?* "At least, she was following him out of the building, the last I saw."

Jane laughed, a short bark without humor. "Sheila won't let him out of her sight—not with those Hoarders." She gripped her empty bowl between taut fingers, and her voice dropped to a harsh whisper. "Darcy scares me more than Trackers."

She's got a point. Aubrey was more than a little surprised by Jane's honest admission. "Garr has his hands full. Sheila's tough, but it's two of them against the Hoarders. And if Don's right about them heading for the Enclave ..."

Don set his empty bowl aside. "Never underestimate the colonel, especially when he's teamed up with Sheila." He pushed back from the table, his chair scraping on the floor. "I've got a good hunch where to find Amos. It'll take us at least a day to get there, unless we can find ourselves another truck. I wonder if Enrico has one he could spare ..."

Doc Simon gathered their empty bowls and stacked them on the weathered counter. "You'll still have to hike through the tunnels, even if you can arrange for a truck. Make sure you refill your canteens. I'm not exaggerating the complications of de-hydration and exhaustion. Headaches may be the least of your concerns."

Aubrey felt her pulse quicken. *We're heading back into the sewer again? I almost wish I hadn't eaten.* She got to her feet, grateful to find her shivering had subsided. *I won't be the weak link on this team.*

"I *was* listening, Doc." Don's booming baritone filled the mess hall. "Dehydration means poor reflexes and sloppy think-ing. I'll take responsibility for my team's health." He rubbed his palms together. "Aubrey, you're staying here. No offense, Doc—you're as tough as they come, but I'm not leaving you by yourself again. Besides, it's time Megan learned how to function as part of the team."

Aubrey caught the glance that passed between him and Doc. *They've discussed this already. While she was stitching Don's arm, probably. I wonder what's up?*

She resented being left behind, but couldn't argue with his logic. Just as she'd had to prove she was ready after her injuries healed, it was now Megan's turn.

Megan levered herself out of her chair to stand beside Jane. She hadn't spoken since they entered the mess hall. Her face was impassive, her body language relaxed and noncommittal. It was impossible to guess how she felt about her new assignment.

Aubrey's nagging doubts resurfaced. *Her speech is awkward, but don't be fooled by that. We've underestimated her before.*

"My go," Megan said suddenly, startling everyone. She nodded her head for emphasis, her remaining eye lighting up with anticipation. Her mouth twisted as she spoke, and each phrase was obviously an effort. "Find Amos."

Doc Simon turned to the door, all business. "I'll get some dried cherries for you, Don," she called over her shoulder as she left the mess hall. "Natural painkiller. I'd say 'go easy on the arm,' but I know who I'm talking to." Her voice faded as she hurried down the corridor to the infirmary.

Don shoved his chair into place, leaning on the back with his good arm. "Let's pack up, Jane. Restock supplies, and grab your combat knife. And one of the prods, while you're at it." He paused for emphasis. "Follow Doc's orders, and get some shut-eye. We leave first thing in the morning."

"Roger that," Snake Lady said cheerily.

"Find Amos," Megan said, nodding. For the first time, Aubrey thought she detected emotion in her voice. Excitement. Eagerness, perhaps. "My go."

NINE ◉

A BROODING SILENCE LINGERED after the departure of Don, Jane, and Megan. Eastside Hub felt gutted, deserted, and far too quiet. Aubrey's nerves refused to settle, and she was grateful when Doc suggested relocating to the infirmary.

Aubrey winced as Doc massaged the scar tissue on her arm, hand, and fingers. The daily routine was a hold-over from her physical rehab after she'd almost electrocuted herself. She'd recovered most of her former strength and dexterity, but Doc insisted on a regular regime of exercise and physical therapy.

"I couldn't believe how arrogant the Hoarders were." Aubrey grimaced as Doc found a tender spot in her forearm. "Darcy, their leader, wouldn't look at us, except maybe Garr. He talked to Mateo as if we weren't even there. Or maybe like he thought we were too stupid to understand. And Mateo says we need an alliance with *them?*"

Darcy. She couldn't disguise her revulsion when she spoke his name. He was a monster. His Implants turned innocent, unsuspecting people into mindless killers. Plus, he'd stooped so low as to Implant a young boy. Aubrey hadn't known she was capable of such stark loathing. Until Darcy.

Doc said nothing, concentrating on the physical therapy, but Aubrey thought she detected a darker frown on her face.

"Darcy's the one who created the Implants in the first place," Aubrey said, emphasizing her point. "He doesn't try to hide it. I think he's actually proud of himself. And once you're Implanted, he assigns you a *number*, like you're not even a person anymore." She knew she was talking too fast, but she couldn't stem the flood of words. "All I could think about were names. Sarah and Thomas, Stephen—all dead because Trackers were after our Implants. Because *Darcy ...*"

Her lips twisted as she snarled his name. She drew a ragged breath, wondering why her eyes remained dry when every fiber of her body wanted to scream.

Doc held her hand, but the massage was over. She leaned forward, studying her with an expression Aubrey couldn't identify and, in that moment, anxiety began gnawing at her.

Doc straightened with a sigh and slid off her stool. "Walk with me, Aubrey," she said, and exited the infirmary without a backward glance.

Curious, Aubrey followed. She assumed Doc's goal was the mess hall, and was surprised when she took the opposite direction, past their sleeping quarters, to a nondescript room at the far end of the Hub.

Doc lit a lantern as she entered, and the wan light danced on the walls. The empty, featureless room was long and narrow, just as Aubrey remembered it.

Doc set the lantern on the floor, gesturing to the wall at the far end. Aubrey recognized the multitude of dark smudges pock-marking the unpainted wall.

"You spent *weeks* in this room," Doc said, gesturing to the smudges. "Over and over, no matter how much it hurt, throwing your little rubber ball and catching it. Hours per day, every day, for weeks on end. You were *determined*. You even taught yourself to be ambidextrous."

"I wanted to contribute," Aubrey said, confused by the unexpected change of topic. "I'd seen what Trackers were capable of—how many people they'd slaughtered. And I almost died when my Implant activated. I knew I had to be a part of Eastside. A *functional* part, not just a rescued Runner."

Doc turned to face her, her eyes boring holes into Aubrey. "I remember. You called them the *Soul-less*. Mindless killing machines who butchered your friends, and ours, in order to 'harvest' their Implants."

Aubrey swallowed hard. Her memories were still raw, jagged, like shards of glass in her chest.

Doc's voice was low and strident, a challenge implied by her words and body language. "You trained long and hard to toughen up and be part of the team. You couldn't *wait* to join the others in the field, no matter the risk."

"It paid off in the long run," Aubrey replied defiantly, as she realized Doc was confronting her. "Maybe you've forgotten, but I saved that boy's life. Megan was about to kill him, even though his Implant was deactivated. I *had* to get tough. Tougher than Snake Lady, even. I won't be the weak link."

Doc stepped awkwardly close, her voice brittle. "And when you stole Jane's gun to kill a Hoarder—in defiance of Colonel Scott's *explicit* orders—were you the weak link?"

Aubrey could only stare, feeling the blood drain from her face. Her fists clenched, fingernails digging into her palms.

Doc's words sank in, hammering against her rationale—her

justification—for stealing the Glock. And her single-minded obsession with killing the monster named Darcy.

"He put Implants into *children*." Tears welled in her eyes and the sudden lump in her throat made it hard to speak. "He said he was probably the one who Implanted me ..."

She retreated an involuntary step, brought up short by the wall behind her, and slid down to the floor.

It no longer mattered what Doc might think. Aubrey didn't care if Snake Lady were to walk in and deliver one of her sarcastic insults. She buried her face in her hands and bawled.

Faces and events raced past her mind's eye without pause or mercy. The boy they'd rescued, the Blackcreek massacre, and her own horror when Sarah and Thomas explained what the Hoarders had done to her. Fleeing from the murderous Trackers, only to come face-to-face with the inventor of the Implants.

Her memories pummeled her like a tidal wave, and she was powerless to control her tears.

It felt like a long time before she looked up, wiping her eyes, to find Doc Simon sitting next to her, also leaning against the wall. As patient as always, she waited for Aubrey to pull herself together before speaking.

"I'm not going to apologize for my harshness." Doc's voice was firm but less confrontational. She shook her head, grimacing. "You came close to crippling an alliance that Garr believes is *critical* to ridding ourselves of Givers, Implants, and Trackers." She sighed, sounding exasperated. "Amos had to learn the same lesson, and there were more than a few times I thought he'd never get it. This *cannot* be about revenge."

Aubrey heard her words, understood them, but she rebelled inwardly. *Darcy deserves to pay for what he's done. How many Runners are dead—slaughtered—because of him?*

Doc waited, watching her with a discerning eye. "Colonel Scott's decision pushed all of you to the edge. I was worried—more than I can describe—before any of you left to meet the Hoarders." She averted her gaze. Lantern light flickered on her face. "But I support the colonel and his leadership at Eastside. If there were any other option, he would've chosen it. He took a huge risk trusting Mateo, and an even larger one by agreeing to an alliance with Hoarders. *Everyone* was stretched to the breaking point."

Aubrey listened, numb.

"You were seconds away from making a critical mistake." Doc took a deep breath, her eyes softening. "But there's more to you than that, Aubrey. You've shown strength and resolve, and you've overcome some daunting obstacles. In my mind, that makes you one of the bravest people I know."

Aubrey managed a watery smile. "I don't feel brave, Doc. And I'm sorry..." Tears filled her eyes, but she blinked them away. "I shouldn't have taken Jane's gun. I wasn't thinking, I was just reacting. I thought I was getting tougher, but I guess I lost it when Garr said we were going to partner with Hoarders."

Doc nodded, looking suddenly tired. "Like I said, Garr's decision—even though I believe he's probably right—pushed the whole team to the edge. You deserve more credit than you're giving yourself. You're tougher than you realize." She looked directly at Aubrey, emphasizing her words. "But you are *not* a murderer. You should thank your lucky stars Megan got there before you crossed a line you can't *uncross.*"

"I know," Aubrey replied weakly. She felt small, miserable.

Doc paused, allowing her words time to sink in. "The Givers take innocent people and turn them into Trackers. Darcy creates numbered 'drones' with his Implants. Don't let that change who you are, Aubrey. Don't let revenge turn you into a cold-blooded killer."

Aubrey took a deep breath and exhaled. "You're right, Doc. I know that, but that doesn't make it easy. If you could've seen the look on his face…" She ran a hand through her hair. "It feels like we've made a deal with the devil."

"Call him whatever you like," Doc replied, watching her with shrewd eyes. "But Darcy, and the other Hoarders, are the key to getting inside the Enclave. We can't do this without their assistance, as distasteful as that might be."

Aubrey squared her shoulders. "I won't make the same mistake twice, Doc, I promise. I won't be the weak link."

"That's all I need to hear." Doc climbed to her feet, arching her back as she stretched. "I'm getting too old to live in a subbasement next to the sewer," she said with a wry smile. "But right now, we've got bigger mysteries to solve."

"Mysteries?" Aubrey sat forward, alarmed by the change in her voice. "What could be worse than Darcy?"

Doc offered a hand and helped Aubrey to her feet. She waited until Aubrey finished brushing the dust off her pants before replying. "Those Trackers knew *exactly* where to find you. There's more going on than we realized." She stooped to retrieve the lantern, and the shadows on the wall gyrated in response. "I think we have a third party involved, one that wants all of us wiped out."

"The Givers." Aubrey felt her heart skip a beat. "That makes sense, I guess, but how did they know where to find us?"

Doc's blunt verdict fell into a sudden silence in the empty room. "Somebody told them."

TEN ◉

"Please tell me you've not that naïve." The mechanic's worried expression spoke louder than his words. Megan decided to categorize Enrico's reaction as *skeptical*. "You already know Mateo can't be trusted."

Megan eyed the mechanic with equal skepticism. She considered Mateo a friend, an ally.

"You weren't there," Jane replied, clearly not intimidated by his pessimistic appraisal. "Why not give Mateo the benefit of the doubt? Colonel Scott seems to trust him."

Enrico threw his hands up in frustration. "Then Garr's lost his mind. I warned him the last time I saw him. Mateo Reyes *is dead*, killed by a Tracker two years ago. Possibly the same one you met in Jericho. I can't believe Garr's so gullible..."

"Mateo claims he's the real deal," Don said, his calm voice a counterpoint to Enrico's agitation. "And it's no secret the Givers use people *outside* the Enclave as raw material for creating redeyes. They'd never dream of using one of the high-and-mighty Citizens of Hoarderville."

Enrico remained unconvinced. "Let's take this conversation inside. This is a small town where everyone knows everyone. I can't be seen arguing with strangers in front of my shop for too long before someone notices. Then the tongues start to wag."

He led them into a small garage, attached to the modest house where he lived alone. Late afternoon sun streamed inside via a single window, illuminating the interior. Don's eyes lit up at the sight of the vintage vehicle stored inside.

Enrico leaned against the truck, arms folded over his chest. He was older than Garr, his hair grayer, but no less in command of his tiny domain. "So, Mateo's the same person, but in Tracker form, and we're expected to take his word for it? A little too convenient, in my sometimes-humble opinion."

"You knew Mateo," Don said, tearing his gaze from truck to owner, "when he was a shopkeeper outside Hoarderville."

Enrico nodded, his expression softening. "He was the most fearless member of the Hub network I'd ever met. No disrespect to Colonel Scott or any of you—Garr's told me some of what you've been through—but Mateo dared to set up in Jericho, right under the Hoarders' noses. Hidden in plain sight? He operated in Cascadia's shadow for a long time. Until one day..." He clapped his hands together, the percussive sound sharp in the tiny shop. "Tracker. End of story."

"Wait a minute." Jane stepped in front of Don. "That can't be right. Garr sent us to Jericho to gauge the Enclave's defenses, look for any way to get inside. If Mateo's been dead for two years, the other Hubs would've heard something. How could Jericho keep functioning as a Hub, unless Mateo is who he says he is?"

Enrico snorted in exasperation. "I wouldn't know. I'm not part of your network. Garr and I served together years ago. Every now and then, I do a few favors for him, but that's it." He scowled, shaking his head. "Why your network would keep using Mateo, or whoever he is, as a conduit for intel is beyond me. Unless everyone just assumed all is well because he's alive and running his guided tours."

"Maybe." Don shrugged. "It's possible we were the first to figure out what Mateo really is. But let's be clear: it was his decision to reveal his Tracker-ness. Why he did it is anyone's guess." Megan caught the glance Don shot her way before he changed tactics. "Tell you what—if you knew the original Mateo Reyes, describe him for me."

The mechanic paused, his combative posture unchanged, and leaned back, arching his spine over the hood of the truck. "It's been at least four years since I last saw him," he said, studying the rafters as if they bore an imprint of Mateo's features. "He's tall—not quite as tall as you, Don—with salt-and-pepper hair, but not as salty as mine. Average build. Dark eyes, laughs a lot. Intelligent and well-spoken. He took to his role like a fish takes to water. He was a natural."

Don and Jane exchanged glances.

"You've just described the Mateo we met," Don said. "During his 'guided tour,' he sounded more like scholar giving a lecture than a shopkeeper, but the locals seem to have accepted him. I think we're talking about the same person."

"Except for the laughter," Jane said, Her foot tapped a nervous rhythm on the wooden floorboards. "When I think of Mateo, a sense of humor isn't the first thing that comes to mind. He's pretty serious, which I guess makes sense, considering what's at stake."

"Or the Givers changed him into a Tracker." Don laughed, seemingly amused by his own words. "I can't believe what I'm saying. Am I actually *defending* Mateo?"

Enrico's skeptical gaze wandered back and forth between them. "You've convinced yourselves Mateo wasn't killed by a Tracker. He *is* the Tracker, and we heard the wrong rumor? Okay, let's go with that, just for the sake of argument." He leaned forward, his defiance clear. "Think of the advantage it would give the Hoarders to have a Tracker *inside* your network. He lives a stone's throw from Hoarderville, so they can keep an eye on him. He gathers intel from unsuspecting Runners, and passes it to the Hoarders. Not to mention the Givers."

Megan felt a burning sensation she identified as anger. Her hands clenched into fists, unseen behind Don's bulk.

Enrico shook his head, frustrated he wasn't getting through. "None of us have the faintest clue what happens when a human is recreated as a Tracker. If the Givers interrogated him, Mateo may have already compromised your entire network. Have you ever considered that?"

"No questions," Megan interrupted. She poked her head around Don, looking up at the mechanic. "Givers. No questions. Only..." Her jaw muscles cramped, and she cursed her inability to complete her thought.

Enrico stared as if he hadn't seen her before. "You're telling me the Givers *don't* interrogate their prisoners before making Trackers out of them?"

Megan frowned, concentrating. Her halting words escaped bit by awkward bit. "No. No questions. No interest. We—our minds—do not matter. Only to obey." She clutched at her throat, as if she could tear the words out. Her next sentence exploded in a frustrated rush. "Givers. They only take."

"Megan's also a Tracker." Don watched for the mechanic's reaction. "Or at least, she used to be."

"Used to be?" He stepped away from his truck, inspecting

Megan with obvious curiosity. "I'll bet there's quite a story behind that." He examined her eyepatch and surrounding scar tissue, speaking as if she wasn't present. "But I doubt we have time. Are you sure she's not taking orders from the Givers?"

"No more voices." Megan reached up to tap the side of her head. "No more Givers," she said, her words clear and unhurried. "My name is Megan." She stepped forward, gazing up at the mechanic with her one good eye. "Your truck. Please."

Enrico raised his eyebrows and turned to Jane and Don. "Direct, isn't she?"

Don glanced at Megan. "She's full of surprises, no doubt about that. But you'd already guessed why we're here. We need to borrow your truck."

"Please," Megan said.

Enrico grimaced and shook his head, but dug the keys out of his pocket and handed them to Don. "This is my favorite truck. My *only* truck. Please bring it back in one piece, if it's not too much to ask."

"Why? What have you heard about Don's driving?" Jane dead-panned as she approached the vehicle. It was smaller than the ones they'd stolen from Hoarders on previous missions, but there was enough room for the three of them.

And space for Amos, if all went well. Jane climbed into the passenger side, while Megan scrambled into the rear seat.

Don started the engine and rolled his window down. "We really appreciate this. It'll save us a lot of time. We should be back in a few hours, sundown at the latest, assuming there's no Tracker-shaped surprises."

"Then I hope you have the dullest trip of your lives." Enrico stole a furtive glance at Megan, and leaned on the driver's door, lowering his voice. "Listen, you're dealing with *two* Trackers now. The damage sustained by this one tells me that's probably how she broke free of the Givers. Nothing you've told me about Mateo suggests he gained his freedom the same way."

"We'll risk it," Don replied. Jane nodded beside him. Megan pretended she wasn't listening.

Enrico hesitated, choosing his words with care. "Trackers don't think like us, Don. Or value what we consider important. They may have been human once, but not anymore." He shifted uncomfortably, his gaze darting to Megan and back. "Whatever these Givers are, they've programmed Trackers to think like they do. An *alien* way of thinking. You can't assume anything, Don. And you can't reason with them."

He stepped away from the truck and opened the garage door, beckoning them through. Don shifted gears, creeping past him with exaggerated care.

"Thanks." Don leaned out the window. "We'll see you in a couple of hours."

"Take it easy," Enrico replied, feigning a cheerful wave for the benefit of anyone watching. "I want my truck back."

ELEVEN ◉

DON COAXED the truck up the steep hillside. The engine groaned in protest, tires spinning now and then on loose gravel. Jane and Megan held on for dear life as they rattled and bounced over the uneven road.

"Not as much torque as a Hoarder truck," Don muttered under his breath, frowning at the speedometer.

"No kidding," Jane replied, as a pothole sent a shuddering vibration through the chassis. "Can't say much for the shock absorbers, either."

Megan braced her foot against the back of Jane's seat. She found the passing terrain fascinating. The overgrown road wove its way up the hillside, a narrow lane lined with thick evergreens and undergrowth.

Why does this feel familiar? How does the wilderness fit into my past? Not for the first time, she was frustrated by her inability to communicate clearly. There were so many questions she wanted to ask, but the effort was exhausting and, more often than not, the results unsatisfying.

Is one of these villages my hometown?

The one memory she had of the wilderness was her recent escape from Eastside. She'd stolen an Implant from the infirmary, intent on regaining the Givers' favor. Her desperate plan now seemed foreign, illogical.

Her memories had begun to resurface, sporadic and unconnected, during her trek through the sewer tunnels. Her perspective on the Givers' silence began to evolve. She wasn't cut off from the aliens—she was *free* of them. She was becoming human again.

Megan pondered the mechanic's cryptic warning. It hadn't taken long to realize that her verbal handicap was often misunderstood. People assumed she was hard of hearing, or too stupid to comprehend what was said.

She resented it at first, but discovered she could learn a great deal if she stayed quiet and listened.

Enrico doesn't trust Mateo, and he's not sure what to make of me. She tried to interpret his words and nonverbal cues. *Words are only a portion of their communication. The timbre of Enrico's voice, the look on his face, the way he stands—all facets that, combined, tell the whole story.*

"Amos came back here?" Jane's skeptical question intruded into Megan's reverie. "The same place he hid his Implant?"

They crested the hill and drove at a modest pace along a high ridge. The road narrowed to a single lane, little more than a beaten-down track between rows of fall-yellowed maples, interspersed with dark evergreens.

Don flashed a confident grin. "The last time I guessed where Amos went, I was right." The words were no sooner out of his mouth when his expression turned somber. "Amos hates this place, but it's a familiar haunt. I'm gambling he's there now."

Jane opened her mouth, but apparently changed her mind. Megan scooted forward on her seat as Don decelerated. He scrutinized the trees to his left, as if seeking a landmark.

"It's a long way from Eastside," Jane said, as if trying to convince herself. "Amos knows the routine as well as any of us —lay low and wait. Muster Estates is our go-to hiding spot, but I think I'll head out this way next time. If there *is* a next time, that is. I don't mind a good hike."

Don braked and the truck skidded to a stop. There was no need to pull off the dirt track, even if the overgrown underbrush would have allowed it. No other vehicles competed for the use of the winding road. They were alone.

Don shut the engine off, and they waited in the cab an additional moment. A gentle breeze rustled the trees, a reassuring sound outside Don's open window.

"You're right. It's a stiff trek," Don said to Jane. "But this is where Amos comes when he's out of options."

He shut his mouth, his lips forming a thin, hard line. Megan had learned enough by observing Don to know further questions would go unanswered. Jane's eyes looked haunted. Megan suspected she wanted to question his cryptic remark, but something held her back. She wondered what and why.

"Let's go." Don opened his door and stepped out of the vehicle. "It's a short walk into the bush, and then downhill about a hundred yards. Climbing up from the valley is a lot harder. Amos will be tired and hungry by now."

He led the way into the forest adjacent to the neglected road, weaving his way through thick underbrush. There was no conversation. Megan felt the tension mount as they neared the brink of the descent.

Don halted near the edge of the precipice and knelt behind

a fallen tree, surveying the steep hillside. The terrain below was rocky and uneven, with a thick covering of pines, but less undergrowth than on the ridge.

"What's wrong, Don?" Jane crouched beside him, squinting downhill. "What do you see?"

Don shook his head, pulling out a pair of binoculars to scan in a wide, slow arc. "We've been here before. We came for the Implant Amos buried out here, after it was activated."

Jane glanced at him, uneasy. "I haven't forgotten. Aubrey's Implant was activated at the same time."

Megan stood beside her, imitating Jane's careful scrutiny of their surroundings. She wished, not for the first time, that her scanning eye still functioned.

"Last time, a Tracker managed to trail us this far," Don said, continuing his visual inspection. "We got lucky. If we hadn't used the prod on Amos's Implant, it might've found us."

Jane jammed her elbow into his ribs. Don looked at her in surprise, and she jerked her head in Megan's direction. *Shut up,* her eyes flashed at him. Don fell silent. Megan pretended she hadn't noticed.

"Trackers have gotten too close to this place before," Don said, in an obvious attempt to cover his verbal misstep. "But I don't see any sign they're patrolling now. Let's not waste any time. This is a quick sortie—either Amos is there, or he's not. Then we head back."

He rose to his feet, stowing the binoculars and leading the way downhill. Megan and Jane followed close behind, picking a cautious path over the rocky ground. A broken ankle, or even a serious sprain, would put everyone at risk.

Don's familiarity with Amos's hiding place made for an uneventful, if strenuous, trek down the steep incline. Within minutes, he halted near an outcropping of rocks, dropping to one knee to peer inside a dark hole. Megan didn't need to hear his muttered comment to know Amos wasn't inside.

Jane crouched next to him, digging into her pack for a small lantern. Leaning forward as far as she could, she shone it into the recesses of the cave.

The cave's small mouth belied the depth of the cavern below, and Jane flashed the light into every nook and cranny. The brief inspection confirmed what they'd already suspected.

"If Amos was here, he didn't stay long," Jane said, dousing the lantern. "And he didn't take the sewer route back. We'd have met him on our way to Enrico's place."

"Or I guessed wrong, and he was never here," Don said heavily. "If so, I've got no idea where else to look. He'll have to find us."

Megan gasped, pointing a shaky finger at a dark mound thirty yards downhill. A tight cluster of carcasses lay scattered in haphazard fashion at the foot of a towering Douglas fir.

One of the bodies was clearly human.

TWELVE

DON CROSSED THE DISTANCE with long strides, a sickened look on his face. Jane and Megan caught up, flanking him on either side. They stared at the vermin-ravaged carcasses at the base of the tree.

Jane ducked her head. Megan sensed her relief. The body at their feet wasn't Amos.

"Tracker," Don growled under his breath. He dropped to one knee, examining the damage to the Tracker's skull. His head had been split open, exposing the alien technology embedded in his brain.

Don pointed to a fist-sized rock beside the corpse, a rust-colored stain marring most of its surface. "Looks like Amos had a visitor. That might explain why he's not here."

Jane circled the base of the tree, examining the scattered carcasses. "What happened here? Look, a coyote—dead. Like it went into convulsions or something."

Don kicked a small object away. "Rats. Also dead." He bent to examine the Tracker, frowning. "Scavengers usually pick a carcass clean but, for some reason, there's almost no damage." He gestured at the head wound. "Aside from the obvious."

Megan crouched beside the Tracker, taking shallow breaths through her mouth, one hand covering her nose. The pattern of destruction was eerily familiar.

"Tracker kill," she managed to say. *He looks like the Tracker I killed for interfering with my Quest.* She felt her insides lurch. "This one. Killed by another."

Don raised his eyebrows. "Mateo? He's intervened before."

Megan didn't answer. She stared at the scraps of alien circuitry in the Tracker's brain tissue, laid bare by the head trauma. She couldn't see the entire device, but she knew exactly what it looked like.

Memories danced before her eyes, half-formed and incomplete, overlaying the body sprawled awkwardly at her feet. She saw a hand, two devices cupped in its palm, larger than the Implants but similar in design. She tried to access more than the single image, but to no avail.

Her breathing became ragged as the hand and the sleek metallic objects grew in size, until they filled her vision. She recognized the paired devices. They were mental processors, which allowed the Givers to communicate with, and control, their Trackers.

Unbidden, emotions erupted inside her. A flashback—to a similar emotional reaction, one she'd experienced the first time she'd seen that hand.

Stark, unreasoning terror flooded her, as real as if she had been transported back to that fateful day. *Processors? No, don't do this. Don't turn me one into of Them!*

A piercing shriek echoed in her mind, a desperate cry born of horror and betrayal. The voice was her own.

Please, no! Why are you doing this to me?

The mental image vanished like a mist, and her senses came into focus. She heard the alarm in Jane's voice, felt Don's hand on her shoulder. She saw the rotting corpse, inhaled its rancid stench.

She collapsed to her hands and knees beside the dead Tracker, vomiting convulsively.

THIRTEEN ◉

"PEOPLE WILL BELIEVE just about anything, if they see it on the Infomedia."

Connor couldn't help overhearing the sarcastic comment as he exited Elemental Beanery.

The patio table nearest the café's exit was crowded. Young patrons had pulled up extra chairs, and their lively banter caught his attention. He recognized a few of them from university. Not friends, or even acquaintances, but faces he knew by sight, if not by name.

He couldn't explain why he'd returned to this spot when there were dozens of available options. Madison and Reagan's deaths hung heavy over the area, although the rest of the bustling crowd seemed to have already forgotten.

Mojo's Coffee Cartel had reopened a few days earlier, under a new name: Elemental Beanery. The proprietors appeared eager to rebrand their café's reputation after the previous month's terrorist attack.

Connor hoped the students wouldn't notice him, but his

desire was short-lived. Several saw him glance their way, and called out to him.

"Let me guess—the new security measures?" Connor raised his voice, feigning nonchalance. "It's all the Infomedia talks about, all day, every day. It's a little over the top, if you ask me."

One of the students pulled out an empty chair, gesturing for him to join them. Connor shook his head, scrambling for a plausible excuse. "Thanks, but I've got to keep moving. Midterm exams aren't that far off."

"They've started implanting people already." The breathless comment came from a girl on the opposite side of the table.

Connor almost dropped his latte. He didn't recognize her, but her barely-contained enthusiasm was jarring.

"The Council's implementing the new security measures," she said triumphantly. "It's about time. The threat from the savages is getting worse."

Connor hid his reaction behind a hasty gulp, and winced as the hot liquid burned his tongue.

There was a murmur of assent around the table, sprinkled with affirming comments. Connor knew what they were referring to. He'd seen the news reports: patriotic Citizens lining up to volunteer for the new security chips. It was the lead story all morning.

The consensus of the Infomedia's panel of self-appointed experts was an enthusiastic endorsement of the new security measures. Every Citizen, district by district, would receive a security chip, implanted in their right forearm.

For the good of the Enclave.

"Have you heard the new label they're giving the security program?" The guy who'd offered Connor a chair laughed as he shared his tidbit of knowledge. "They're calling them 'anodynes.'"

Or nodes, for short." He leaned back in his chair, laughing again. "I guess they thought 'security tracking chip' sounded too clinical. So they're promoting it as the 'Anodyne Initiative.' It's all just a marketing ploy."

"What's wrong with that?" The girl was ready to take up the challenge. "Anodyne means soothing, or relaxing. It's a reminder we don't have to live in constant fear of savages sneaking into Cascadia. Nodes are for our protection."

"Doesn't it also mean *bland*?" Connor felt his blood boil at her unquestioning acceptance of Council propaganda. He tried but couldn't disguise his sarcasm. "As in, 'hey, no big deal, but we're going to monitor your every waking moment'?"

"It's for the good of the Enclave." Chair Guy glowered at him, all traces of friendliness gone. His body language was angry and combative, ready to rise to the Council's defense.

Connor struggled to control himself. The patio was under video surveillance, as was much of Cascadia. He clenched his teeth and managed to bite back an angry retort.

Another student across the table—Connor had never seen him before—bolted forward, spoiling for a fight. "Citizens have the right to be safe inside Cascadia. The savages would jump at the chance to invade if we let our guard down. They're getting through our borders far too often, as it is."

"Are you a Citizen of the Enclave, or not?" The ultimatum came from the girl, who was beginning to eye Connor with suspicion. "Everyone has a responsibility to protect our way of life. Complying with the Anodyne Initiative is our civic duty. It's a simple as that."

Connor took a deep breath, clamping down hard on his frustration. *Don't make a scene. The eyes of the Givers are everywhere.* "You're absolutely right." he said, hoping to distract from his earlier gaffe. "The savages need to learn their place. That's *outside* Cascadia."

At least we're on the same page about savages.

He managed, with effort, to keep his voice light and conversational. "If that means getting a node for the good of the Enclave, then so be it." He saluted the group with his latte. "I've got to go. Sorry if anything I said came across wrong…"

His apology was lame and insincere, and he knew it, but several heads nodded around the table. They were bored with the topic already. Chair Guy was the lone exception, his shrewd look of appraisal unchanged.

Connor turned his back on him and strolled toward the nearest travelator, feigning an interest in his latte. There was a brief pause, and the students resumed their animated conversation. He could still pick out the girl's eager voice.

"Hey, I've got an idea! Tomorrow—why don't we all meet here? We can go downtown and get our nodes together."

FOURTEEN ◉

CONNOR'S LATTE WAS COOLING OFF, but he knew better than to drink while riding a travelator. The problem wasn't with the moving sidewalks. Travelators were designed with meticulous attention to detail.

No, the problem was other Citizens, jostling each another as they crowded on and off. The most annoying were those who insisted on using their wrist-coms, more focused on their petty chats than their fellow Citizens.

His run-in with the students had thrown him off-balance, more than he wanted to admit. It had been a mistake to visit the former Mojo's. The memories were too raw. He needed a neutral space to think, to sort out this "alliance" with the savages. And Megan ...

His eyes felt hot, and he realized tears were welling up. He ducked his head, drawing one deep breath after another until his emotions were under control. No one around him seemed to notice, too absorbed in their own private worlds.

Connor edged his way to the travelator's outside boundary,

eager to remove himself from the moving thread of humanity. He was still several blocks from the Museum of Science, Technology and History, but walking the remaining distance was more appealing.

He stepped off the travelator, adjusting his gait as he made the transition from moving surface to stationary concrete. The Museum was within sight, its massive walls as impressive as a mini-Enclave.

He quickened his pace, anticipating some peace and quiet in the familiar surroundings. He could lose himself among the exhibits, finish his latte, and think.

Memories of his last meeting with Darcy crowded into his conscious mind. It hadn't been much of a conversation. Over the years, Connor had learned to view his foster father with a complicated mixture of respect, admiration, and fear.

He was grateful Darcy adopted him after savages murdered his family. Nothing would ever change that.

At the same time, Darcy's chronic tantrums were escalating in number and intensity. The pressure of leading their clandestine rebellion against the Givers and their human stooges was taking its toll.

Connor jogged up the front steps. His hand was on the door handle when he noticed the words etched into the tempered glass, "No Food or Drink." He looked from the door's prohibition to his latte, thwarted, and retraced his steps to the sidewalk. He chose a bench at the foot of the stairs and sat down, his back to the Museum, sipping his lukewarm beverage.

There had been nothing lukewarm about his argument with Darcy earlier that morning. Connor respected his adoptive father, feared him at times, but this business about an alliance with the savages was driving a wedge between them.

Normally, he kept his opinion to himself, but ever since he'd seen Megan—alive but under the savages' control—he seemed unable to control his emotions. Or his mouth.

You want us to play nice with savages? Connor winced as he recalled his impetuous outburst. *Lure them inside Cascadia so we can Implant them? Fine. That doesn't mean we have to pretend they're our equals.*

Darcy gave him a strange look, unaccustomed to Connor contradicting him, let alone with such hostility. His hesitation didn't last long.

Use your head, Connor. Darcy's rebuke had been swift and withering. *We've just acquired two new drones, but we need more. The savages aren't going to waltz back to their ghetto and herd their group into Cascadia out of the goodness of their hearts. We need them to trust us, to see us as their allies.*

Connor closed his eyes, resting the disposable cup on his knee. He was right, of course—Darcy was always right. His analytical mind could assess data and strategize faster than anyone Connor knew.

His foster father wasn't swayed by Connor's contempt for the savages. The long-range strategy was more important. They couldn't allow emotion to contaminate their resolve.

Until the Givers are destroyed, Darcy had replied when he demanded to know how long he'd be required to play his part in deceiving the savages. *Cascadia belongs to us—to humans. Nothing will change until the aliens are gone. The savages share our common goal. We can use that to our advantage.*

Connor opened his eyes, gazing across the boulevard. The Arts and Culture Gallery, directly opposite the bench, dominated his view. Its unorthodox design was a dazzling counterpoint to the dignified columns adorning the Museum edifice.

A sizable crowd had gathered in front of the Gallery, milling around in the artificial amphitheater. Waiting for an outdoor performance of some kind, Connor supposed.

He downed the last of his tepid latte in a prolonged gulp, wishing he could drown out the memory of his foolhardy response as easily. *The savages are smarter than you think. What happens if they realize you're targeting collaborators, instead of the Givers?*

He grimaced at his own folly. No one talked to Darcy like that. He wasn't known for his warmth, even in his best moods, but Connor felt his blood freeze at his foster father's patronizing expression.

Are you that stupid? Have I raised an idiot? The Givers use Trackers as bodyguards, but their real protection is the councilors who shield them. To get to the Givers, we have to remove the collaborators. Please, tell me that's not too difficult to grasp.

Tony's arrival brought a merciful end to their verbal sparring. He lingered just inside the door, looking uncomfortable as he picked up on the tension in the room. He kept his place, saying only what was necessary.

Drones DR-57 and DR-58 are ready, sir.

Darcy had held his position, his icy gaze drilling into Connor. Their standoff ended when Darcy spun on his heel and stalked to their front door. He paused to look over his shoulder, addressing Connor on the threshold of heir villa.

By the time we return with our new drones, you will have thought long and hard about your commitment to the cause.

And then he was gone. Tony hastened to catch the door before it closed, ducking out on Darcy's heels. Connor didn't miss the shrewd smirk Tony shot his way as he exited.

Connor sighed and set his empty cup on the bench. He

leaned forward, propping his elbows on his knees. The crowd across the street was growing larger. The imminent performance, whatever it might be, must be close to curtain time.

He reached inside his shirt and pulled out the archaic locket on its silver chain. The tiny picture inside smiled back at him. Megan, in happier days, wavy blond hair tousled by the breeze on the summer day the picture was taken.

A cold rage washed over him, a bottomless pit threatening to engulf him. *Darcy expects me to ignore what the savages did to Megan. For the "good of the Enclave."*

A commotion across the boulevard caught his attention. He roused himself, annoyed by the intrusion, and was puzzled by the scene unfolding outside the Gallery. Curious pedestrians trotted past him, chattering as they crossed the street to gawk at the developing spectacle. A confrontation appeared to be brewing between a small group on the front terrace of the Gallery, and a much larger crowd gathered in the amphitheater.

Connor snapped the locket shut and stowed it inside his shirt. More people streamed past his bench, intent on learning what the noisy disturbance was about. He jogged across the street, halting at the edge of the sidewalk.

The outdoor amphitheater boasted an assortment of tables and benches, rapidly filling with curious onlookers. A block-wide concrete staircase descended below street level, providing public access and additional seating. Connor chose to remain on the sidewalk, gazing over the heads of the crowd, to the terrace in front of the Gallery.

A small cluster of people gathered there, some waving placards. Others distributed leaflets but, judging by the crowd's growing hostility, their message was not well-received. The hair on the back of his neck bristled. Trouble was brewing.

FIFTEEN ⊙

A PROTEST. HERE, IN CASCADIA? Connor was familiar with the concept of protestors—he *was* a history major, after all—but an actual protest was unheard of, a direction contradiction to the Enclave's smooth-running society.

And with all the surveillance, the protesters will be identified before they sit down for supper.

He shivered in spite of himself. *I wouldn't want to draw the Givers' attention.*

The protestors' placards made their purpose clear: opposition to the Anodyne Initiative. Connor was intrigued. Were other Citizens waking up to the implications of the security chips?

"Punish the offenders, not the innocent." One protester raised his voice, striving to be heard above the murmuring of the restless crowd. His voice carried loud and clear, aided by the amphitheater's natural acoustics. "No one has the right to monitor me like a criminal."

His listeners were growing agitated.

"If you're not doing anything illegal, you've got nothing to worry about," a voice called from the crowd. "Unless you're hiding something."

Connor marveled at how easily the question morphed into an accusation.

A second protestor answered the challenge before the first could respond. "I've never gone outside the walls—not *once*—and I have no intention of leaving Cascadia. Why bother? Everything we need is right here. *So why do I need a node?*"

The crowd closed in, the mood morphing from curiosity to belligerence. Connor had read about mob mentality, studied it in class, but the speed at which it developed was both mesmerizing and alarming. He scanned the nearest faces, fascinated and repelled by what he saw.

A new voice rose from the crowd. "Enclave security is the responsibility of every Citizen."

Others shouted their agreement, taunting the protesters, who clustered close together as the crowd advanced. Connor could tell they hadn't anticipated such a strong reaction to their message. Their frightened expressions were clear to see, despite the distance between them.

"You're either for the Enclave, or against it." A female voice rang out above the buzz of the crowd. Connor stood on tip-toe, trying to spot her. She sounded like the girl who'd argued with him at the Beanery. "True Citizens will have nodes."

They've swallowed the propaganda.

The first protestor dropped his placard, raising his hands above his head to get the crowd's attention. He needn't have bothered—all eyes were on him. "If Cascadia's walls aren't secure, or if savages are forging documents to get inside, that's what the Council should focus on. How does monitoring *us* put a stop to that?"

"Haven't you heard the Infomedia?" A tall figure pushed his way to the fore, climbing the steps to confront him. He stared the protestor down for a long moment, and whirled to address the crowd. "When every Citizen has a node, it'll be child's play to isolate the terrorists. The savages will be the only ones unable to enter any public building—no node to scan, no entry." He raised a fist in triumph, and the crowd fastened on his every word. "No access to anything. They won't be able to buy a cup of coffee. No node, no Citizenship!"

The crowd, riled up, shouted in solidarity with his declaration, applauding and hurling abuse at the protestors. The beleaguered group retreated to the far side of the terrace, cowed and fearful.

The spokesman followed them, clearly enjoying himself. "The Council's already made their decision. If you don't want a Citizen's responsibilities, go live in Parasite City. The Enclave doesn't need your kind."

The crowd reacted just as Connor could have predicted. He was taken aback by the level of animosity the spokesman was able to provoke in a span of minutes.

Connor took a step or two back, wary of the fickle crowd. Things could get out of hand at a moment's notice. He glanced around, covertly checking for potential escape routes if the situation deteriorated any further.

He froze when he caught a glimpse of the newcomer. About fifty feet to his right, another figure stood on the same step, peering in all directions.

But not for an escape route. He was roughly Connor's age, standing stock-still as his gaze swept back and forth over the crowd. Connor averted his face at the last second, but not before catching sight of the red glow around his eye.

A Tracker—here? Connor's mouth went dry, and he heard his heart pounding in his ears. *We haven't activated any of our drones yet. There's nothing for him to scan.*

Connor moved to his left, anxious to remove himself from the volatile situation, and stopped short, eyes widening. A second Tracker, her scanning eye alight, stood an arms-length away, an over-stuffed backpack slung over one shoulder.

What—who—are they looking for? None of this makes sense.

The second Tracker, so close that Connor could see the pulse in her neck, jerked back without warning, her stoic expression morphing into stark terror.

Connor whipped his head around to see the first Tracker plowing across the crowd. His fixed stare, outlined in ominous red, didn't waver as he shoved people aside, ignoring their furious cries.

He's going to start a riot. Mob mentality is ready to boil over.

The first Tracker increased his pace, driving with relentless purpose through the human sea—in Connor's direction. If the second Tracker was terrified, the first possessed confidence to the point of recklessness.

Connor recognized the Tracker's predatory look, and his stomach knotted. *They're not spying on the protest. They're scanning for each other.*

The female Tracker clawed her way through the crowd, angling deeper into the amphitheater toward the terrace. The first Tracker altered course to intercept her, becoming more violent as he fought through the crowd. Indignant rebukes deteriorated into cries of pain and outrage.

Connor backed away, almost tripping over his own feet. He caught his balance, avoiding a fall at the last moment. His reaction was purely instinctive. He had to get away—*now*.

Two Trackers racing into the volatile crowd, converging toward the terrace and the protesters cornered there—the inevitable collision didn't bode well.

The first Tracker, slicing diagonally across the crowd, caught up to his target. His hand snaked out, claw-like, seizing the female Tracker by the shoulder.

Connor watched as the Tracker buried his fingers into her flesh and yanked her backward. Connor was sure he heard the sound of bones cracking.

The female Tracker half-turned, her face contorted by fear and agony. She swung her free arm at her assailant, but didn't strike him. Instead, she pulled him close in a fierce embrace. She squeezed her eyes shut, ducking her face against her fellow Tracker's shoulder.

Twin detonations rocked the amphitheater, the concussive explosions echoing between Gallery and Museum. The echoes died away, and stunned silence hung over the carnage for a suspended moment in time ... and then the screams began.

The crowd, panic-stricken and unreasoning, stampeded outward from the epicenter of the blast.

Connor fell to his knees, hands clasped over his ringing ears. *She blew herself up—caused a chain reaction.* He reeled as the implications of the two-pronged atrocity sank in. *How many Citizens died? Are the Givers trying to create hysteria?*

He struggled to his feet, sickened by the calculated slaughter, but savvy enough to join the fleeing throng. It was vital that he blend into the crowd, for the sake of the inevitable video review by the authorities.

Adrenaline and fury fueled his headlong flight, but his mind was remarkably clear. The Givers' heinous actions gave him all the answers he needed.

I'll play nice with the savages, at least until the aliens are gone. His stride lengthened, and his lips tightened into a grim smile. *And then, if any of the savages survive, they'll pay for what they did to Megan.*

SIXTEEN

"ARE YOU SERIOUS?" Amos hunched his shoulders and tucked his chin into his jacket collar, trying to stay warm. "*This* is your so-called secret entrance into Hoarderville?"

Mateo crouched beside him, taking shelter behind a wind-swept outcropping of jagged rocks. "Not *my* secret entrance, no," he replied, his voice a terse monotone. He gestured down the man-made channel, filled with churning ocean waves, to a gate at the far end. "This is one of Cascadia's main shipping seaports."

Cascadia's western boundary faced the Pacific Ocean, and a stiff offshore breeze magnified the pre-dawn chill. It had taken the better part of an hour, on foot, to reach their current vantage point. They'd followed a service road running parallel to the Enclave's southern border—abandoned, Mateo said, after construction of the wall was complete—until it terminated at the ocean. They'd camouflaged Mateo's truck as best they could before picking their way north over the rocky shoreline, to a marine gate.

"Shipping is a vital factor in Cascadia's economy," Mateo said, his voice barely audible over the pounding surf. "This port has existed since construction first began, two generations ago. I'm surprised it never occurred to you that Cascadia needs to import goods and raw materials."

"Of course, it occurred to us," Amos replied, resenting his patronizing remark. "We also know the marine gates are well-guarded. There wasn't any reason to waste time hiking over rocks just to remind ourselves."

"Cascadia has always taken advantage of the sea routes to facilitate the importing and exporting of goods," Mateo said, continuing as if he hadn't heard. He seemed content to settle into his favorite instructor role. "Some Enclaves don't have the good fortune to be situated on the coastline."

Amos rolled his eyes. "I hope this doesn't come as a shock," he replied, raising his voice to be heard, "but I've never been interested in *how* Hoarders do their hoarding. On the other hand, I *have* noticed its effect, up close and personal."

Mateo ignored his bitter comment. "You'll no doubt notice some similarities between the marine port and Gate Seven." He dug into his pack and pulled out a pair of binoculars, offering them to Amos.

"Not necessary," Amos said. He found his antique spyglass in his pack and trained it on the marine gate.

Steep rock walls flanked the channel on either side, a stark contrast to the pearl-smooth surface of Cascadia's walls. The sides of the passage were steep and devoid of vegetation, with the exception of a few stunted pines, clinging defiantly here and there on the rocky slopes.

Amos peered through his spyglass, adjusting the focus. The gate zoomed closer, revealing the stark details he expected to see. "It's got the same security as any other gate, which means guns. Lots of guns. What are they afraid of—a mutiny on one of their supply ships?"

"It was attempted once," Mateo replied, as if he relished answering the question. "A ship was commandeered, and its crew was more than willing to join the mutineers—the level of animosity toward the Enclave has always been high. Their attempt at storming the gate was an utter failure, and Cascadia's brutal retribution has been a most effective deterrent."

"And you expect us to work with people like that?" Amos lowered his spyglass, resentment simmering at Mateo's dispassionate recounting of yet another Hoarder atrocity. "I don't trust them, and I doubt they trust us, either. You've met Darcy—the guy's a psycho."

I saw it in his eyes. It's always in the eyes.

"The Givers are your common enemy." Mateo defaulted to his favorite mantra. "Why is this such a difficult concept? The Givers are preparing to embed security chips in every Cascadian Citizen. As a result, Darcy and his followers are desperate. They'll no longer be able to move about freely. They'll be totally dependent on your assistance."

A wave broke on the rocks, showering them in salty spray. Mateo continued as the water receded. "I brought you here to infiltrate the Enclave. But once inside, where will you go? Do you know the Givers' exact location, or the stronghold they've built—their 'Citadel'? Not every Citizen, or their Councilors, will appreciate our opposition to the Givers. Quite the contrary. People, in general, do not release their grip on power once they have it. The Council is no exception."

Amos bit back a hot retort.

Mateo cocked his head to one side. He sounded irritated.

"I could go on, but I believe I've made my point. Citizens and Runners need each other. This small-minded bickering is a distraction from focusing on our true enemy, the Givers."

"So, what's your plan?" Amos stowed his spyglass and shielded his eyes as the rising sun peaked over the Enclave. "If a ship full of mutineers couldn't get past the gate, I'm not sure what the two of us can accomplish on foot."

"Your tone of voice suggests a certain lack of confidence in my abilities," Mateo replied, his dark eyes unwavering. "Or at the very least, the absence of basic respect between us. Do you think I *haven't* taken all variables into account?"

You picked a fine time to stop talking in riddles. Amos looked away, biting his tongue to avoid an unhelpful jibe. He squinted at the sun's reflection on the ocean waves.

"Okay, okay, I get it," he said at last, lifting his hands in mock surrender. "The Givers are the real enemy. But we've got good reasons to hate Hoarders—between Implants and Trackers, we've lost friends and family. You can't expect us to stuff those memories as if they never happened."

And my brother's death is none of your business.

Mateo lifted his chin, looking at him from an odd angle, his expression unchanged. Amos spied a faint glow of red around his left eye.

"I was content in my life as a shopkeeper," he said, not breaking eye contact. "I was changed into a Tracker, against my will, to serve the Givers or be executed." The red circle winked out, restoring his human appearance. "Your craving for revenge is an enemy equal to the Givers. I ask nothing of you, that I do not also require from myself."

The wind gusted, bringing with it another dousing of spray. They remained at an impasse, crouched behind the rocks.

"I guess I owe you an apology," Amos said at last, finding it difficult to put into words. "I never ..."

Mateo stopped him with an upraised hand. "I do not seek an apology. You pay lip service to my belief that the Givers are our common enemy, but we are about to enter their fortress. Your distrust of me is an impediment. Once we're inside, the danger increases. Second-guessing my every move is as risky to me as it is to you."

Amos felt his cheeks burn. *Busted, mid-apology.*

"Maybe I owe you two apologies." He exhaled, watching for Mateo's reaction. He gave none. "All right, here's the short version. Garr's right—this can't be about revenge. And you and I need to present a united front inside the Enclave." The words were difficult to speak with conviction. "I'll do whatever's necessary inside Cascadia, and you and I will act as a team. I give you my word."

Mateo dipped his head in a slight bow. "Agreed."

Amos looked past him, peeking over the craggy ridge at the formidable weaponry above the gate. "Since you've considered all the variables, what's the plan for sneaking into Hoarderville, if not by sea?"

Mateo eyed him, not turning to look down the channel. "I trust your ability to feign sincerity will improve with practice."

SEVENTEEN ⊙

MATEO TURNED HIS BACK on the channel, gesturing for Amos to follow. He scrambled over the algae-slicked rocks, splashing ankle-deep in seawater.

Amos followed, surprised they were retracing their steps. In less than a minute, the fortified gate was no longer visible, hidden from view by the rocky terrain.

If we can't see the gate, Cascadia Security can't see us. The thought did little to reassure him.

Mateo crept along the water's edge, testing each step. The rocks were coated with algae, strands of kelp, and sharp-edged barnacles—the perfect recipe for a disastrous injury.

Amos noticed, for the first time, small pockets and clefts worn into the rocks by years of erosion. At high tide, everything would be submerged. Mateo seemed particularly interested in the exposed cavities. Amos's pulse quickened as his imagination suggested a reason for Mateo's studious inspection.

Mateo pulled off his pack, clutching it to his chest as he squatted and crab-walked under a starfish-covered ledge. Amos crouched to peer inside, and hunched low to make his own awkward way into the gap.

A few yards inside, he discovered he could stand upright. He took two quick steps and almost collided with Mateo in the semi-darkness. Waves washed against the shoreline, creating a hollow, muted echo. The dripping alcove reeked of seaweed and decaying marine life.

To his amazement, he found Mateo standing before a barnacle-encrusted wall, clearly of Hoarder design. An oblong hatch, with a circular handle set dead-center, glistened wetly in the subdued light.

Mateo pointed at the sealed portal, no trace of gloating in his voice. "*This* is our secret entrance into Cascadia."

Amos was surprised at how easily the handle spun under Mateo's coaxing. He noticed the hatch's smooth metal surface, a marked contrast to the crusty wall surrounding it.

This is a recent addition.

Mateo tugged on the handle, and the hatch swung outward into the tiny cavern. He signaled to Amos, who ducked his head and stepped over the high threshold. Mateo followed, pulling the hatch shut in one fluid, soundless motion. He spun the handle, and the clandestine entrance was secured.

Amos inhaled the humid air, grateful to be away from the malodorous seaweed. His eyes adjusted to the gloom and he realized they were in a natural fissure in the bedrock. The edges were smooth, obviously due to machining, leaving a narrow crevice, just large enough to squeeze through.

"The marine gate is just around the corner," he said, unable to contain his curiosity. "How could the Hoarders not know about this?"

Mateo twisted as if to squeeze into the crevice, but paused

to face him. He cocked his head to one side, studying Amos in the cavern's murky twilight.

Amos was startled to realize their only light source came from Mateo's scanning eye. He hastened to add, "I'm not second-guessing you. I'm just curious."

Mateo nodded at the crevice. "This geological formation has existed since before the earliest construction of the Enclave. If you'll follow me, all will become clear."

"That hatch is new." Amos jerked a thumb over his shoulder. "There's no way it's been here, underwater, since Hoarderville was built. It'd be covered in seaweed and starfish."

Mateo gave no reply as he entered the crevice, navigating a sloping descent over the rough-chiseled stone. Amos hurried after him, suddenly aware he had no artificial light source of his own.

He felt, and heard, a metallic surface under his questing foot as he exited the crevice. He looked past Mateo's silhouette and his mouth dropped open. They stood on a metal catwalk, high above a massive cavern that housed Cascadia's power plant.

The lighting system—blue-tinged and set in a narrow grid just below the catwalk floor—provided scant illumination, but enough to reveal row after row of generators, turbines, and other machines Amos couldn't begin to identify.

The catwalk stretched along a machine-tooled wall, fading gradually into the murky twilight. Amos tore his eyes away to find Mateo studying him, his scanning eye extinguished.

"The rationale for not sealing the crevice is unknown to me." He spoke before Amos could ask. "We're fortunate to have discovered it." He slung his pack over his shoulder and adopted a brisk pace along the catwalk. Amos was left, once again, with no option but to follow.

"How did *you* find that hatch?" he asked as he caught up, matching Mateo's longer strides.

Mateo slowed, glancing at him with mild amusement. "I'm a Tracker. I followed them."

"Followed who?" Amos frowned. His question was sharper than he intended, and he cringed at the echoes he raised.

Mateo didn't seem to notice or care. "Runners with active Implants," he replied without inflection. "They must infiltrate Cascadia in order to carry out their assignments. This is their entry point. The location of the hatch is programmed into them when their Implants activate."

"Assignments. You mean, assassinations." Amos quashed a surge of renewed bitterness. "Programmed? You mean Darcy knows about it? Why aren't the Givers guarding it? You'd think they'd station a Tracker here, to take out anyone using it."

Mateo resumed his pace, his footsteps evoking no echoes. "Darcy is on the Council," he replied cryptically.

Mateo the tour guide—he loves laying out the clues. "You're saying Darcy knows about it, and uses his Council position to make sure it *stays* secret—and unguarded. The Givers know nothing about the hatch."

"Darcy ordered its installation," Mateo replied. "The average Citizen holds the maintenance level in cultural contempt. The existence of the hatch is quite secret."

Amos nodded, impressed in spite of himself. The cavern was huge, and obviously not natural. The sheer number of complex installations visible below the catwalk's metal grating was mind-boggling.

"I'm pleased to see your improvement in assimilating new information," Mateo said, resuming his previous pace. His footsteps were silent on the metal grating. "Colonel Scott must be congratulated on his team. When your emotions are kept in check, you've each shown a remarkable ability to think."

"You're not very good at giving compliments," Amos replied with a wry smile. "Assuming that's your intent. I guess Trackers have their own secret exit when they're hunting us."

"Not necessary," Mateo replied he arrived at a set of stairs, little more than a steep ladder, and began climbing. "Trackers conduct 'official business' on the Council's behalf. They enjoy the same access to numbered gates as any freeborn Citizen." He paused to look over his shoulder, a rare grin lighting his face. "The newest recruit in Cascadia Security knows better than to interfere with a Tracker on a Quest."

EIGHTEEN ◉

AMOS CAUGHT UP to Mateo at the base of a second short staircase. He paused to catch his breath, glancing at the humming machinery, and frowned. "It's not as dark as before. Does that mean what I think it means?"

"Another workday is about to commence," Mateo replied, his expression neutral. He surveyed the complex maze below. "We have a narrow window of time between low tide and the beginning of the day shift. Those fortunate enough to secure work permits will soon arrive to begin their service to the Enclave."

Amos bristled at the idea. *The Hoarders must enjoy watching them beg for work, and then sending the "lucky" ones into this dungeon to do jobs they won't.* "Let's not forget the Hoarders also throw them back outside once their shift's over. Anything to remind us they hold all the power."

"The economic and social inequities are secondary concerns." Mateo waved an arm in the general direction of the machinery. He resumed his relentless journey. "Don't allow your emotions to distract you."

Amos took a deep breath and scrambled after him. The lighting grid emitted a series of pops and clicks, and the luminance increased at an accelerated rate. They came to another landing, and Mateo set a punishing pace along a second catwalk, following the curve of the wall.

This route is familiar to him. Amos frowned as he weighed the implications. *I'm not the first Runner he's snuck into Hoarderville.* His mouth was dry as he jogged after Mateo, his earlier suspicions reawakened.

The sounds of human activity wafted up to his ears. Muted conversations, orders issued, the trudge of many feet, and an ever-increasing mechanical cacophony as the power plant scaled up to a higher operational level.

The lighting grid flared to near-daylight intensity, illuminating rows of hulking machinery. Shift supervisors invaded the cavern, leading a steady stream of day-permit workers across the massive space—in their direction. There was nowhere to hide on the catwalk. They were exposed.

Sweat broke out on his forehead. *The day-permit workers might not betray us, but their overseers—the ones barking orders— must be loyal to the Enclave.*

He said as much to Mateo, finding it necessary to raise his voice over the steadily-rising noise as additional machines were brought online.

Mateo didn't slow his brisk gait. "This catwalk is inaccessible from below. The workers, and their overseers, will assume we've been sent on some official errand. It is unlikely they will raise an alarm."

Amos was not expecting Mateo's sudden halt, and barely avoided a collision. Mateo faced a closed panel in the wall, the tight seal rendering its outline all but invisible. The panel hissed as it slid back and away. The narrow opening provided just enough clearance for Mateo to squeeze through, followed immediately by Amos.

Mateo closed the door panel, muffling the industrial noise. Amos found himself in a long room, adorned on either side by storage lockers. The interior lighting was cold and artificial, underlining the room's sterile pragmatism.

Eastside Hub is more welcoming. Amos felt a familiar tension between his shoulder blades. *The stakes just got higher. Again.*

"Say nothing." Mateo fixed a stern gaze on him. The red circle under his skin flared to full intensity. "No questions, no comments, nothing. I am a Tracker, and you must play the part of my prisoner. We may encounter a few minor Citizens between us and our goal. We cannot arouse suspicion."

"And our goal is what, exactly?" Amos's temper flared. He was *inside Hoarderville*. "Feel free to be specific."

Mateo cocked his head to one side, his posture as abnormal as the red circle around his eye. "A parking garage, several levels above this one," he said, as if their destination should be obvious. "The Enclave is far too large to travel on foot. It's necessary to commandeer transportation to facilitate our foray."

"Translation: we're going to steal a Hoarder vehicle." Amos nodded. "And go where?"

"To pay Councilor Peterson a visit." Mateo seemed surprised by the question. "Garr and Sheila guided the Citizens to safety after the Tracker ambush. Darcy would insist on reciprocating by bringing them into Cascadia." He paused, looking pensive. "He would also be inclined to keep them here indefinitely, but our arrival should loosen his grasp."

Amos stared at him, pleasantly surprised. "I'm relieved to hear you don't blindly trust Darcy."

Mateo grimaced. "This alliance must survive. That doesn't mean we're required to walk blindfolded into a snake pit." He pulled his cap lower over his face, gesturing for Amos to copy his action. He complied, dreading the prospect of seeing Darcy again—on Hoarder turf.

"Keep your eyes on the ground in front of you," Mateo said as he strode to the far end of the room. He opened the door, peering cautiously in both directions. Satisfied, he seized Amos by the arm and dragged him into the corridor. "The eyes and ears of the Givers are everywhere. Keep your head down, and say nothing unless I permit it."

Amos pulled his cap lower, finding it easy to imitate a prisoner accompanying his captor. *Next stop, Darcy's living room. There's no anti-venom kit for that.*

* * *

THE ELEVATOR ROSE—smooth, silent—hauling them skyward to the twentieth floor. Amos shoved his hands deep into his pockets, keeping his gaze on the carpeted floor.

So, this is what a functioning elevator feels like.

His stomach fluttered as the elevator car came to a stop, the momentary weightlessness catching him unaware.

Their journey through the maze of corridors beneath the Enclave had been completed without incident. Amos lost all sense of direction as they took multiple twists and turns. They might be traveling in circles, but he had no choice except to trust Mateo. The few Citizens they encountered ignored them, acting as if both he and Mateo were invisible. Amos suspected the red glare around Mateo's eye could account for their studied indifference.

Mateo needed less than thirty seconds to steal a Hoarder vehicle from an underground parking garage.

Amos was unable to stifle a gasp when they exited the garage and joined the mechanized insanity that was the vehicle level. He counted twenty lanes of traffic, each vehicle locked in maniacal competition with their equally aggressive counterparts. The contrast to the Old City's empty and pot-holed streets was jarring.

Mateo kept to the outer lanes, beneath a massive overhang. He called it a "pedestrian level," in response to Amos's breathless inquiry. The overhang prevented him from seeing more of the bustling anthill of humanity inside Cascadia.

Just as well. Amos hated to admit it. *I looked like a gawking savage until Mateo reminded me to keep my head down.*

The elevator doors parted and they stepped into a climate-controlled hallway. Plush carpet cushioned their footsteps, and indirect lighting fixtures gave the polished wood a gleaming warmth.

Mateo guided him to one of the many look-alike doors lining the opulent hallway. A small digital panel glowed faintly beside the door, waist-high. Mateo pressed a button, clasping his hands behind his back as they waited.

Relax. Amos inhaled several slow, steady breaths, resisting the urge to hunch his shoulders. *Sure, you're about to step into Darcy's personal domain, but hidden in plain sight still applies.*

The door hissed open, retracting horizontally into the wall, and his jaw dropped.

"Good welcome, Citizens." Sheila stepped away from the open door, waving them inside with a wide sweep of her arm. "Won't you come in?"

NINETEEN ◉

THE STEEP ASCENT was daunting. Megan's leg muscles burned by the time they gained the crest of the hill. She was grateful when Don signaled a halt to catch their breath.

She leaned against the rough bark of the nearest tree, filling her lungs with the brisk air. Any distraction was preferable to the nightmare triggered by the dead Tracker.

Don straightened without comment, turning away from the brink of the cliff. Their brief respite, it appeared, was over. Jane followed in his wake, pushing aside low-hanging branches. Megan trailed just far enough behind to avoid the branches as they swung back.

The rocky valley they'd scaled was forested primarily with evergreens. The plateau, in contrast, boasted an eclectic profusion of maple, hemlock, and dogwood trees, interspersed with a few jack pines and cedars.

Megan noted the botanical change in a detached manner, as if another part of her mind was at work—categorizing, sifting, and evaluating new data. Analyze. Adapt.

No. Her face twisted as she rebelled against Tracker thinking patterns. *No more Givers. I am Megan.*

She spat on the ground. Her action was, in part, a symbolic rejection of her former programming. It was also an attempt to purge the aftertaste of vomit.

"You okay, Megan?" Jane pushed a branch aside for an unobstructed view. She seemed suspicious, although Megan also detected a note of feigned concern in her voice.

"Fine." Megan waved a casual hand as she pushed through the underbrush. *Don't patronize me. I'm not fragile.*

Jane studied her as she drew near, and then continued on Don's trail. Megan quickened her pace, anxious to prove her breakdown by the Tracker's corpse was behind her.

The truck engine bellowed to life as she emerged from the bushes. She sidled up beside Jane, who ignored her as they waited for Don to turn the truck around.

The overgrown brush on either side of the unpaved road forced him to execute a series of incremental turns, raising a choking swirl of dust. She held her breath against the gritty cloud as Don skidded to a halt.

Jane took the passenger side in the front. Megan scooted across the rear bench, seating herself behind Don. The big man shifted into gear, and the truck crawled forward.

"Well, Enrico can start breathing again," Jane said lightly. She grinned, turning to face Don, one arm flung casually over the bench seat. "He'll get his truck back before sundown, and all in one piece."

Don grunted. His thoughts appeared to be elsewhere.

"Lighten up, Don. That was a joke." Jane punched his shoulder. "And it was funny."

He glanced at her and focused on the dirt road. "Amos is

too smart to engage a Tracker single-handed," he said. "And judging by the angle of the wound, the Tracker was struck from above. If I was a gambler, I'd wager Mateo was involved."

Megan's stomach lurched at the mention of the deceased Tracker. She swallowed hastily.

He died serving the Givers. She struggled to reconcile the conflicting emotions. *But in a way, he was dead long before his life ended.*

She flexed her hand, fascinated by the opening and closing of her fingers. She regretted the loss of her enhancements—the strength, the speed, the stamina. Her body functioned much as it once had, before …

She frowned as the image of the anonymous hand, twin processors cupped in its palm, invaded her thoughts.

"Megan? Are you okay?" Jane's interruption rasped on her nerves. Megan shifted position to evaluate her.

Jane's body language was casual, one arm flung across the bench seat, but her eyes were watchful, attentive. She'd seen the expression on Megan's face, observed the beads of sweat breaking out by her hairline.

How can I explain myself? Frustration gnawed at her. The nightmarish recollection of the day she'd become a Tracker—even if merely an incomplete fragment—how could she possibly describe it? Megan concentrated, willing her thoughts into coherent speech. She reached up to touch the side of her head.

"Same. I have." She ground the words out in short, sharp bursts. She hoped Don or Jane could fill in the blanks, make sense of what she said. "Not working, but same."

"The dead Tracker," Jane said, her voice remote, her gaze shrewd. "The tech we saw inside its head—you have the same, but it doesn't work anymore."

Megan nodded and Jane eyed her with new interest. "I'll bet seeing that tech brought back a few memories."

Don growled something under his breath. Jane shot him a resentful look, but fell silent.

Megan nodded again. Her wavy hair feel forward, partially obscuring the patch over her scanning eye. She decided against trying to explain the nightmare memory—the concept was too complex. There was something else her companions needed to know. *Let's see if this works.*

She pointed to her eyepatch, flexed her bicep, and indicated her eye a second time. Jane frowned, shaking her head as she tried to interpret her improvisations.

"Givers. Change," Megan said, repeating her actions. "My eye, body …"

Jane nodded. "You mean your Tracker enhancements? To make you stronger, enable your body to repair itself?"

Megan pointed at her with an enthusiastic nod. So far, so good. She forced her uncooperative lips to form the words, hoping for a sudden burst of clarity. "Change. Animal dead—wrong change."

Don stiffened noticeably. Jane twisted sideways, leaning over the seat, her eyes searching Megan's face. "The animals were changing. Into what—Trackers?" Jane frowned, her skepticism plain. "Do you mean the Givers are experimenting on animals, too?"

Megan shook her head. No. Emphatically, *no.* In a flash of inspiration, she opened her mouth as wide as she could, and brought her teeth together in a sharp *bite*, hoping against hope Jane would make the connection.

"Animal, change," she said, and snapped her teeth together a second time.

Jane's eyes widened. "The scavengers died because they tried eating the Tracker." She caught her breath at Megan's relieved smile. "You're saying the enhancements killed them."

Megan tapped the side of her head. "Not complete," she said, pleased she was getting through. *If I had paper and pencil, this would be a lot easier.*

Don spoke for the first time. "The enhancements must be a package deal." The truck's sudden acceleration underlined his reaction to the news. "Whatever the Givers put into a Tracker's blood was too much for the animals. It's possible the tech in a red-eye's brain acts as a regulator."

Jane looked to Megan for confirmation, but she gave a noncommittal shrug.

"I don't think Megan knows *how* it works, just that it does." Jane settled into her seat, massaging the back of her neck. She bolted forward without warning, pivoting to stare at Megan. "Blood." The connection was made. "Darcy designed Implants based on the same technology the Givers use to make Trackers. We've always said 'it's in the blood.' Doc saw it under her microscope, but no one could figure out how it worked."

Don lifted one hand from the steering wheel and brought it down with a resounding *thump*. "And Garr expects us to partner with a psycho like Darcy? It's like inviting the Grim Reaper over for Thanksgiving."

The miles flew by, and they arrived at the highway sooner than expected. Don slowed to make the turn from gravel to pavement. The aging highway was devoid of traffic. He accelerated, and the chassis rattled in protest.

"The Givers use their tech to control the Trackers," Jane said, staring out the windshield as if she hadn't heard Don's bitter remark. "And Runners, once their Implants activate, are driven to assassinate specific targets. In both cases, it spreads through the blood. But for animals, it's lethal." She leaned forward, dropping her head into her hands. "Darcy is pure evil. Brilliant, but evil."

Don's only response was an inarticulate growl as he drove the aging truck down the highway. Outlying farms became visible as they neared a small town. They weren't far from Enrico's shop.

"So, in other words, never turn my back on Darcy." Don's somber gaze found Megan in the rearview mirror. "Or take a bite out of a Tracker. You'll be relieved to hear I have zero intention of doing either."

Megan said nothing, recalling Darcy from their meeting in the Old City, and the blond teenager at his side. The one who'd called her by name.

She wondered what the connection was.

TWENTY ⌖

KENASTON MILLER, "Kenny" among his coworkers at the office, awoke slowly. He felt groggy, lethargic. He moved to swipe a hand over his face, his motion instinctive.

Annoyance flared when he failed to complete the gesture. Annoyance gave way to apprehension. His arm—no, *both* arms —were pinned, motionless, at his sides. He forced his eyes open, squinting into a blurry haze of light above his head.

He lay on a bed. Or a table, Kenny decided, after the unyielding surface refused to adapt to his body weight. He tried but couldn't move. Restraints of some kind achored his arms and legs to the table. Apprehension escalated quickly into panic, and his heart thundered in his ears.

He heard voices speaking nearby, muffled, indistinct, almost as if he were underwater. A cloying odor—honey mixed with sulfur—filled his nostrils. He fought dizziness, struggling to regain his mental equilibrium. His vision began to clear, bit by bit, as well as his hearing.

Am I in a hospital? Why can't I move?

His narrow victory over blind panic was short-lived. A new and terrifying sensation invaded his body, as if hundreds of burning insects crawled with military precision under his skin. He opened his mouth to scream, but no sound escaped.

The crawling sensation accelerated, circling his torso, and ceased abruptly. A refreshing coolness flooded from his shoulders to his feet, and he gasped in relief. The lights above his head gradually resolved into focus. A ring of surgical lamps, harsh and revealing.

I was right. I'm in a hospital.

Panic erupted anew at the sudden clamor inside his head. It seemed to come from within, a jumbled cacophony of discordant notes. It was like hearing voices without knowing the language, interspersed with odd clicking noises that sounded remotely mechanical.

Bile surged in his throat, and he swallowed several times in quick succession. Sweat beaded on his forehead, and he willed his rebellious stomach to settle.

His hearing was improving. He understood the sharp, exasperated outburst just to his left. In precise, clipped English. "This one's defective. The Givers—he can't hear them." A woman's voice, dour, her words clear but incomprehensible.

What—who are the Givers?

The speaker leaned over him, an angry scowl twisting her features. She wore a physician's attire, but her surgical mask was pulled below her chin, revealing a down-turned mouth as she examined him.She was not pleased.

A second figure appeared to Kenny's right, gazing down at him. He was also outfitted for the operating theater. His surgical mask, with its accompanying cap, hid most of his features from view. He seemed less volatile than the first speaker.

"Not another one." His voice was flat and dismissive, his eyes cold and distant.

She glared at him, as if he were accusing her of malpractice. "I'm the surgeon. I didn't invent the technology, I just perform the procedure. If the manufacturers made a production error, take it up with them."

"Perhaps you'd like to inform them yourself, Dr. Campbell," the man replied calmly. He inclined his head, indicating the opposite end of the operating table.

All eyes—including the table's restrained subject—shifted to the foot of the table. The surgeon stiffened and fell silent, averting her gaze.

A cluster of alien creatures stood in stoic silence, observing. They wore no surgical gear. Kenny's stomach heaved without warning. His reflexes failed, and the surgeon dodged away, her voice raised in disgusted protest as he vomited over the side of the operating table.

Kenny stared into the circle of lights, silently pleading, as if the glare could somehow purge the nightmare image of the creatures. A new resurgence of alien voices—poking, prodding, crawling like mechanical spiders over his brain. None of the words made sense, and he collapsed in limp relief when the sensations abruptly ceased.

"There's no point," a new voice said, detached and clinical. A young male, dressed in a white lab coat, consulted a handheld device with an expert's eye. "His brain appears incapable of accepting the programming. Everything else seems to be in working order, except he can't hear the Givers."

The alien nightmares pivoted in perfect synchronicity and departed in a vertigo-inducing swirl of motion. No one spoke until after the unmistakable *click* of a door was heard.

The technician made a series of adjustments on the device in his hand, frowning at the results. "Maybe it was a mistake to try this on a Citizen." He hesitated, as if expecting a rebuke. "He can't be controlled."

"Then he's useless." Dr. Campbell turned away, removing her surgical gloves with short, angry motions.

"Not necessarily," the older man replied, his features still hidden behind the surgical mask. "The rest of the tech is functional, correct, Ethan?"

His question was directed to the young technician, who nodded twice. Yes.

The masked man gave Kenny an appraising look. "Take him somewhere public, the more crowded the better." He spoke with the casual confidence of a man accustomed to having his orders obeyed without question. "Another protest, if possible. Plant him in the crowd. Push the button."

Ethan tucked the device into a pocket of his lab coat. "As you wish, Councilor."

TWENTY-ONE

AUBREY TUGGED THE HOOD of her jacket forward, thankful for the light drizzle of rain. *Bad weather gives me an excuse to cover up. Plus, there's less people on the street to notice me.*

She was grateful that Garr had included her on his regular rounds in Eastside's neighborhood. She knew the exact location and protocol for accessing the dropbox. She was careful to make the customary stop at the market, browsing and chatting with a few merchants before resuming her casual route.

Eastside Mission, a block ahead and across the street, appeared gray and lifeless in the rain. The usual crowd of regulars were indoors today, seeking shelter from the cold and damp.

Doc Simon wasn't thrilled about the idea of Aubrey visiting the dropbox alone, but she'd argued, successfully, that it was unwise to break their routine. Doc relented, albeit with obvious reluctance.

Garr has a bad cough. Aubrey rehearsed her alibi, in case anyone asked. One of the shopkeepers they knew, perhaps. *I'm going to make him some hot soup.*

They were always careful to follow the same routine. Garr's patient coaching came to mind. *Look casual, but never let your guard down. Trackers look normal unless they're hunting.*

Aubrey quickened her pace. A bag of vegetables she'd purchased weighed her arm down. The dreary weather painted the neighborhood with stifling, claustrophobic hues. She'd made this trip before, several times, but this was her first solo.

There weren't many people out and about, but she watched diligently for any telltale signs. The Tracker raid had occurred more than twelve blocks from the Mission, but her nerves were still on edge.

Rain seeped through the fabric of her hood, plastering her bangs to her forehead. She shivered and brushed the hair away from her face, cupping her scarred hand over her eyes. She tightened her grip on the produce bag and slipped into the alley, darting toward the boarded-up doorway.

She ducked under the overhang as if seeking refuge from the drizzle. *Hidden in plain sight.* She mouthed the words. *Just taking a little break out of the rain.*

She crouched, balancing on the balls of her feet, and placed her bag of produce on the slick pavement. Out of the corner of her eye, she spied a dark figure moving at the end of the alley. She held her breath, mindful to lower her gaze so she wasn't staring. *Easy, Aubs. Don't draw attention, don't stand out.*

The figure shuffled out of sight, and the patter of rain obscured his or her footsteps. Eastside Mission was a block further north—was that the anonymous walker's goal?

Aubrey waited, counting off three seconds under her breath, as she'd been taught. The rain droned on, pattering on the uneven paving stones. She waited, motionless, until she was confident the other was a safe distance away.

She edged the brick out, her action shielded from view by the deep entryway. As she expected, a small, leather-wrapped package lay nestled inside. *See, Doc? This trip was necessary.*

She extracted the package and maneuvered the brick back into place, wiping away any trace of her actions. The package was thinner than usual, and Aubrey hesitated, doubt eroding her earlier confidence. *What if it's empty? Doc won't be impressed if I made this trip for nothing.*

She ignored the inner clamor of warning and, disregarding their usual protocol, opened the package right then and there. Inside was a single sheaf of parchment, its lettering bold and ragged. The message was short and blunt. She felt dizzy as the words sunk in. She swallowed convulsively, sealed the package and stuffed it inside her jacket for safe-keeping.

She glanced down the alley, half-expecting to find the shuffling figure had returned. No, her luck continued to hold—the alley remained empty. She was alone, at least for now.

She leaned against the doorframe, feigning nonchalance for a few additional seconds, and set off at a brisk pace for the opposite end of the alley. *Walk, Aubs, don't run.*

She risked a quick, furtive look in both directions before rounding the corner. Pedestrians ignored her as they scuttled across the street to various dry destinations. She kept walking, pulling her hood forward to disguise the number of times she gauged her surroundings.

Is that thunder? Aubrey slowed to listen, her nerves frayed. No, the rumbling noise wasn't natural. It was mechanical—the roar of a heavy engine. And it was drawing closer. *Hoarders.*

She broke into a run, splashing through the puddles.

The roar of over-charged engines reverberated off the dilapidated buildings. Aubrey—every survival instinct in play—

dodged into another alley and flattened herself against a brick wall. She cringed, wondering if she was the Hoarders' target.

Bulky all-terrain vehicles, windows tinted black and opaque, roared past her, oversized tires splashing gouts of water over the sidewalk. The water splattered not far from her feet.

Aubrey counted three—no, *four*—Hoarder vehicles in an ominous convoy, each identical to the one preceding it. Their occupants were safely anonymous, hidden behind tinted windows. The convoy careened, one by one, around a corner some six blocks away, accelerating toward their unknown destination. She listened with bated breath until the guttural engine noise faded.

Her jacket succumbed to the persistent rain, and a cold rivulet of water snaked down her spine. She stepped timidly out of the alley, still unsure if she was the object of pursuit.

The steady drone of rain greeted her. She was alone.

She tightened her grip on the produce bag, relieved to find she hadn't dropped it. After one last stealthy look, she slipped out of the alley, intent on the hidden access for Eastside Hub.

She took her time, mindful to watch her back trail.

* * *

AUBREY RUSHED into the infirmary. She expected to find Doc Simon puttering at her worktable, but the room was empty. She trotted down the corridor, her waterlogged shoes squishing in sodden protest.

She heard voices ahead, and her spirits lifted. Don, Megan, and Snake Lady had returned during her absence.

Don's boisterous laugh greeted her as she burst through the half-open door to the mess hall. "Wow, and here I thought *we* looked like drowned rats."

Jane cradled a cup of the chicory root beverage they called

"coffee," warming her hands without actually sipping the steaming liquid. Her eyes widened when she saw Aubrey. "Something happened. I can tell."

Aubrey pulled the package out of her jacket. The leather felt damp, but its contents were untouched by the elements. She unwound the strap with trembling fingers and read the blunt message, her words rushing together. "South Central overrun by Trackers. Trust no one. Risk no contact." She brushed her damp hair away from her eyes. "It's unsigned."

An aura of crippling dread filled the mess hall.

Jane broke the silence. "Unsigned … so we can't confirm the source. What if it's a trick, to isolate the Hubs from each other?"

"Whoever left that message knew where to find our dropbox," Doc Simon said, crossing her arms. "That means one of two things. Either the source is legitimate, or the location of our dropbox has been compromised."

"There's more," Aubrey said. "I saw a convoy of Hoarder trucks—four of them—just a few blocks from Eastside Mission. They're up to something."

"South Central overrun." Don's hand dropped to the hilt of his combat knife. "Trust no one, eh? And Hoarders running a convoy not far from here." He exhaled heavily. "Looks like we're on our own."

Aubrey slumped into a chair, her soggy attire forgotten. *And Garr, Sheila, and Amos are still missing.*

TWENTY-TWO ◎

HERE WE GO AGAIN. Amos steeled himself for a second stand-off with the Hoarders.

He recovered from the initial shock of seeing Sheila dressed like a high-and-mighty Hoarder, welcoming them into Darcy's apartment—or villa, as the Hoarders called them. Questions flooded his mind, but the mere sight of Darcy quenched any desire to ask.

"Amos." Garr bolted forward in his chair, his look of shock morphing into genuine relief. "How did you get past Gate Seven security?"

Everything about the scene was surreal. Garr sat in a comfortable chair, opposite Darcy, before a massive stone fireplace. The flames weren't natural—the hearth was sealed behind tempered glass. Garr was also dressed in Hoarder attire.

Mateo pushed past Amos, raising his hands in a cautionary gesture. "Good welcome, Colonel Scott. My apologies for preempting Amos's reply. I must insist on a certain level of privacy regarding my visits to Councilor Peterson."

Amos kept his mouth shut. *This isn't a typical Eastside debrief. We're in enemy territory.*

"Ah, the voice of the all-knowing Tracker speaks." Darcy's mild voice was edged with contempt. He stood to his feet, his pale eyes alive with malice. "Is there no 'good welcome' for me, as well, Mr. Reyes?"

Mateo ducked his head in a slight bow, a show of deference that caught Amos by surprise. "I meant no disrespect, Councilor. Privacy is my best defense against the Givers."

Very smooth. Amos gave him credit for a strategic answer. *Remind him about the Givers, our common enemy.* He couldn't help but be impressed by Mateo's dogged insistence in bolstering their uneasy alliance.

He also made a mental note to question Mateo later. For some reason, the cagey Tracker didn't want Darcy to know they'd found his secret entrance to the maintenance level. *He wants Darcy to think there's more than one way to sneak into Cascadia. Why—to keep him off-balance?*

He tensed when he realized Darcy's eyes were now on him.

"You're the one they call Amos," Darcy said, as if confronted with a problem requiring a solution. "Garr and Sheila have told me some *fascinating* stories about you. Carving out your own Implant—I didn't think your kind were capable of such dramatic action."

Amos gritted his teeth, feeling heat rise in his cheeks at Darcy's undisguised scorn. "Would you like to see what kind of drama I'm capable of?" He took a step forward, hands balled into fists. "I thought you Hoarders were desperate for help from 'my kind.'"

An enraged voice interrupted from the opposite side of the room. "Mind your tongue, *savage*."

Amos whirled to locate the speaker, and spotted the gray-haired Hoarder who'd been at Darcy's side during their ill-fated meeting. He occupied a straight-backed chair, one hand resting casually on a Hoarder rifle. The muzzle of the weapon was angled midway between Amos and Mateo.

"Stand down, Tony." Darcy's command had the effect of a whip on bare skin. "That's no way to speak to our new allies."

Amos whipped his head around, his blood boiling at Darcy's open smirk. Sheila caught his eye, shaking her head imperceptibly. Beneath her serene expression, Amos sensed anxiety, saw it in the subtle tightness around her eyes.

Bide your time. His inner voice jumped into the fray. *You've got no idea what progress the colonel's made. Don't blow it for everyone.*

Amos unclenched his fists. *Good advice, Gabriel. For once.*

Garr lanced the festering tension. He remained seated on the edge of his chair, his calm demeanor bringing equilibrium to the volatile standoff. "Amos, what happened to the rest of the team? Sheila and I were preoccupied with getting the Citizens out of harm's way—"

"Where *are* my manners?" Darcy interrupted, spreading his arms in a magnanimous gesture. "Please, come and sit with us. We have much to discuss."

A psycho and a narcissist. Amos eyed the him warily. *He can't stand not being the center of attention.*

Darcy returned to his chair, opposite Garr, reaching for a large bottle of an unknown liquid. He tugged at the stopper, and it acquiesced with a wet *pop.* Darcy refilled his glass and glanced at Sheila with a sly grin. "Sheila, would you be a dear, and bring us some ice? You *do* remember how to find the kitchen, don't you?"

Amos watched as Sheila, eyes averted, walked stiffly out of the gathering room and into the kitchen. Mateo took a chair across from the two sitting by the fire. Amos noticed Mateo subtly maneuvering his chair to a spot between Garr and the trigger-happy Tony.

Sheila returned, placing a tray on the table. Darcy used a pair of tongs to add ice to his drink, as well as Garr's. He didn't offer anything to Mateo. Amos moved to join them.

"Not you, Amos." Darcy held up an imperious hand. "Forgive my bluntness, but this is *my* villa. Sheila can show you where the shower is, and provide you with clean clothes. *Then* you have permission to sit on my furniture." He leaned back in his chair, twirling the amber liquid in his glass, watching Amos with a cunning smile.

Stung, Amos looked to Garr. Colonel Scott returned his gaze with steady calm. "Perhaps you should take him up on his offer," he said, his soft voice at odds with the sharp look in his eyes. *Later*, Amos could almost hear him say.

He acquiesced with a curt nod, and followed Sheila out of the gathering room.

"Nice Hoarder outfit," he said *sotto voce* as he caught up to her. "How does it feel to be Darcy's personal servant?"

Sheila halted, pivoting to face him, her eyes fiery.

Amos knew he'd gone too far. "Sheila, I apologize. I shouldn't have said that." He gestured around the opulent villa. "Everything about this has me on edge. Darcy—"

"Is the enemy," she interrupted, cutting his fumbling apology short. "And as long as the Givers are around, he's also our ally. Have you ever heard of 'hidden in plain sight,' Amos? Well, it looks a little different *inside* the Enclave."

Amos nodded, chagrined. *I deserved that one.*

She led him to a closet, pulling out a shrink-wrapped set of clothes and measuring it against him. "This should come close. Leave your clothes in the washroom. I'll get them cleaned for you. Darcy owes us that much, at least." She gave him a tired smile, her mood lightening slightly. "It's been an unusual couple of days, to put it mildly. I'll fill you in later. Just get cleaned up, and don't keep our 'host' waiting."

She ushered him into a washroom nearly as large as Eastside's mess hall.

"Darcy's not stupid," Sheila said as she pulled the door shut. "You don't have to pretend you like the alliance. But whatever you do, don't cross him. Darcy's not just an average Hoarder. He's the twisted genius who invented Implants by reverse-engineering tech he stole from the Givers."

The door was open a mere crack. All Amos could see was one of her eyes, and for a disturbing moment, he pictured Megan's disfigured face.

"And he's nuts," Sheila whispered. "A raving sociopath."

The eyes. Amos felt a familiar quiver in his gut as she closed the door with a firm click. *It's always in the eyes.*

* * *

SHEILA WAS WAITING in the hall when he finished cleaning up. Amos felt awkward in the clothing provided by the Hoarders, like an actor dressed for a role that wasn't his. He said as much to Sheila, embarrassed by his appearance.

"You look fine," she said, straightening his collar. "If we're going to do any reconnaissance inside the Enclave, we've got to blend in." She flashed him a grin. "Just imagine if the average Citizen knew actual *savages* were running loose on their streets. Hidden in plain sight, Amos, Hoarder-style."

Amos was about to reenter the gathering room, but she

caught his arm just above the elbow, pulling him back. Startled, he pivoted to face her.

"The kid's back," she whispered, stealing a furtive glance around the corner. "The blond guy who called Megan by name. His name's Connor. Watch your step. He's almost as unstable as Darcy."

"Thanks for the warning." Amos nodded, inhaling deeply. "I guess we shouldn't keep the Hoar—*Citizens* waiting."

TWENTY-THREE

CONNOR TAPPED HIS FOOT in a nervous rhythm, but betrayed no other outward sign of unease. He affected a bored expression, watching as the floor numbers crept upward on the elevator's display pad.

Elevators are the eyes and ears of the Givers. Darcy had repeatedly hammered that lesson home. The bombing at the Arts and Culture Gallery protest will be all over the Infomedia by now. *Darcy needs to know Trackers are behind it.*

Connor felt a growing excitement as he imagined how they might enlist the protesters to join their cause. Failing that, perhaps Darcy could devise a way of using the protests to stir up further unrest. Anything to buy additional time before the Anodyne Initiative went into full implementation.

The doors parted at the twentieth floor, and Connor strode down the hall, his expression carefully neutral. Just a typical Citizen heading home after a typical Cascadian weekend. *Why was I present at the protest? University classes resume Monday, and I was researching a term paper at the Museum across the road.*

He hid a smile. *My perfectly legit alibi.*

He fidgeted outside the door to their villa, chafing impatiently at the few seconds it took to key in his personal entry code. The locking sequence disengaged in a flurry of lights, and the door slid open. Connor stepped over the threshold and came to an abrupt halt. The door hissed shut behind him. He stared wordlessly, feeling slow and stupid.

To his left, Darcy lounged in front of the hearth with DR-57 and Mateo, the Givers' traitorous pawn. On his right, Tony sat in a stiff armchair, one arm leaning on a decorative table beside him. The chauffeur toyed with a rifle resting on the table. He wore the smug, self-important expression that Connor was beginning to despise.

Before Connor could say anything, DR-58 swept past him, trailed by a scruffy savage, and continued down the hall, disappearing around a corner. Neither of them acknowledged his presence, and the scruffy savage—judging by his scowl—was in a foul mood. Connor vaguely recognized him.

"Connor." Darcy smiled, raising his whiskey glass in salute, as if nothing unusual was happening. "How good of you to join us. I trust you remember Mateo, and also our esteemed guest, Colonel Scott."

Connor recovered, shut his mouth, and swallowed hard before he dared reply. *Darcy's coaching me. From now on, we refer to DR-57 by name, not number.* He ground his teeth, wanting more than anything to pounce on the "Colonel" and force him to confess what he'd done to Megan. Then, he remembered the decision he'd made in the aftermath of the protest.

"Have you seen the Infomedia?" Connor managed to keep his voice even. "Do you know about what happened during the protest at the Arts and Culture Gallery?"

Darcy's brow furrowed. "What protest?"

He has no idea. Connor hesitated, unsure how much to divulge in front of the savages. "Sir? Could I have a moment to speak with you, alone?"

He saw the look of instant suspicion on DR—Scott's—face. Mateo raised his chin, analyzing Connor from an odd angle. "I know we promised to share information," he said for their sakes. "But I'd like to talk to Darcy first."

Darcy stood, leaning over to set his whiskey on the glass-topped table with a firm *clink.*

"Gentlemen." He addressed the traitor Mateo, and the savages' leader, with surprising civility. "My son and I would like a private moment, if you don't mind. We will, of course, share any pertinent information with you."

Connor caught movement in his peripheral vision. The scruffy savage was back, accompanied by DR-58. *I'll have to ask Darcy what her name is, again.*

The scruffy savage were now dressed, as was Garr, in the proper garments for a Citizen of the Enclave. Connor had trouble reconciling the incongruity. *After they're done with those clothes, we'll need to burn them.*

Darcy barely acknowledged their return, addressing his comments to Garr alone. "Colonel, why don't you and your team wait on the balcony? I think you'll find our view of the Cascadian skyline inspiring."

Garr didn't reply at once, favoring Connor with a shrewd and appraising look. *Not used to people telling you what to do?* Connor fumed at the savage's presumption. *Well, get used to it, "Colonel."*

Mateo broke the brief stalemate, rising to his feet and heading for the balcony. "Very well, Councilor. We will anticipate hearing your update. Your foster son appears barely capable of restraining himself."

I'm restraining myself right now. Connor sneered behind his back. *Tony's rifle. Your arrogance. Do the math, Tracker.*

One by one, the savages filed out after Mateo. Tony locked the door with an exaggerated flourish. He hefted his rifle, pointing it to the ceiling, clearly enjoying the sensation of power he thought the weapon gave him. Connor ignored him.

Darcy sprang into action, changing the opacity setting to *obscure*. The floor-to-ceiling windowpanes darkened, throwing the gathering room into semi-dusk and preventing the savages from spying on them.

Darcy activated the flatscreen over the hearth, and surfed quickly through his favorite Infomedia channels. As Connor suspected, the lead story on every news outlet was the "terrorist incident" at the Gallery.

Surveillance footage cycled in an endless loop of smoke, chaos, and fleeing Citizens, narrated by a dramatic voice-over, describing the scene in graphic and sensationalized detail. The video footage was then supplanted by a panel of talking heads, debating back and forth while edited snippets of the carnage replayed behind them. A scrolling chyron at the bottom of the screen was apocalyptic hyperbole, at best.

Connor wasn't surprised to hear the panelists turn the crisis into a marketing campaign for the Anodyne Initiative. Their consensus was unanimous—the sooner, the better. For the good of the Enclave.

And the entire sequence would begin again.

Darcy watched the report in silence, absorbing every possible detail from the footage segments. He made no comment on the talking heads' insistence on accelerating the Initiative, obviously not deeming it worthy of debate. Connor understood his guarded reaction. This was the Givers' doing, aided and abetted by their collaborators on the Council.

After watching the news cycle for a third time, Darcy turned the flatscreen off, staring at its blank surface for a long moment. At last, he tilted his head in Connor's direction, his gaze fixed on the fireplace.

"You were there." It was not a question.

"Yessir." Connor took a quick breath, squaring his shoulders. *Stick to the facts, no wild speculations.* "There was an anti-node protest in front of the Gallery. I was curious, so I went to see what people were saying about the Initiative. A couple of Trackers showed up and detonated in the middle of the crowd. I escaped when everyone else ran."

Now Darcy *did* turn to face him, his eyes demanding a truthful accounting. "I saw only *one* explosion, from multiple camera angles." His challenge was clear.

"A chain reaction, sir." Connor gulped, his pulse quickening. "That's what I didn't want the savages to hear before I could tell you. There were two Trackers, *hunting* each other. One tried to make a break for it, but the other caught up. When she realized she couldn't escape, she grabbed the other one and blew herself up. The other Tracker exploded a split-second later. It only *looks* like a single detonation on the flatscreen."

"Trackers hunting other Trackers?" Tony sounded skeptical. He sauntered next to Connor and lowered his weapon. "That doesn't sound like the kind of strategy the Givers would authorize, if you ask me."

"No one asked you." Darcy dismissed him with a wave of his hand, turning to face the balcony. The glass remained opaque. The savages couldn't be seen, but neither could they see inside.

"A house divided against itself," Darcy mused aloud. "What are the Givers up to?"

"What do we tell the savages?" Tony seemed unfazed by his earlier rebuke. "The less, the better, in my opinion."

Darcy whirled to glare at him. Tony cowered, sweat breaking out on his forehead.

"We'll tell our *allies* everything, do you understand?" Darcy took a menacing step forward. "For the sake of our cause, we have to risk a dangerous level of cooperation. Their *names* are Garr, Sheila, and Amos. We need more drones, and they're the key to bringing more of their kind into Cascadia."

Connor nodded. Darcy always saw the big picture. The collaborators, and the Givers, were their first priority.

Avenging Megan would be his victory lap.

TWENTY-FOUR

Amos watched the windows darken, hiding the Hoarders from view. He was getting numb to the outlandish technological advancements in Cascadia. The disparity between life inside and outside the Enclave was breathtaking.

"Very nice. Locked out, stuck on a balcony, twenty floors above ground." He shrugged in resignation. "Looks like we're not going anywhere until the Hoarders say so."

Garr stood with his back to the balcony rail, ignoring the sights and sounds. "Let's make this quick. We don't know how long their private little chat will last."

"For starters, how did you end up inside the Enclave?" Amos turned his back on the opaque panels, ignoring the twitch between his shoulder blades. "Don and Jane escaped the Tracker ambush with me, but we got separated."

"I was able to procure Megan and Aubrey's safety," Mateo said. "They met Don and Jane, *en route* to Eastside."

Garr and Sheila exchanged relieved glances.

"Garr and I escorted the Hoarders back to their vehicle, as

crazy as that may sound." Sheila smiled without much humor. "It was Darcy's idea to sneak us into the Enclave. Even the guards seem intimidated by him."

"Not surprising," Garr said dryly. "Darcy's a member of the ruling Council." He exhaled a deep breath. "Believe it or not, since our arrival, we're been sitting in their gathering room, discussing potential strategies against the Givers."

"Just like that." Anger and disbelief clouded Amos's voice. "You sat down for drinks with the guy who's responsible for Implants and—boom—he's part of the team? I don't know how you expect us to trust him. I still can't believe *you* trust him."

"Who said anything about trust?" Sheila laughed bitterly. "If there's a line between genius and insanity, Darcy crossed it a long time ago." She tapped her fingers on the balcony rail. "I never would have guessed I'd be able to sleep in a Hoarder's haunt, but exhaustion said otherwise."

Rain began to fall, gently at first but escalating into a steady downpour. They edged away from the balcony rail. The rain foreshortened their view of the Enclave, cloaking the surrounding apartment towers in mist.

Garr raised his voice over the pattering rain, eyes warm but his voice cold. "We don't have much choice about partnering with Hoarders. No one said it was going to be easy. Sheila and I had to sit in the back of their vehicle and pretend to be good little Citizens, just to get inside Gate Seven. *That* was an unnerving adventure. Those guards were packing an impressive amount of firepower." He paused, chuckling with genuine humor. "I don't think young Connor enjoyed the return trip, sandwiched in the back seat between Sheila and I."

"He probably took a bath in disinfectant later," Sheila said, snickering at the memory. Her laughter faded, and she became serious again. "Once this is over, I wouldn't turn my back on the Hoarders, especially Darcy."

"That would be wise." Mateo crossed his arms, gazing from one Runner to the next. "Darcy needs you. That's the only thing restraining him. If we succeed, there'll be nothing to hold him back. You're already well-aware of their deep prejudice against 'savages.' I daresay it rivals your own knee-jerk stereotypes for those you deem Hoarders."

"What about Megan?" Amos changed the subject, ignoring Mateo's jibe. "The Hoarders obviously recognized her. The blond kid called her by name."

"Correction. Darcy and Connor recognized Megan," Mateo said in his instructor's voice. "Their driver, Tony Moretti, is a recent recruit and has no memory of her. His rather obvious reaction made that plain."

"I don't think Megan recognized any of them," Sheila said. She pondered for a moment before adding, "Then again, with all the damage she's sustained, that might not mean much."

"Does that mean she might take their side?" Amos glanced over his shoulder, keeping a wary eye on the opaque windows. He shook his head, embarrassed by his impulsive question. "No, forget I asked that. Darcy's responsible for the Implants, and Megan is—was—a Tracker, trying to 'harvest' them. If anything, they should be enemies."

Sheila snapped her fingers, her thoughtful frown giving way to an astonished grin. "Wait a second—that's the missing piece. Garr, remember when Darcy told us they only Implant people from *outside* Cascadia?"

Garr nodded, his eyes haunted. "By Darcy's twisted logic, it makes sense. They'd never Implant a Citizen of the Enclave. It's like an unwritten rule."

"How noble," Amos muttered, recalling the afternoon he'd removed his own Implant.

Sheila acted as if she hadn't heard him. "Just yesterday, Connor made an off-hand comment about that being the only thing they had in common with the Givers—neither side would ever use a Citizen as raw material. That's sacrilege."

Garr's eyes lit up. "I remember him saying that. And yet, it's obvious that both Darcy and Connor recognized Megan. If that's the case..."

"Megan was a Citizen." Amos exhaled in a long, slow whistle. "The Givers broke the unwritten rule."

Mateo quelled their growing enthusiasm with a sharp gesture. The dark tint on the windows was beginning to fade. Tony's bulky frame could be dimly seen through the glass. He was coming to open the door.

"It wouldn't be in the Givers' best interests to antagonize their allies on the Council." Mateo turned toward the balcony rail, hiding his face from the villa's occupants. "If that's true— why the needless gamble? What is it about Megan that made such a risk seem like a good idea?"

Amos caught his breath, suddenly alarmed. "You're not speaking in riddles for once. You *don't* know what's going on with Megan, do you?"

The door latch clicked behind them.

"No," Mateo said quietly, his words oddly rushed. "And that is a matter of some concern."

TWENTY-FIVE

"ARE WE GOING to tell them everything?" The question seemed innocent enough, but Darcy bristled when Tony asked it a second time. Connor saw the look on his foster father's face and was thankful he hadn't been the one to ask.

The savages were sequestered on the balcony, isolated behind a locked door and darkened windows. Suspicion nibbled at Connor over the idea of them having any unsupervised time together. Mateo could be concocting any number of betrayals.

We're twenty floors up. He forced himself to relax. *It's not like they can go anywhere.*

"Are you deaf?" Darcy glowered at Tony, who blanched and fell silent. "We need more drones—it's as simple as that. How many times do I have to repeat myself?"

He whirled to glare at the blank screen over the hearth, as if he could pry the Givers' secrets from its uncooperative surface. He bottled his temper with a visible effort and gestured to Tony without looking at him. "Stow your weapon, and bring the savages in. The bombing incident at the Gallery—we'll let them watch the Infomedia report and draw their own conclusions. Then we'll escort them to CSMD and give them access to the raw footage."

He stooped to toggle a switch. The windowpanes began to return to the default *unfiltered* setting. Tony hastened to the door, eager to placate his employer's wrath. Connor dared to ask one last question during the short interval before the savages returned.

"Is there any topic we should avoid?" He kept his voice neutral, hoping Darcy would catch the subtle difference between his query and Tony's. To his relief, Darcy understood.

"Excellent," Darcy replied. "You're learning, Connor." He seemed pleased. "Treat the savages as though their opinions and insights are valuable. Allow them to believe we're interested in their perspective on the Gallery protest."

Connor nodded surreptitiously—the balcony windows were by now almost completely translucent.

Darcy leaned in, lowering his voice as Tony unlocked the door. "But nothing about your sister." His icy gaze bored into Connor. "Nothing to tip them off about the price they'll pay for what they've done. The savages will bring Megan into Cascadia of their own accord, with no suspicions."

Busted. Connor met his gaze, swallowing hard. He knew Darcy was right. *Do nothing to jeopardize the cause.*

"Yes, sir," he whispered as the savages edged past the belligerent Tony. "Not a word."

TWENTY-SIX ◉

THE SAVAGES WATCHED the Infomedia report with avid interest. Darcy allowed the cycle to loops several times before he stopped the replay.

Connor split his attention between the footage and observing their reactions. The savages tried to be coy, but it was clear they were impressed and belittled by Cascadia's superior technology. *As you should be.*

"Protesters inside the Enclave," Garr said, rubbing his jaw. "That's a new phenomenon. What are they protesting?"

"Trouble in paradise?" Amos made no attempt to hide his sarcasm. Connor couldn't decide which of the savages he detested more. Garr, the leader responsible for Megan's abuse, or the cocky Amos. *You both need to learn some respect.*

Darcy answered, ignoring the bait in Amos's snide remark. "The Anodyne Initiative, of course. They've got more common sense than the average Citizen." He stood behind the savages, nursing his glass of whiskey, compelling them to ask questions by volunteering no additional information.

Reinforcing dominance. Connor smiled to himself. *Darcy knows what he's doing.*

Sheila eyed Darcy with obvious skepticism. "Are you withholding information for any particular reason? Keeping us in suspense, perhaps?"

Her insolent question wiped Connor's smile from his face. It took a great deal of self-restraint to stay silent. All three savages were getting on his nerves. Mateo, even more.

"Forgive me, Sheila," Darcy replied, aiming a pitying look at her. "I forget, sometimes, how unsophisticated life can be outside Cascadia. You have so little access to information—beyond gossiping over the back fence, I suppose." He pressed on, not giving her an opportunity to respond. "The Anodyne Initiative is the latest treachery from the Givers and their boot-licking sycophants on the Council." His voice rose as he warmed to his favorite subject. "Every Citizen will be given a security chip, capable of transmitting their exact location—anywhere, inside or outside Cascadia—to the Peace Wardens, our elite security force."

"That's supposed to make us feel safer." Connor made no effort to dilute his contempt. He continued, mimicking the Infomedia report they'd just watched. "'Imagine the peace of mind you'll enjoy, knowing Peace Wardens can be at your side the moment you need them ...' As if the increased surveillance wasn't enough."

For once, his foster father didn't reprimand him for speaking out of turn. If anything, Darcy seemed pleased Connor was bolstering his argument.

Darcy took control of the narrative. "After the Initiative's implementation, entering Cascadia will be impossible, unless you have a security chip. The same will be true for any public place, or even to purchase groceries." He paused, jaw clenched, radiating hostility. "According to the Council's reasoning, if a terrorist incident occurs, or border security is breached, it will be child's play to isolate the perpetrators."

Garr propelled himself out of his chair, pivoting from the flatscreen to confront Darcy. "And by 'terrorist,' you mean someone from *outside* Cascadia. Because no true Citizen would ever betray the Enclave."

"You mean *us*." Sheila's accusation was no less biting for its low volume.

"We have to protect our way of life." Tony's bitter voice drew their attention to him. He'd retreated to the far side of the room, sulking after Darcy denied him his weapon. "Border security is the only thing keeping the rabble outside, where they belong."

Darcy silenced him with a wordless exclamation, pivoting to glare with obvious menace. The blood drained from Tony's face and he sat down, staring at the floor.

Connor wondered privately if Tony had crossed the line, and was now a liability in Darcy's eyes. *We know how that ends, don't we, Tony?*

The other savages jumped out of their seats, crowding together in a tight cluster, their backs to the hearth. Connor edged closer to Darcy, putting distance between himself and the unpredictable trio by the fireplace.

Mateo roused himself from his vantage point beside the balcony door. He'd lingered there, watching with shrewd attentiveness ever since the savages returned from their exile on the balcony. Connor had kept a wary eye on him—it was no secret Mateo possessed all the enhancements the Givers bestowed on Trackers.

"The security chips are enjoying the benefit of some rather brilliant marketing," Mateo said. He positioned himself in front of the savages, shielding them behind his body. "I daresay one of the most effective propaganda campaigns in years. The Infomedia nicknamed them 'anodynes,' selling the premise that they'll improve border security and restore peace to the Enclave. The Council adopted the nickname, and belatedly rebranded their 'Enhanced Security Measures' as the 'Anodyne Initiative.' A cunning PR move."

"They call them 'nodes' for short," Connor said, unable to hide his disgust. "You should hear the university crowd—they act like it's the latest hot trend."

He caught the look Darcy shot his way and shut his mouth, chagrined to realize Mateo had baited him into speaking out of turn. The savages—he could never think of them as anything else—arranged themselves opposite Darcy in a combative formation. Their actions reminded Connor of cornered animals, which made them even more dangerous.

"It wasn't enough for you Hoarders to seize control of all the resources." Sheila's eyes flashed with indignation. Mateo's wordy speech hadn't been enough to distract her from Tony's outburst. "Or that you built Enclaves to hoard everything for yourselves. You just *had* to drag us into your private little war against the Givers."

Darcy rewarded her with a scornful look. "Are you suggesting we Implant our fellow Citizens instead?" He punctuated his reply with a mocking laugh. "For the record, the *Givers* were the first to make use of your kind. In any war, there are always expendable foot soldiers. Ask Colonel Scott to explain the concept of 'cannon fodder,' if you're really curious."

Garr lurched forward, eyes blazing. He held himself in

check with great effort, thrusting one arm out to block Amos. Darcy met the colonel's gaze with equal fire, neither one willing to back down.

Mateo stood apart from either group, figuratively and literally, looking back and forth at their tense faces. "I'm sure the Givers would be pleased by your current level of cooperation," he said, his calculated placidity giving way to exasperation. "I remind you—the Anodyne Initiative is already underway. We have a limited window of opportunity. You've got the rest of your lives to vilify each other. Perhaps you've heard of the old adage, 'first things first'?"

"Enough with the lame quotes." Amos glared at him before turning to address Darcy. "But he's got a point. We're wasting valuable time. Any suggestions, *Councilor*?"

Connor marveled at Darcy's self-control. The belligerence of the scruffy savage—incongruously clothed in a Citizen's attire—was inexcusable. Connor decided which of the rabble he hated most. *I'll be there, Amos, when Darcy gives you a fresh Implant. Count on it.*

Darcy studied the hostile trio with calculating eyes, the muscles along his jawline clenching and unclenching.

"The Infomedia has limited access to the raw video," he said at last. "We have a friendly resource inside the Cascadia Security Monitoring Division. It's possible we'll learn more about the Gallery bombing by paying them a visit."

TWENTY-SEVEN ◎

DARCY'S CONTACT INSIDE the Cascadia Security Monitoring Division eyed them with wary suspicion as she ushered them into her private office.

Amos caught a glimpse of the plastic ID card pinned to her lapel: Tara Lindholm CSMD. He tried not to stare at the impressive array of sophisticated technology, guessing that the less she knew about their identities, the better.

"The Gallery footage, unedited." Darcy didn't waste time or bother to introduce them. Lindholm gestured to the various screens, apparently unfazed by Darcy's pushy demand or the anonymous group crowding into her personal domain.

I wonder if it's respect or fear. Amos was sure he knew the answer as they clustered around her workstation.

The trip from Darcy's villa in the Oceanview district to the bustling downtown, if there was such a thing in Hoarderville, was eye-opening. There was little conversation on the way. They couldn't fit everyone into a single Hoarder vehicle, and were forced to take the subway instead.

Darcy's instructions were specific. Say as little as possible —the eyes and ears of the Givers are everywhere. No one felt like making small talk, and aside from minimal verbal directions from one of the Hoarders, they were left alone with their own thoughts.

The subway afforded a limited view of the Enclave, and the high-speed transportation reduced what little they could see into one big blur.

Amos hid a sardonic grin as they were whisked through the subway tunnels, surrounded by dozens of unsuspecting Citizens. *All blissfully unaware that the dreaded savages walk among them.*

Lindholm's voice jarred him back to the present. She sat at her workstation, the rest of the group gathered around her in a tense semicircle, fixated on the various screens. "Would you like to review the protest itself, Councilor, or are you more interested in the terrorist attack?"

Darcy crossed his arms, glaring at the multiple screens. "The whole thing, but slow it down as the attack begins."

For the next several minutes, they watched the footage in silence, alert for any extraneous detail. There was a great deal of additional footage, compared to the Infomedia broadcast. Multiple camera angles, each providing a unique perspective, made for a much more complete record.

"Wait—freeze it." Connor pointed to one of the monitors. Lindholm complied. All eyes were on the screen he indicated, top right in the panel. "You can see the moment the Trackers began chasing each other. Look at the trail they leave when they start pushing through the crowd."

"Slow motion from this point," Darcy said, leaning on the back of Lindholm's chair.

She acquiesced with an irritated look, not appreciating the way his weight offset her balance.

Amos leaned forward, intent on the video feed as the pair of Trackers threw themselves among the protestors. The first Tracker—a female—traveled in a straight line, while the second angled through the crowd on an intercept course. Their paths converged a few yards short of the Gallery's front doors. Just beyond, the beleaguered protestors huddled together, seeking shelter from the surly mob.

"*There.*" Connor pointed, triumphant. "Two explosions, one right after the other, just like I said. It wasn't a coincidence. The female Tracker meant to take the other one out."

"One more time, as close as you can magnify," Darcy said, squinting to make out the details. Lindholm obeyed, but the video was already close to maximum magnification. The scene played out as before, slow and choppy, until the overlapping explosions. Dust clouds and fire-tinged smoke filled the screen, obscuring their view.

"Trackers hunting each other." Darcy stared at the murky screen. "What's the Givers' strategy? What possible advantage could this give them?"

Amos glanced covertly at him. For once, it sounded like Darcy was asking a legitimate question.

"To silence the protesters?" Garr stared at the screen as the smoke began to clear, revealing the human carnage in the blast radius. "There's no point—not with the Anodyne Initiative already underway. A handful of protesters aren't going to sway public opinion that much."

"What's this?" Sheila interrupted, pointing to a separate screen, set on its own console against the wall. Unlike the cluster of screens Lindholm monitored, this instrument panel was overlaid with a grid-like pattern. *A street map.* Amos squeezed past Tony to examine the console. *Probably the Enclave.*

"New technology," Lindholm replied crisply. She glanced over her shoulder, waiting for Darcy's approval. At his curt nod, she continued in her clipped monotone.

"It was installed just a few days ago. See the red outlines?" She reached over to adjust the tech, and the screen zoomed in to highlight a smaller subsection of the grid. "Those are vehicles, and the dots inside represent the precise number of Citizens in each one." She stabbed a finger at the icons, tracing their progress. "These Citizens have already received their nodes. They've also voluntarily registered their vehicles. Once the Initiative is up and running, we'll be able to pinpoint anyone's location, what vehicle they're in, and who their traveling companions are."

Amos frowned, puzzled by the Givers' convoluted strategy. Beside him, Sheila uttered a startled gasp. "So, if you see a vehicle on the grid, but none of the occupants have nodes..."

Lindholm nodded, a predatory look in her eyes. "Then it's a stolen vehicle. No node, no Citizenship. We could isolate and eliminate them within *minutes*." She waved a nonchalant hand at her other screens. "We'll still use video surveillance, but the *real* security will be the nodes. And this new tech."

"What about the protesters?" Garr asked. "Citizens who decide, for whatever reason, they don't *want* to join the Initiative?"

Lindholm snorted. "They'll be given nodes anyway, for the good of the Enclave. Exile is the only alternative. If they want to live like savages, they can live *with* the savages. That's just my off-the-record opinion, of course."

Darcy leaned over her shoulder. "This meeting never took place," he breathed in her ear, the implied threat chilling. "And you've never seen these people."

Lindholm froze, and Amos saw her eyes widen in fear. She stared straight ahead, her hands limp at the controls. "As you wish, Councilor."

Darcy pivoted to face the rest of the group, his pale eyes boring into each one in turn. Even Connor, Amos noticed, wasn't exempt from his withering gaze. "Tony will rendezvous with you on the parking level. He'll transport you outside the gates. It's time you returned to your Hub." He paused before opening the door, turning to issue a final warning. "The Anodyne Initiative is moving ahead. You must return, with reinforcements, before it's complete."

TWENTY-EIGHT

REINFORCEMENTS. AMOS FUMED, staring out of the passenger window as they waited in line at Gate Seven. *After all the people he's Implanted, Darcy expects us to forget it ever happened and rush to his aid.*

He was being petulant, and he knew it. He understood the logical necessity of the alliance, but his emotions—fueled by too many memories—had a different view.

Like it or not, he's our ticket. Mateo can sneak us into Cascadia, but only Darcy can give us access anywhere else.

Amos shifted position in the rear seat, impatient to be under way. He couldn't wait to change out of the ridiculous outfit the Hoarders gave him to wear. He glanced over his shoulder at a small duffle bag in the cargo area. Tony had assured them their regular clothes were inside.

Amos settled into his seat, his restless eyes wandering to their driver. Tony exuded stress—drumming his fingers on the steering wheel in an uneven rhythm, stealing furtive glances at their surroundings, whistling a discordant melody.

Mateo sitting right beside him probably doesn't help. Amos hid a smirk.

"This line-up's taking forever," Sheila said. She sat between Amos and Garr, watching the slow procession ahead.

Garr spoke for the first time since they'd descended to the vehicle level. "What are the odds of Lindholm betraying us to the Givers?"

Amos knew he wasn't serious, but Tony jerked as if he'd been shot. He twisted sideways, mumbling something incoherent into his collarbone.

Mateo leaned over the console, a bemused look on his face. "Mr. Moretti, your new allies have a saying they're fond of— hidden in plain sight." He tipped his head to one side, watching for Tony's reaction. "Unfortunately, you seem to be achieving the opposite. We're far too close to the checkpoint for such conspicuous behavior."

Tony flushed a dark crimson. He stole another glance at the guardhouse—two vehicle-lengths ahead—and snarled a quick response under his breath. "I *said*, don't mention the Givers. Everyone knows they exist, but only a few Citizens have ever seen them. And, in case you've forgotten, until we've cleared the gates, we're under surveillance."

Mateo leaned back, glancing over his shoulder to wink at Amos. "Ah, yes, the vaunted Cascadia Security forces, keeping the good Citizens of the Enclave safe behind their walls."

Whatever retort was in Tony's mind was never spoken. The vehicle in front of them shifted into gear and advanced to the checkpoint. Tony coaxed their vehicle forward, braking to a nervous stop. He reached a shaky hand into the console between the front seats to retrieve the small packet of permits Darcy had prepared.

The vehicle ahead of them roared, tires squealing as it accelerated. The guards on either side of the exit brandished their weapons, relaxing only after Gate Seven dropped into place with a *thump* that Amos felt through their vehicle chassis.

The sergeant waved an impatient hand. Tony maneuvered their vehicle into place. He said nothing, opening his window to hand their permits to the guard.

Amos expected a closer inspection, but the sergeant's eyes widened in astonishment as he perused their permits. He wasted no time in handing them back to Tony, affecting a crooked smile as he waved them through.

Darcy's signature carries weight. Here's hoping Garr can come up with a way to take advantage of that.

Gate Seven lifted with a heavy groan, revealing the bustling shantytown outside, warmly lit by the midday sun. Tony gunned the engine, and they lurched forward. Cascadia Security guards stood at attention on either side of the exit, weapons held ready, flanking the vehicle as it plunged into the open country beyond.

Gate Seven slammed down as soon as they cleared the exit, raising a cloud of dust. Tony stomped on the gas, and the tires spewed dirt and small stones as they raced over the hard-packed earth outside the Enclave.

They reached Jericho's outer perimeter in less than a minute. Mateo's gaze flickered to his former shop. Another merchant had already taken over his space, like a hermit crab laying claim to a vacant shell. Jericho's precarious marketplace carried on without a hiccup.

Mateo said nothing.

Tony drove as far as the Old City's outskirts, slowing to a stop in the middle of an anonymous intersection. He left the engine idling and looked at Mateo for the first time since they'd begun their journey.

"End of the line, Tracker." He tried, and failed, to sound authoritative. Mateo smiled, cocking his head to one side as if listening to the demands of a pampered child.

Tony bristled at his lack of response. "Didn't you hear what I said? Get out."

Mateo held his gaze without flinching. Amos, Sheila, and Garr took advantage of the opportunity and exited the vehicle. Once they were clear, Mateo opened his door and disembarked. His gaze never left Tony's. He seemed to be enjoying his ability to agitate the chauffeur.

Amos slipped behind the vehicle, opening the tailgate to retrieve the duffle bag. *The sooner I get out of this Hoarder outfit, the better.*

He slammed the tailgate shut, slung the duffle bag over his shoulder, and joined his companions on the sidewalk.

"Five days." Tony spoke through his open window as he revved the engine. "This intersection is our rendezvous spot. Bring the rest of your group here. I'll pick you up and sneak you back into Cascadia."

"Five days isn't much," Garr replied mildly, ignoring his attempt at intimidation. "We'll be on foot for at least part of the trip. If we have to hike both directions, there's no way—"

"*Find* a way," Tony interrupted, scowling. "The Initiative isn't going to wait, and neither can we. We'll probably all have nodes by the time you get back. You'll be the only ones able to travel in Cascadia without being tracked."

Mateo leaned his arm on the door. "Are these your words, or those of the esteemed Councilor?"

Tony glowered and revved the engine again. "Five days,"

he said, rolling his window up. Mateo stepped back as Tony reversed direction.

Tires squealed on the pavement, and he was gone.

"You heard the man," Garr said dryly, as the Hoarder vehicle disappeared in a cloud of dust. "Five days isn't much time. We've got a lot of strategizing to do, not to mention a long hike ahead of us."

Amos exchanged glances with Mateo, and he thought he detected a glint of amusement in the Tracker's eye.

"We might be able to help with that," Amos said, shifting the duffle bag on his shoulder. "As long as nobody minds hiking back to the ocean." He glanced at the sun, estimating. "We've got plenty of daylight left."

TWENTY-NINE ⊙

"LAUGHTER. NOW, *THERE'S* A SOUND I don't often hear around this place." Doc Simon leaned against the doorframe in the mess hall, a pleased look on her face as she took in the euphoric atmosphere.

Don turned from the counter, feigning indignation and pointing a wooden spatula at her. "I don't know what Sheila's been telling you about my culinary skills, but it's all lies." He shook his spatula for emphasis, splattering drops of sauce on the floor. "I'll have you know I'm a highly respected chef. In certain circles."

Sheila swatted his arm with a dish towel. "I think you're confusing 'respect' with 'dread.' There's a reason field rations are popular whenever you're on kitchen duty."

Aubrey shook her head, grinning widely as she sliced the vegetables. Doc Simon nodded to herself, pleased to observe the lighter ambiance.

The unexpected return of Garr, Sheila, Amos—and even Mateo—lifted everyone's spirits. The brooding tension, hanging over Eastside like a dark cloud since the Tracker ambush, dissipated the moment Amos poked his head in the mess hall to utter Don's signature greeting.

"Did anyone miss us?"

Bedlam erupted, as boisterous as it was uncharacteristic. What followed was an afternoon crammed with stories and dialogue, as Colonel Scott convened a rigorous debriefing session. Doc candidly referred to the debrief as a "rollercoaster," although it took several minutes to explain to her younger colleagues what that meant.

She listened intently to the overlapping stories about the Tracker ambush, and took detailed notes on individual accounts of their escapes. On a separate page, she jotted down a hasty bullet-point list of their impression of the Hoarders, in particular their leader, Darcy.

She set her pencil aside when the conversation shifted to descriptions of Cascadian culture. She found the idea of protests and their effectiveness fascinating, and was equally puzzled by the significance of Trackers hunting each other.

"That enough for today," Garr said at last. He leaned back, stretching his arms. "Don, Sheila, you're on meal prep."

Aubrey raised her hand. "I can help."

Doc raised an eyebrow and jotted an additional note. Aubrey wasn't usually a fan of cooking. Volunteering was a good sign. Doc smiled to herself and closed her notebook. Debrief was over and the mess hall reverted to a working kitchen. She noticed Mateo speak quietly to Garr before leaving the room.

"What *is* that incredible smell?" Jane's voice was oddly upbeat, accented by a genuine smile. She squeezed between Doc and Garr to join Don at the cooking unit, sniffing with gusto.

"What—you've never tasted meat that wasn't raw?" Don

tossed his spatula on the counter, looking down at Jane with affected pathos. "This may come as a shock, but many civilizations have been known to cook their food."

"Was this your idea, Sheila?" Jane asked, ignoring him. Doc Simon couldn't recall the last time she'd seen such an open, carefree look on her face.

Sheila shook her head, tending to the sizzling contents of the frying pan. "The credit belongs to the Colonel. We hiked to the far side of Hoarderville to get Mateo's truck, and Garr insisted we pick up some fresh meat on the way back. I guess he started planning this during the ride."

"Thank you, Garr," Aubrey said over her shoulder, spying him in the doorway beside Doc. "I don't think this mess hall's ever smelled so good."

Garr sketched a small salute, smiling easily. "You've earned it. That aroma might even convince me Don isn't the kitchen menace I thought he was."

Don performed an exaggerated bow.

"Don't let it go to your head, big guy." Sheila poked him in the ribs. "Stirring a pot of sauce isn't the same as cooking a full-course meal."

"Is that so?" Don scowled at her, resuming his task. "You don't want to see what happens if I stop stirring. For the record, my role is *crucial*."

Amos appeared in the doorway, craning his neck to see over Doc's shorter frame. "Let's go check the dropbox, Jane. I want to be back by the time supper's ready."

Jane dared to dip a spoon into the Don's pot, nodding with approval after tasting the sauce. The big man waved his spatula at her with an indignant protest, and Jane ducked her head, dodging out of reach.

"Just checking," she said, laughing as she squeezed past Garr and Doc. "Had to be sure Don wasn't trying to poison us." She joined Amos in the corridor, and they set off at a brisk jog, their footsteps lighter than usual.

Doc chuckled again, watching the camaraderie from the doorway. She glanced up at Garr and lowered her voice. "This is one of your better ideas, Colonel. They've been under so much pressure lately. They needed an excuse to unwind."

"It's the calm before the storm," he replied, "and everyone knows it. But you're right. They needed this." His shoulders rose and fell in a self-deprecating shrug. "Who am I kidding? I need this as much as they do."

Doc eyed him with concern. "I won't ask whether or not you trust this Darcy character, because that isn't the right question. Judging by everything I heard today, he's a predatory sociopath. Once Darcy gets what he wants, he'll discard you without a second thought. And I shudder to think what 'discard' means to someone like him." She shook her head. "You're playing a dangerous game, Colonel."

Garr didn't argue. "It's like dancing with a scorpion," he said, a faraway look in his eye. "But he's our only chance to get to the Givers. We have to strike quickly, before the Anodyne Initiative takes effect. If we wait too long, we won't be able to move around the Enclave undetected. Darcy needs us. He can't afford to jeopardize the alliance."

"That's exactly what I mean." Doc turned to face him, hands on her hips. "Right now, Darcy needs you. But if you succeed, none of you will be necessary anymore. Win or lose, it might not make much difference."

"No more Givers means no more Trackers. Or Implants," Garr replied, meeting her gaze with steady resolve. "No more innocent people kidnapped by Hoarders as raw material for their private war. We've been their expendable pawns far too long. I've buried too many good people…"

Doc watched him closely. "The body count could go up, if Darcy stays true to form."

"This is a risk we have to take." Garr caught himself, looking away for a moment. "Don't worry, I won't let my guard down." He inclined his head to indicate the cooking crew. "And I promise you, I'll bring them back. This won't be our last celebration together."

Doc nodded, breaking eye contact with a sigh. "I'll hold you to that, Colonel," she said, a brief smile lighting up her face. "I might even risk some of Don's cooking."

Garr chuckled, and then became serious again. "I almost forgot … your presence is required in the infirmary. Mateo has an idea he wants to run past you."

He did an abrupt about-face and strode down the corridor. After a final look at the cheerful company in the mess hall, Doc followed in his wake.

"Mateo," she muttered under her breath, shoving her hands into the pockets of her lab coat. "Still not sure what I think of him, either."

THIRTY

THUNDER RUMBLED, adding an ominous soundtrack to the overcast streets. Amos kept an uneasy eye on the weather. Gray clouds contributed their part, brooding over the worn buildings near Eastside Mission. A chill breeze gusted now and then, warning of an impending storm.

Despite the threatening weather, people filled the streets, wandering in and out of a variety of shops. Amos waited, with as much patience as he could muster, by a clothing merchant's open door. Jane was purchasing something inside. He could hear her haggling over the price.

Hurry up, Jane. Amos fidgeted, unsettled. He felt exposed. *If a storm hits now, everyone will scatter, and 'hidden in plain sight' won't mean a thing.*

Moments later, Jane joined him on the sidewalk. She showed him the cap she'd purchased, looking pleased.

"You inspired me to get myself one of these," she said, molding the brim of the cap before donning it. "This, combined with my hoodie, and I'll be practically unrecognizable."

"The Enclave has security cameras everywhere," Amos replied as they resumed their roundabout route to the dropbox. "The cap and hoodie helps, but they won't make you invulnerable. You still need to be vigilant."

"This isn't my first time in the field." Some of Jane's old fire flared. She nodded in the direction of an alley—just ahead and to their right. "Follow my lead. There's something I want to check out before the dropbox."

Amos navigated the turn with her, curious in spite of his unease. His inner voice fought to make itself heard, but he stifled it. His mouth felt dry, and he kept a diligent eye on their surroundings.

The narrow alley was typical for the Mission district. Aging bricks crumbled at the corners, and the few doors and windows were boarded up or nailed shut. A rusted garbage dumpster squatted in an intersection between back alleys.

Jane ducked behind the dumpster, using it as a shield. Amos followed suit, dropping to one knee to look over her shoulder, wondering what had piqued her curiosity.

Rancid odors stung his nostrils. Regular garbage collection in the Old City had ceased not long after the Enclaves were built. Waste disposal was forced to adapt, rendering dumpsters obsolete. Despite years of disuse, the dumpster had managed to retain a foul smell.

It took Amos less than a second to spot the anomaly—a Hoarder truck, parked in the alley. No, *two* trucks. He spied the second vehicle further down the alley, and felt for the knife under his jacket. *I'm literally bringing a knife to a gunfight.*

"I saw something black and shiny through the back door of the shop," Jane whispered, taking stock of the scene. "And my guess was right—Hoarders. I wonder what they're up to? They usually avoid the Mission district, and they certainly don't park in back alleys."

Amos opened his jacket to retrieve his spyglass. He focused on the nearest truck. The tailgate was open, and there was something odd about the cargo area ...

"Here they come," Jane said, elbowing him in the ribs.

A pair of Hoarders exited the back entrance of a shop opposite their position. They supported an unconscious woman between them, her limp arms slung over their shoulders. They lifted her into the cargo area, shoved her further inside, and closed the tailgate. One of the Hoarders wiped his palms on his breeches and they shared a laugh.

Amos lowered his spyglass, sickened, and stuffed it inside his jacket.

Jane watched the Hoarders through narrowed eyes. "See anyone you know?"

"No." Amos shook his head. "Whoever they are, they've got three people stowed in that truck."

Jane's face hardened, and she spat on the ground.

The Hoarder vehicles slipped into motion, creeping down the alley at minimal speed—and noise—until they reached the next side alley. The parade of vehicles executed the turn, bumper to bumper, and disappeared from view.

Amos counted under his breath. Three seconds elapsed before they heard roaring engines and squealing tires, marking the return of typical Hoarder driving habits.

Jane turned her head, eyes wide. "Maybe it's the Givers."

Amos pictured the crude sketch Megan had drawn, their first clue to the Givers' alien origin. "I doubt it. Darcy's not the only Hoarder collecting Implant fodder."

Jane shook her head emphatically. "This may have nothing

to do with Darcy, or Implants. The Givers lost a lot of Trackers during the ambush. What if these Hoarders were sent here to collect replacements?"

Amos remembered the convoy Aubrey had described. "If you're right, the Hoarders must be getting desperate." His stomach felt abruptly hollow. "Kidnapping people in broad daylight … they've never taken risks like that before."

Jane rose to her feet, dusting off her hands on her pants. "The dropbox." She glared daggers after the Hoarders. "And then back to Eastside. Garr needs to know about this."

They made their way back to the street, resuming their trek to the dropbox and blending in with the other pedestrians. Another low rumble of thunder underlined their need for haste. Amos glanced at the clouds, trying to estimate how much time remained before another downpour.

"Watch where you're going, Amos." Jane's brusque warning coincided with his near-collision with an elderly couple exiting a grocer shop. Amos mumbled an apology and skirted around the nervous couple.

He glanced ahead and spotted a glint of red light. It winked out a fraction of a second later, restoring the Tracker's benign, human appearance. He was about the same height and build as Amos, perhaps within a year or two of his age.

He strolled, calm and nonchalant, in their direction.

Jane's wiry fingers closed in a punishing grip on his hand. She'd seen it, too. His heart raced, and adrenaline spiked as his flight-or-fight instincts took hold.

He clutched Jane's hand with equal fierceness, nudging her subtly toward to the curb. He forced himself to keep his breath normal, his steps unhurried and steady.

It was the most difficult thing he'd ever done.

My Implant's long gone. Jane's never had one. He's not scanning for us. He's not scanning for us...

The Tracker passed by without a glance in their direction, weaving his way through the human traffic. Amos didn't dare turn to see where the creature went. He kept to the same pace, and Jane matched his steps.

"The dropbox will have to wait," he said under his breath, and Jane squeezed his hand to signal her agreement.

THIRTY-ONE ◉

MEGAN LEARNED A GREAT DEAL during the rollercoaster debrief. There was little she could add to the conversation, even if she wanted to. She hid her exasperation well, but the *aphasia*, as Doc called it, was driving her crazy.

When questioned, she answered as best as she could. The Hoarders they'd met—did she know who they were? Any recollection of the teenager, Connor, who appeared to recognize her? Any memories of her pre-Tracker life?

Meagn shook her head each time. No words were needed to augment the simple gesture, so she bottled her frustration and kept her mouth shut.

And listened.

Now, seated on the gurney—once her prison—she watched Mateo prodding at the deactivated Implant on Doc's worktable. The same Implant she'd stolen less than a week ago, in hopes of currying favor with the Givers.

"A remarkable piece of reverse engineering." Mateo held the Implant up between them, admiring it. She had no reaction.

"Whatever else one might think of Councilor Peterson and his self-appointed 'cause,' his ability to use the Givers' technology against them is extraordinary."

"Tracker kill," Megan said, her words clear enough. She clenched her hands into fists, twisting handfuls of the blanket between her fingers. She managed to force her uncooperative lips to form the words. "Animals. In the blood. Dead."

"I concur." Mateo leaned against the worktable, setting the Implant down with painstaking care. He crossed his arms over his chest. "The creatures were incapable of assimilating what our blood carries. It was too much for them."

"What was too much?"

Megan hadn't heard Garr and Doc approaching until the door swung open. The colonel's question hung in the air between them. Doc Simon crossed to her worktable, casting a protective look over her instruments.

Mateo obliged her unspoken hint and retreated to a respectful distance. "Have you ever observed the unique properties of Tracker-enhanced blood, Dr. Simon?"

Doc bristled. "I know how to use a microscope." She laid a hand on her prize instrument and took a breath before continuing. "Which 'unique' property were you thinking of?"

Megan waved a hand to catch her attention, and managed to choke the words out. "Dead scav … animals."

Mateo nodded, explaining on her behalf. "Megan deduced a new aspect of the Givers' enhancements. To employ a crude metaphor, the human cardiovascular system is a pipeline for nanotechnology. The scavengers we found near Amos's rustic refuge died because they were unable to assimilate enhanced blood. The results were, I'm afraid, rather grotesque."

"What's that got to do with your asking me to bring Doc

here?" Garr interrupted. "This is all very interesting, Mateo, but if you've got something more pragmatic to offer, I'm ready to listen."

Mateo lifted his chin. "My apologies, Colonel. My brief explanation for the scavenger casualties is very much connected to my request, I assure you."

Doc scooped up the Implant, using it as a pointer. "Connected to this, in some way?" She watched him closely. "You seemed quite interested in it a moment ago."

"All Giver technology is connected, Doctor," he replied without hesitation. "Darcy's invention of the Implants, however distasteful we may find it, is simply an extrapolation of their pre-existing technology. Crude, in comparison to the originals, but effective." He eyed Garr as the latter approached. "Allow me to answer your earlier query. The scavengers' freakish demise got me thinking. Implants and Tracker enhancements share a common denominator. Specifically, the delivery system."

"You mean blood." Doc looked from the Implant in her hand to Megan and back again. Her eyes widened, and she stared at Mateo. "What are you suggesting?"

Mateo straightened, unperturbed, and stepped away from the worktable. "You said it yourself, Doctor. Most of Megan's physical injuries were repaired by her enhancements, but only partially. I think the phrase you used was 'fits and starts.' She would not have survived otherwise." He crossed the limited space to stand beside his fellow Tracker. "I propose a simple experiment: a blood transfusion. Perhaps that will reactivate her self-repair subroutines."

Fear stabbed Megan as the implications sank in.

The Givers had violated her body with alien technology, stolen her humanity, and reduced her to an anonymous—and expendable—pawn. She was free of them now, and the specter of losing her identity again left her weak and shaking. She saw the resolve in Mateo's eyes and lowered her gaze to the floor.

Gar rubbed his jaw, frowning. "What if kick-starting her subroutines backfires? Megan is free of the Givers' control for the first time in years. Why take the risk, based solely on your 'theory'?"

Mateo didn't back down. "She has no memory of Darcy or his companions. We've focused on Connor, since he spoke her name. But have no doubt—Darcy recognized her as well, and that is the only time I've seen him at a loss for words. Understanding the connection may give us a tactical advantage. We'd be foolish to ignore it."

"Megan is not a *tactical advantage*," Doc interrupted harshly. Her fist tightened on the Implant. "She's part of this Hub, an Eastside family member."

Megan placed a hand on Doc's shoulder, interrupting her tirade, and eyed Mateo. "My ... talk?" The words emerged haltingly, plaintive, hopeful.

Mateo studied her, his expression evasive. "I can't promise that. As I indicated, a blood transfusion is an experiment, but one I feel is worth the attempt."

Doc stepped between them, her back to Mateo. She took Megan's hands in her own. "Are you sure about this?" She spoke slowly, spacing her words as if Megan was slow-witted.

Megan felt a flash of resentment, but forced herself to relax. *She wants to be sure I understand the risk. But if there's even a chance of speaking normally, or unlocking my memories ...*

Garr intervened, addressing Mateo. "Is there any danger of the Givers taking control again?"

Mateo shook his head. "A Tracker's processing center is

located directly behind the scanning eye. Aubrey's impetuous use of her prod, admittedly in self-defense, rendered Megan's processor useless and irreparable. There is no reason for concern." He angled his neck to the right, pointing to a spot just below his left collarbone, near the shoulder joint. "There are numerous locations where the enhancements can be accessed, Dr. Simon. This area will suffice."

Doc locked eyes with Megan. "It's your decision."

A shiver ran down Megan's spine. Fear or anticipation—she couldn't decide. She managed a weak smile and nodded.

Doc chose a standard hypodermic needle and, after a moment's hesitation, extracted a full syringe of blood. "Would I be right in assuming that I should inject Megan in the same spot?"

Megan tugged at her shirt collar, exposing her shoulder in anticipation of his reply.

Mateo shook his head. "Any blood vessel will do. The elbow, I believe, is the traditional favorite in the medical profession."

Megan shoved her sleeve up, as high as the fabric would allow. Doc swabbed the area with disinfectant. She hesitated, lips pursed, before injecting the needle.

Megan held her breath as Doc depressed the plunger, and the dark liquid disappeared into her vein. She met Doc's gaze, wondering how long she'd have to wait.

The reaction hit hard and fast, virtually instantaneous. A burning sensation raced up her arm like a marauding wave of acidic insects. She gasped, lurching forward, and clung desperately to the gurney frame.

The insects circled her ribcage and arced across her abdomen, spreading fire and agony in their wake. Up her spinal column, into her neck, and ...

Megan threw her head back as acidic fire invaded her skull.

Scalding needles pierced her brain, questing, probing, burning. Her vision blurred, cleared, and blurred again. She fought to focus.

Mateo stood at the foot of the gurney, impassive. Garr and Doc Simon flanked him on either side. Doc stretched a hand toward her, looking stricken.

A second spike of pain lanced through her skull, finding its epicenter behind her ruined scanning eye. Megan screamed. The infirmary spun out of control, and she collapsed on the gurney, writhing, unable to escape.

"What did you do to her?" Doc's outcry was muffled, barely discernible.

An obsidian cyclone opened hungrily in Megan's mind. She tried to resist its magnetic pull, but her strength evaporated and the vortex claimed her.

THIRTY-TWO ◉

KENNY MILLER regained consciousness with great effort. Lethargy held him in stasis, body and mind, and he fought to free himself from under its weight.

Sunlight warmed his face, but his body felt cold and stiff. The surface beneath him was hard and unyielding. He squirmed, seeking a more comfortable position, and rolled over. He was rewarded by an unexpected sensation of free-fall, shattered abruptly by the unforgiving ground. The jolt drove the breath from his lungs, and for a few precious seconds, his world shrank to a desperate craving for air.

The bruising impact helped clear his mental fog. His lungs mercifully filled with oxygen, and he forced his eyes open. A wave of vertigo threatened to engulf him, but he resisted, levering himself into a sitting position. He appeared to have landed on a large patch of uncut grass.

"Do you need help, sir?" A voice Kenny didn't recognize spoke nearby. He looked up to find a cluster of young people standing nearby. University students, most likely.

Two of them bent down and took him by the arms, lifting him gently onto a park bench.

I must've fallen off. He peered at his surroundings, trying to pinpoint his location. Dozens of people milled around him, and he vaguely realized he was in a park ... somewhere. *Why was I sleeping on a park bench in the first place?*

"I'm okay." His voice sounded weak and fuzzy in his ears. "I guess I dozed off, or something."

One of the students laughed as if they shared a private joke. "Yeah, I've fallen out of bed, myself, once or twice. Frat parties are like that. You sure you're okay?"

"I'm fine, I'm fine," Kenny replied, arching his sore back. *Why am I so stiff?* "Serves me right for napping in a park." He grinned with more cheerfulness than he felt.

How did I get here, and why can't I remember?

"Good thing you woke up when you did." A young woman patted him on the shoulder, beaming an enthusiastic smile. "It's just about to start."

Kenny squinted up at her, the sunshine still too bright for his eyes. "What's about to start?"

"The protest," she replied, waving to a spot he couldn't see over the crowd. "Everyone's here, even the Infomedia."

"The Anodyne Initiative is a *terrible* idea," said one of the young men who'd helped him up. His voice was serious, his eyes alight with burning indignation. "The Council should force security chips on savages, not Citizens."

Protest. Kenny's mind sluggishly absorbed the word. He'd heard something about a protest, not long ago. What was it?

Heat encircled his left eye, barely perceptible at first, but growing warmer. Images flooded his mind—an operating room, a gurney, invisible restraints around his wrists and ankles, a pair of hideous creatures keeping a silent vigil over him. And the councilor, his features hidden behind a surgical mask.

Find a crowd. Push the button.

"Sir?" The young woman sounded worried. "Is there something wrong with your eye?"

Kenny ducked his head, raising a hand to his face. A reddish glow reflected on his palm. The burning sensation intensified, and he grimaced in pain.

With an inarticulate cry, he sprang to his feet, scattering the concerned students. He pivoted in a frantic circle, eyes wild. He was stranded in the middle of a crowd—protestors, counter-protestors, curious bystanders. A mixed cocktail of humanity, all gathered to witness the spectacle. And he realized, in equal parts fear and horror, what his role was to be.

Kenny filled his lungs, raising his voice above the chattering onlookers. "Out of my way!" He flailed his arms, shoving people aside in his desperate attempt to flee. "You're all going to die—I don't want to hurt anyone!"

The crowd resisted his frenzied efforts, their instinctive reaction increasingly hostile. Kenny shouted louder, flailed harder, insistent and terror-stricken.

He didn't see the blow coming. A fist crashed against his jaw and he stumbled to his knees, pitching headlong on the grass. Indignant voices surrounded him on every side.

"What's your problem, buddy?"

"I don't know what happened. He just went crazy."

"Look—what's happening to his face?"

The burning sensation lanced into white-hot fury. Kenny whimpered in silent agony. *Please, just run. Please ...*

A click echoed inside his skull, and he knew it was too late.

THIRTY-THREE

"What's the deal with this?" Tony's plaintive question broke into Connor's train of thought. The chauffeur sounded more anxious than usual. He took his foot off the accelerator, straining to see a block ahead. Traffic slowed to a sympathetic crawl around them.

Connor leaned forward, peering over his shoulder. A large crowd had gathered in one of the many urban parks dotting Cascadia's business district.

"That's a lot of people crammed into one place." Connor turned to Darcy, uneasy. "Another anti-node protest, maybe?"

"It won't last long, if it is," Darcy replied bitterly, gesturing at the park as they drew abreast. "See all those Peace Wardens? They'll shut it down at the first sign of trouble, real or fabricated. The Givers won't allow anything to interfere with their precious Initiative."

Tony muttered something under his breath, glancing out his window at the growing crowd. A line of sweat beaded his forehead, and his hands clasped and unclasped the steering wheel in nervous spasms. Everything seemed to put him on edge these days.

Connor shifted in his seat as they crept past the park. The green space, sandwiched between imposing business towers, was all but overrun with Citizens, many waving placards, some in favor of the Initiative and others against.

What a waste of time. He watched the fractious crowd with a sick feeling of futility. They were clearly oblivious to the latest propaganda. *No node, no Citizenship.*

He faced forward, ignoring the pointless gathering as Tony navigated the clogged traffic lanes. Connor gazed out his window, seeing but not registering the buildings they passed. He toyed with his locket, slipping it back and forth on its silver chain.

"This isn't a tourist outing, Tony." Darcy consulted his wrist com, noting the time with an exasperated sigh. "The Council doesn't call an emergency session often, but when they do, they expect everyone to drop everything."

"Something to do with the Initiative, you think?" Connor forgot for a moment that, in Darcy's world, it was best to wait until he was spoken to. "There's never been protests like this, not since the Enclave walls were finished. I wonder if that's rattling the collaborators' nerves."

Darcy sneered at the mention of the traitors.

Tony slammed the brakes without warning, bringing them to a skidding halt. The sudden stop threw Connor against the back of the driver's seat.

Darcy caught himself against the dashboard and lashed out, eyes blazing. *"What are you doing?"*

Connor fell back into his seat, dazed. He caught sight of Tony's reflection in the rearview mirror. Tony breathed in short, shallow gulps, hands clenched on the steering wheel. Sweat poured down his face, and his gaze was riveted on the mirror. Fear, or perhaps horror, had frozen him in place.

Traffic on all sides came to a haphazard standstill, horns blaring. Here and there, a driver skidded into the wrong lane. Tires squealed and metal crunched, testifying to multiple collisions. Darcy spun in his seat, looking behind, and his rage instantly evaporated.

He's rattled. Connor twisted in his seat. A quick survey drew his attention to the urban park, now several blocks behind. A chaotic scene greeted him.

Smoke billowed out of the park, spilling past the corner of the nearest office tower. Fear-crazed Citizens poured out of the park and into the street, scattering in all directions. Mass hysteria, mob mentality operating on survival instinct alone, resulting in a human stampede of fear.

The Peace Wardens responded with prompt and devastating competence. Connor stared, uncomprehending. *They're firing into the crowd. They're shooting ... anyone.*

He fought a battle with nausea, appalled by the cold efficiency of the slaughter. The majority of Wardens directed their aim into the park, while a smaller contingent targeted anyone fleeing the scene. They appeared unaffected by the carnage they created. *They're headed our way.*

Darcy's voice lanced the paralysis inside their vehicle. "Get out. Stay low, and follow me."

Tony's grip on the steering wheel tightened even further, if that were possible. He screwed his eyes shut, blocking out the atrocity in the rearview mirror.

Darcy uttered a wordless exclamation and cuffed him hard on the shoulder. He didn't wait, opening his door and sliding to the pavement. Tony's eyes popped open. He killed the engine and crawled awkwardly over the middle console after Darcy.

Connor slid across the rear seat, easing his door open. He dropped to the pavement, mirroring Darcy's crouching position. Curiosity ate at him, but he knew better than to poke his head up for a look.

He addressed Darcy in a harsh whisper, looking past the trembling Tony. "Did you see?"

Darcy nodded once, and gestured sharply. *Follow me.*

Connor gave Tony a shove to get him moving, and the chauffeur crawled on hands and knees after Darcy. Wide-eyed Citizens sat frozen in their vehicles, ignoring them. Connor was tempted to warn them, but realized he'd only expose himself to the advancing Wardens.

They think they're safe if they stay put. A part of his mind flinched, and he scrambled after Darcy, pushing the deluded Citizens out of his mind.

They wove their way to the curb, putting as much distance as possible between themselves and the Wardens. They halted near a financial tower, taking refuge behind one of the ornate pillars framing the entrance. The guttural hissing of weapons was less frequent but, judging by the sound, the Wardens were not far behind.

The Givers equipped them with the latest weapons. Connor swallowed hard against the lump in his throat. *As if shooting unarmed Citizens wasn't easy enough.*

Darcy lay on his belly, edging forward to peer around the base of the pillar. Connor went to one knee behind him, careful not to jostle his foster father. "Can you see anything?"

Darcy shifted position, angling his neck for a better vantage point. "They've stopped advancing," he said guardedly, not looking at Connor. "Take a look for yourself. Circle around to the far side of the pillar."

Connor edged past the petrified Tony. His range of vision was not as panoramic as Darcy's, but he spied three Wardens nearby. They stood at attention, weapons held ready, facing his direction. *What are they searching for—or who?*

There was no obvious signal. The Peace Wardens pivoted as one, with classic military precision, and retreated toward the park. Connor scrambled to his knees, peering over the grid-locked traffic for a better view.

Smoke wreathed the street bordering the park, teased back and forth by the breeze. Connor sank down, his back to the pillar. Darcy rose to his knees, a grim look on his face as he watched the departing phalanx of Wardens.

"I don't understand," Tony said, speaking for the first time since the chaos began. He leaned against the pillar, his trembling hands draped across his knees. He spoke in a monotone, and his eyes stared vacantly. "The Peace Wardens ... why shoot everyone?"

Darcy shot him a look, his expression unreadable, and directed his words at Connor. "There's a subway entrance down the block to your left. We'll never get our vehicle out of this traffic jam in time."

His cryptic comment seemed to jar Tony out of his stupor. He looked at Darcy as if just waking from a deep sleep. "In time for what?"

You're losing it, Tony. Connor had no sympathy for him. "He means we've got no time to waste." He glanced at Darcy. "You saw it too, didn't you?"

Darcy nodded grimly, his pale eyes ablaze. "Some of those Peace Wardens were Trackers."

THIRTY-FOUR

TARA LINDHOLM GASPED when she opened her office door at CSMD. She stumbled back, raising a hand to cover her mouth as if disbelieving the evidence of her eyes. Connor's imagination supplied several dire scenarios to explain her reaction.

Darcy missed nothing. He saw his long-time ally's jittery reaction. There was more to the story than a simple unannounced visit. He stepped into her office. Connor crowded in after him, Tony trailing morosely behind.

Darcy morphed smoothly into his networking charm. "I apologize for our unexpected visit." He extended a hand, his most sincere smile lighting up his face. After a moment's hesitation, Tara grasped his hand with trembling fingers. Connor wondered if she noticed, as he did, the unchanged ice in Darcy's eyes. "There's been a disturbing incident in the financial district this afternoon, and we're in need of your services."

Tara retreated another step and collapsed into her chair, beckoning frantically. Connor dragged Tony into the office and closed the door.

She's already seen the slaughter. He watched Tara raise a shaky hand to shield her eyes. She took several deep, slow breaths, and faced Darcy directly.

"I should've known. If anyone survived, it'd be you." The worry lines around her eyes gave her a bleak appearance. "Forgive me, sir, there's been so much chaos, all in a single afternoon. I had no way of knowing whether or not you'd been killed."

Connor felt the tension rise at her cryptic report. There was a missing piece, something they weren't aware of. Tony seemed to have shrunken into himself, reduced to a passive spectator.

"I'm not sure I follow. You thought I'd been killed?" Darcy kept his voice modulated, calm and reassuring. "I was on my way to the Council meeting, and something terrible happened at a protest against the Initiative. I was in the wrong place at the wrong time, nothing more."

Tara stared at him for a long moment, her pale hands clasping spasmodically. She found some reservoir of strength and rotated her chair to face her bank of viewscreens. Connor and Darcy gathered around, looking over her shoulder. Tony recovered sufficiently to shuffle behind them.

Tara pointed to a screen showcasing the carnage in the park. "You're referring to this, I take it? The anti-node protest and the police action to contain the 'rioters'?" She shot a troubled glance over her shoulder. "That's how the Infomedia's been spinning this footage ever since it happened." She didn't wait for Darcy's answer before pointing to a second screen. "Were you aware of this?"

They crowded closer, staring in shock at a video clip set on a repeating loop. Aerial footage showed a skyscraper near the center of Cascadia.

Clouds of black smoke engulfed an entire floor just below

the penthouse level. Tongues of red flame licked out of the burning structure at irregular intervals.

"That used to be the Council Chamber," Tara said woodenly. "Ninety seconds after the 'riot' began, the entire floor exploded. Multiple detonations, clearly a chain reaction. The Council calls for an emergency session, and then this..."

Darcy studied the video. Connor knew he was turning evidence over in his mind, alert for clues, inconsistencies.

"Where's the video from inside the Chamber itself?" Darcy straightened, seemingly energized by the new threat. "How many councilors had arrived before the explosion, and which ones?"

Tara hung her head. "It gets worse, Councilor."

She added nothing else before switching video feeds. The interior of the Chamber filled the main viewscreen. The ornate conference table was unoccupied. Only the cleaning crew was present, tidying up before the meeting. As they watched, one of the cleaners rose in front of the camera, obscuring their view, and then the video went dark.

Sabotage. The single word echoed in Connor's mind. *The collaborators?*

"That's everything," Tara said with resigned finality. "We have no idea how much of the Council was present when the bombs went off. Whatever happened, it was planned well in advance. And the timing of the riot is suspicious, as well. Look here."

She redirected their attention to a viewscreen showing the riot footage. Her fingers moved deftly across the controls, and another image emerged. A close-up of the protestors, taken prior to the 'intervention' by the Peace Wardens.

Tara leaned back in her chair, gesturing to the still image.

"If you think the protest *isn't* connected to the Council Chamber bombing, watch this."

She activated the video, and the image transformed into a flurry of action. Tara zoomed in to focus on a solitary figure fighting his way through the throng, lashing out at protestor and counter-protestor alike. The mob turned on him, and he was knocked to the ground. Tara jabbed a finger at the console, freezing the image in place.

"He was screaming something about people dying, and not wanting to hurt anyone, and then he exploded." She recited the facts with clinical detachment, with no attempt to explain the incongruity between her words and the anonymous man's lethal actions.

"Look at his face," Tara said, increasing the magnification. "He's not *behaving* like a Tracker, but that's an active scanning eye. He wasn't in that park by accident. He was in the perfect position to instigate panic."

"And the CSPW opened fire on innocent Citizens." Darcy inhaled sharply in a rare display of unease. "And a number of the Wardens have been replaced by Trackers, who never disobey orders."

"Exactly." Tara sighed, looking defeated. "The protest was a setup, same as the Council Chamber." She shook her head, fear deepening the lines around her haunted eyes. "The Givers have gone on the offensive."

THIRTY-FIVE ⊙

DR. CAMPBELL SIGHED AND STRETCHED her weary limbs. She'd performed so many surgeries in the past few days. It was hard to keep track. She tugged her surgical mask down and stepped away from the operating table.

Her latest Tracker patient lay supine on the operating table, eyes wide, staring at nothing. Campbell nodded to herself, recognizing the signs. The Givers had initiated the recoding sequence in the girl's mental processors. Her lips moved silently as she acquiesced to the alien programming. The conversion process was on track.

The alien cluster had exited the room several minutes earlier. It wasn't necessary for them to be physically present when they invaded the mind of a new recruit. Privately, Campbell preferred it that way. Despite her many years of service, she still felt an awkward queasiness whenever the Givers were in close proximity. Their distinctive aroma didn't help.

She glanced up to catch Councilor Sterne's eye. He hadn't bothered to don surgical attire today, opting instead to observe the procedure from an antiseptic distance. He gestured, beckoning her to join him and Ethan, his personal assistant.

Dr. Campbell sauntered toward the pair with studied nonchalance, tugging her surgical gloves off, finger by finger, the snapping sound underlining her refusal to be intimidated by him. "A new Tracker, Councilor, prepped and ready for its first assignment on behalf of Cascadia."

Her statement was redundant. Sterne was well-aware of the successful surgery. She was simply taking advantage of an opportunity to remind him of her strategic importance.

Sterne didn't take the bait, ignoring her insolent tone. "You'll be pleased to learn, I'm sure, that we were able to find a use for your most recent surgical failure." His benign expression, coupled with a benevolent tone, made the barbed insult all the more biting. "By now, you've probably seen the results on the Infomedia."

Campbell glared silently and tossed her wadded-up gloves into a nearby recepticle.

"Well done, Mr. Jacobs," Sterne said to his assistant. "The Givers have noted your service."

"Thank you, sir." Ethan fidgeted awkwardly, not glancing at the livid surgeon. "The edited riot footage was pretty convincing. The Initiative should proceed at an accelerated rate."

A satisfied smile flitted across Sterne's face. "The pieces are falling into place."

Dr. Campbell edged closer, curiosity outweighing resentment. Despite the lingering sting of his snub, she couldn't hide her eagerness. "Everything's on schedule, then?"

"Yes. The Givers will be pleased." Sterne clasped his hands behind his back, a look of hungry anticipation on his face. "I'll alert Mateo."

THIRTY-SIX

MEGAN'S SCREAM WAS a call to arms, and Don led the charge down the corridor. Aubrey had never seen him more incensed. He shoved the infirmary door violently open. It rebounded off the interior wall and he lunged inside. Sizing up the crisis, he snatched one of the prods from Doc's worktable and pivoted to confront Mateo.

"You want to see how much damage I can do with this?" He brandished the prod in his massive fist. "Aubrey tells me the left eye is a good spot. Go ahead—light up your scanner, give me a good target."

Garr intercepted him, blocking the big man from reaching Mateo. Aubrey halted just inside the door, Sheila crowding in beside her. Adrenaline set Aubrey's nerves on fire—Megan's scream awakened her worst nightmares.

Mateo stood alone on the opposite side of the infirmary, calm and unflappable. He cocked his head to one side, studying Don as if he were a new specimen to be catalogued. "Must I really repeat myself, Mr. Benoit? Your penchant for emotional overreaction continues to undermine your ability for rational decision-making."

Don growled something inarticulate, and Garr was hard-pressed to prevent him from acting on his threat.

You don't make it easy, Mateo. Aubrey was floored by his audacity. *You don't earn trust with insults.*

Megan sprawled in a graceless heap on the gurney, the only barrier separating Mateo from the rest of the Runners. Doc hovered over her, an anguished look on her face.

"What did you do to her?" Doc glared over her shoulder. "Megan *trusted* you."

"I did precisely what I said I would, Dr. Simon. What each of you agreed to, including our unconscious colleague," Mateo replied, observing his fellow Tracker with detached curiosity. "An experiment, in hopes of reactivating Megan's subroutines. Experiments, of any kind, entail a certain amount of risk. As a person of science, you should be well aware of this."

"Megan isn't a lab rat," Sheila interrupted hotly.

"That's enough, all of you." Garr released his grip on Don, but stayed firmly planted between him and Mateo. "Megan knew it was risky, but she gave her consent. Stop with the blame game —no one's at fault."

Don reluctantly lowered the prod, flicking the power off with his thumb. He tossed his prod on the worktable, his scowl unchanged.

Sheila slipped past Aubrey, hovering beside the gurney opposite Doc Simon. Doc lifted Megan's limp arm, fingers pressed against her wrist. Aubrey held her breath until Doc nodded. She'd found a pulse.

"If I may…" Mateo approached the foot of the gurney. He hesitated, uncharacteristically, at the baleful look Doc aimed his way. "Dr. Simon, my ability to scan the patient is more efficient than your primitive methods."

"Be my guest," Doc replied icily, glaring at him. "But from a distance, do you understand me?"

"I recommend you do as Doc says." Garr crossed the floor to stand beside Sheila. "We're aware that a Tracker's scanning range isn't dependent on close proximity."

Mateo gave him a curious look. "When we're scanning for Implants, yes. That's what we were designed to do. Megan is a different matter."

His gaze shifted from Garr to Doc. Neither showed any inclination to budge. Don coughed into his hand, glancing with exaggerated significance at the prod. Mateo acquiesced with a slight nod, stepping away from the gurney.

Aubrey couldn't repress a shiver as he activated his scanner. The reddish glow gave his gaunt face an alien aspect. She tried not to stare, but couldn't help herself. *That circle of light means death.*

If Mateo was bothered by Doc's furious glare, he hid it well. He scanned Megan from head to foot and back again, taking his time. His expression was difficult to read.

"I see no evidence of additional damage," he said at last. The red circle pulsed under his skin with a steady, mechanical rhythm. "Nor is there any indication whether or not our experiment succeeded. Only time will tell."

"And we can't tell whether or not you're lying," Sheila said coolly, studying him with shrewd eyes. "Your reputation for coy deception is well-earned. You've got a serious lack of transparency, unless it suits you, of course."

"You should have a chat with Amos about the value of not second-guessing your allies," Mateo replied, not looking at her.

He scanned Megan's limp form again, and the red glow faded, restoring his human appearance. He cocked his head to one side, sniffing deeply, and an odd expression crossed his face.

"Am I the only one who smells something burning?"

THIRTY-SEVEN ◉

"WHAT A WASTE." Aubrey wrinkled her nose as she scraped the blackened cooking pot. "I was looking forward to something besides trail rations for a change."

"I guess we'll never know whether Don was going to poison us or not." Garr grimaced as he helped the big man wrestle the cooking unit away from the wall for a thorough cleaning. Don stooped to yank the power cord out. Aubrey noticed that he didn't respond to Garr's attempt at lightening the mood.

The door opened and Sheila strode in. She made a show of holding her nose as she frowned at what remained of the feast that might have been. "Good thing we're in the subbasement. The locals will assume the Mission's cooking crew burned the evening meal."

"Lucky for us," Garr replied, scrubbing the surface of the cooking unit. "We've had too many close calls already. Let's not tempt fate."

"How's Megan doing?" Aubrey paused her scraping. "Has there been any change?"

Sheila shook her head, dropping the pretense of plugging her nose. "Still out cold. Doc's keeping an eye on her, but it looks like we're going to have to wait." She tried, and failed, to repress a smile. "And, for the record, Mateo's been banned from the infirmary, until further notice."

Aubrey finished cleaning the pot, grinning in spite of herself. *I can imagine the expression on Doc's face when she did it. And the look on Mateo's face, too.*

The door opened again, this time to usher Amos and Jane into the mess hall. They halted abruptly, sniffing the air. Amos recovered first, crossing the room to speak with Garr, Jane close on his heels.

Something's up. Aubrey's grin faded. Her chest constricted, matching the sinking feeling in her stomach. *What else can go wrong today?*

"The dropbox." Garr straightened from his task. "Any updates, pigeon posts?"

Amos shook his head. "We didn't make it that far."

"Not even close," Jane said.

"Trackers?" Don spoke for the first time since leaving the infirmary. He wiped his hands on a towel. "Or another Hoarder convoy?"

"Both," Amos and Jane said in unison. They glanced at each other, and Amos gestured for her to continue.

"Two Hoarder trucks," Jane said, "parked in the alley behind a clothing shop." She removed her cap and crushed it between her palms. It looked new. "We saw three people—sedated—in the truck closest to us."

"We couldn't see inside the other vehicle," Amos said before anyone could ask. "We also don't know what the Hoarders' plans for them are—more Implants, or more Trackers." He paused uneasily. "Speaking of Trackers, we caught one scanning the street about a block away."

"He passed within three feet of us," Jane said, fiddling absent-mindedly with her cap. "Between Trackers and Hoarders, it's getting crowded out there."

Amos shrugged. "We've seen Trackers prowling near Eastside before. Hoarder abductions are the bigger worry. Any time an adversary changes tactics..."

Aubrey's heart sank. Her hands were trembling. *Textbook symptoms of anxiety.* She recalled one of Doc's many explanations. *Hold it together, Aubs. You're not the weak link.*

Garr ran a hand through his hair. "The Hoarders could be deploying extra Trackers in the area because they suspect we're located nearby. Their ambush failed last week, and they lost a number of Trackers in the process."

"Or this new Tracker was tipped off somehow," Sheila replied, stuffing her fists into her pockets. "If he knew Hoarders were kidnapping locals to Implant—don't they return them to the same area, post-Implant?"

"To avoid arousing suspicion, yes." Aubrey was glad for a topic she could speak to with authority. "Take me, for example. I've got no memory of being abducted, or Implanted. I had no idea what they'd done to me until..."

Her voice trailed off as she visualized her final evening in Thomas and Sarah's kitchen, before one of the Soul-less broke down the door. A farmhouse, engulfed in flames...

"It may not make much difference, either way," Sheila said, fixing her gaze on Garr, driving her point home. "Between extra Trackers in the vicinity, plus kidnappers from the Enclave, Eastside's no longer a safe haven."

"Evacuation protocol." Garr's terse announcement fell into

a somber silence. He stooped to plug in the cooking unit, and Don helped him shove it into place against the wall. Their task complete, Garr pivoted wearily and leaned against the counter. "Pack what you need, and get a good night's sleep. Tomorrow, we head for Cascadia."

"So much safer." Don laughed without much humor. "Back to Hoarderville, everyone's favorite tourist destination."

The walls seemed to close in as he spoke.

Aubrey bit her lip. *The feast was a temporary distraction. We all know what's next—the Enclave, Darcy, and the Givers.*

"Trail rations for the road." Don heaved a heavy sigh. "And trail rations before bed. Let's all remember to thank our good friend Mateo for that."

"Where is Mateo?" Amos glanced around the mess hall. "Is he with Doc?"

The question seemed to startle Sheila. "No, Doc told him to stay clear of the infirmary."

There was a moment of stunned silence. A quick search of the Hub confirmed Aubrey's suspicion.

Mateo had disappeared.

THIRTY-EIGHT ◎

CHAOTIC IMAGES FLASHED through Megan's mind at dizzying speed, with no discernible connection from one to the next. She fought to focus on the spinning images, desperate to catch one in her hands and force it to hold still, long enough to identify and comprehend.

She floated, weightless, flailing uselessly. An image sailed past, just out of reach. She lunged for it, hands out-stretched, but gravity tripled without warning. Megan's stomach heaved and she plummeted like a rock.

No matter how hard she tried, she couldn't capture any of the spiraling images or slow her tumultuous descent. *This is all just in my mind.* She tried to impose control, to no avail. *Mateo did something to me...*

Mateo. The name became an anchor in her swirling vision. A face attached itself to the name, and she clung to it. *Mateo. He's one of us—one like me—a Tracker.*

Another part of her mind erupted in furious protest. *No more voices, no more Givers. I am Megan.*

A change—was her precipitous descent beginning to slow? Had her single, defiant assertion of identity somehow allowed her to assert a modicum of control? She tried concentrating on a single image in the whirlwind. She was rewarded at last, but not as she'd expected.

Megan landed hard on an unyielding surface, and a heavy weight settled on her chest, pinning her mercilessly. She panicked, unable to breathe, and her limbs refused to obey. Her heartbeat thundered, rattling her bones.

Her ears popped loudly, as if she'd fallen down a steep mountainside. The whirlwind winked out of existence, with one exception. A solitary image refused to disappear. On the contrary, it expanded, dominating her mind's eye, and abruptly asserted control.

She was *inside* the image. It wasn't a hallucination, it was a *memory*. Two technological devices, cupped in the palm of an unknown hand. Mental processors. She heard afresh her cries of panic and despair. *We didn't betray you. Please, don't turn me into one of Them!*

"Will someone *please* shut her up?"

Megan fastened eagerly on the exasperated voice. This was more than she'd remembered before.

A second voice—female—replied to the first. "As you wish, Councilor."

The image of the twin processors flickered and vanished. The crushing pressure on her ribs lifted, and Megan felt almost weightless with its departure.

She gasped, gulping in great drafts of oxygen, and found herself in the infirmary again. Her vision cleared. Doc Simon leaned over her, brow furrowed with worry.

"Megan? Can you hear me?" Doc repeated the question

over and over. Megan heard the anguish in her voice. "Don't try to speak. Just nod if you understand me."

Megan levered herself up on her elbows, grimacing at the pain in her joints. *Everything hurts. Like I've run a marathon or something.* She nodded and managed a weary smile. "I hear you fine, Doc."

Doc's eyes widened, and Megan bolted upright. *That was me. That was my voice.* "Doc, you heard me, didn't you? I'm not hallucinating?"

Doc laughed, her worried expression melting into delighted relief. "Yes, Megan, I heard you, loud and clear. And if you're using words like 'hallucinating,' I'd say you're just fine."

Her laughter was contagious. Megan's grin stretched wider. "It worked. Mateo's blood transfusion, I mean. Listen to me —I can *talk*."

Doc placed a hand on her shoulder, her eyes full of merriment. "Yes. That crazy Tracker's idea succeeded, after all. We've all been worried sick about you. We thought Mateo killed you—Don almost took a prod to him. Wait here. I'll go tell everyone you're okay." She paused at the door, looking over her shoulder with an impish grin. "I'll just tell them you're awake. You can surprise them when they get here."

Megan nodded, grinning, and Doc was gone.

She sat cross-legged on the gurney, gazing at her hands. She flexed them, over and over, grateful as the stiffness faded. It felt like she'd been run over by a truck.

A lock of hair fell forward, covering her good eye. She pushed it back, tucking it behind her ear. She felt lighter than she had in weeks, despite the still-receding stiffness.

She stretched her arms and legs. As she'd guessed already, the enhancements no longer affected her strength.

She remembered how the sensation felt, but there was no evidence of it now. Still, to be able to speak—that was worth everything. The nightmarish vision she'd been forced to endure was a small price to pay.

She fastened on one specific memory. The final moments before the Givers stole her humanity and transformed her into a Tracker.

Her lips curled in a darker smile.

That voice she'd heard in her nightmare/memory. The one they called "Councilor."

She knew him.

THIRTY-NINE ◉

"YOU'VE GOT A VISITOR, Colonel," Sheila said, poking her head into the mess hall. Garr looked up in surprise, pried away from the scraps of paper on the tabletop.

We don't get many visitors. Aubrey was intrigued, mirroring his reaction. *Eastside Hub isn't exactly a tourist attraction.*

Before Garr could respond, Sheila pushed the door open and Enrico Torres took a tentative step into the mess hall. He seemed ill at ease, and Aubrey recalled hearing about the mechanic's reluctance to be associated too closely with the Hub network. Garr stood, motioning for his long-time friend to join him at the table.

"You've never visited Eastside before." Garr shook Enrico's hand and they sat down, facing each other. The colonel leaned forward, elbows on the scuffed table, studying the mechanic with probing eyes.

"I've never had a compelling reason," Enrico replied, removing his weathered cap and twisting it nervously between his hands. "Until today, that is."

Aubrey thought she could guess the reason for the heavy silence following his cryptic remark. "Should we make ourselves scarce, Garr?" She half-rose from her seat and gestured with one hand at Don and Sheila.

"You must have an opinion." Garr cocked an eyebrow at his guest. "Is this a private conversation?"

Enrico settled into his chair with an audible sigh. "That won't be necessary. In fact, I'd prefer if everyone heard what I have to say." He glanced at Don, who'd just finished cleaning the cooking unit. "Would you mind closing the door? I'd feel better knowing it was shut."

Don wiped his hands on a towel, returning Enrico's gaze as he shut the door. "I thought you wanted everyone to hear whatever it is you're itching to say." Sheila joined him at the foot of the table, arms crossed. She could look intimidating, when she wanted to.

"Yes, of course." Enrico leaned back in his chair. "My concern is having unexpected guests drop in without warning. My reflexes are pretty sharp. All it takes is the sound of a door opening, and I'll switch topics on the spot."

"That sounds like overkill." Don tossed his towel on the counter behind him. "Paranoia isn't needed at Eastside."

"Is that so?" Enrico didn't sound convinced. He folded his hands on the table and addressed Garr. "You've got a mole, Colonel Scott."

Don lurched into motion, seizing a chair and reversing it before sitting down. He crossed his arms over the back of the chair and fixed an uncompromising stare on the mechanic. "We'd guessed as much after the Tracker ambush," he said, his voice gruff. "You're a little late to the party, my friend."

Garr laid a hand on Don's arm. "The one thing he swore

he'd never do," he said, nodding at Enrico, "was set foot in our Hub. He wouldn't be here, if there wasn't something we need to know."

Enrico nodded, stealing a nervous look at the door. "I've heard rumors. South Central's been sacked, and you've been warned to avoid contact with the other Hubs. You found an anonymous warning to that effect in your dropbox."

"Your intel's pretty good." Don drew the words out, his drawl more pronounced than normal. "Who's your source?"

Enrico shrugged sheepishly, looking at Garr. "I did some repairs at the Mission a few days ago. Uncle John and I had a chat. He filled me in." He leaned over the table, lowering his voice. "Were you also aware there's a new Tracker scanning in the area? A young man, about thirty years old, I'd guess. Medium build, brown hair, green eyes."

Garr nodded. "A couple of our people spotted him. We think he's scanning for new Implants. The Hoarders seem to be intensifying their efforts—"

Enrico shook his head emphatically, raising both hands to interrupt. He jabbed a finger at the scraps of notepaper in front of Garr. "Who do you think put that anonymous note in your dropbox? I saw him—with my own eyes—right after I left the Mission."

Sheila stifled a gasp. "A *Tracker* left the note?"

Don snapped his fingers. "To isolate us from the rest of the Hub network. Divide and conquer—an oldie, but a goodie."

Aubrey's heart dropped. *Was I followed? Am I the weak link after all?* "We took every precaution, Garr, I swear."

Enrico locked eyes with Garr. "You're pawns in someone else's game. If I were you, I'd figure out whose."

FORTY ⊙

AUBREY RUBBED her tired eyes and tried to sort out her thoughts. *The past two days have been an emotional—what did Doc call it?—an emotional rollercoaster.*

After Garr announced the evacuation protocol, she'd retreated to the relative privacy of the dreary room she shared with Sheila and Jane. At some point, she fell asleep, but didn't have much energy when she woke early the next morning.

She sat on her lumpy mattress, leaning against the cinderblock wall behind her, and recalled Doc's vivid description of a rollercoaster. She understood why Doc chose the antiquated metaphor. The giddy preparation and dashed expectation of their hoped-for feast, the discovery of Hoarder abductions, Enrico's cryptic warning, Megan's dramatic recovery…

I think I'd rather ride a real rollercoaster. At least I could disembark once the ride was over.

Her stomach tightened as she caught sight of the pack at the foot of her bunk, stocked and ready. Their rollercoaster ride was far from over.

"You ready, Aubs?" Sheila slipped into the room, leaving the door open. Dim light snuck inside from the corridor, dispelling a portion of the oppressive atmosphere. Her pack dangled from one hand. She hefted it, as if gauging its weight.

Aubrey leaned away from the wall, gesturing at her pack. "As soon as Garr gives the word, I'm packed and ready to go." She tried to shake the sense of foreboding that had settled over her like a damp blanket. "I'd rather sleep for a week, but Doc might call that *avoidance*. Or denial, maybe."

Sheila sat on the edge of her bunk, elbows propped on her knees. "Waiting is the worst, isn't it? I'd rather be on our way, even if it means the Enclave, Hoarders, *and* Givers. Just sitting here, waiting, drives me crazy."

Aubrey arched her stiff spine, feeling with satisfaction an answering twinge of muscle and bone. "The Cascadia Enclave —what's it like? I don't mean how sophisticated, or wealthy, or anything we discussed at debrief. I mean, what's it actually *like* to be there, surrounded by Hoarders?"

Sheila took a moment to ponder, gazing at a spot just over Aubrey's shoulder. "It's hard to put into words. On the surface, I'd say it's a society that prides itself on being superior to the rest of us. At the same time, they're paralyzed with fear over any threat to their way of life, so they're fanatically obsessed about border security. And as far as they're concerned, *anyone* outside Cascadia is a potential invader." She stretched out on her bunk with a self-deprecating laugh. "You'll have your own opinions, soon enough. And my observations are *not* neutral. I had to play nice with a sociopath, remember?"

Aubrey laughed, glad for an excuse to let her emotions out —any emotions. "I can't imagine what that must've been like. Do you think Darcy's forgotten that I almost shot him?"

Sheila sat up, a sly smirk on her face. "Is that what you're worried about? Okay, I guess if I were you, I'd be wondering the same thing." Her smirk morphed into a grin. "It's probably safe to assume a mad genius like Darcy *just might* remember the 'savage' who stuck a gun in his face."

They both dissolved into laughter.

"Keep a low profile." Sheila's eyes turned serious as their laughter faded. "Stick close to me, or Garr, or Jane. The Hoarders are desperate. Darcy needs our help, and he knows it. He won't make any moves against you. At least, not until *after* we've dealt with the Givers." She leaned closer, taking Aubrey's hands in her own. "Doc Simon told me about your little chat. Listen, Aubrey, we're going into the Enclave as a team, and I have no doubt—none at all—about you having my back. You're *not* going to be the weak link. You're too tough for that."

"Thanks, Shiela." Aubrey leaned over to retrieve her pack from the floor. "I don't know if I'm tough, or just too dumb to know when to quit. But I'm going to see this thing through, no matter what. And you're right—waiting is the *worst.*"

They stood, adjusting their packs. Sheila winked mischievously. "Let's round up our fellow Runners. We don't want to keep the Hoarders—I mean, our *allies*—waiting."

FORTY-ONE

"You'll be safer once you're away from Eastside." Garr repeated his explanation as Doc assembled a pair of packs, taking her most precious instruments with her. Enrico, waiting outside in the corridor, had agreed to shoulder one of the packs, and Doc would take the other. "With all the increased traffic in the area, Hoarders *and* Trackers, I'm not comfortable leaving you behind. Not alone."

"I won't argue with you, Colonel," Doc replied, sealing the second pack. "On a personal note, I could probably do with a little fresh air and sunshine after living in this artificial cave for so long."

Garr grinned, reaching for the second pack. "I'm relieved to hear you've still got your sense of humor."

"It's a coping mechanism," Doc replied without inflection, abandoning her pack on the worktable and blocking his exit from the infirmary. "Garr, listen to me," she said, her eyes pleading. "You've pushed our team about as far as you can. I know what we're up against. I'm not second-guessing your strategy or trying to change your mind. But I wouldn't be much of a doctor if I didn't sound the warning. Your team's stretched, almost to the breaking point. That makes everyone vulnerable."

Garr leaned against the worktable, eyes roaming aimlessly around the infirmary. "I won't argue with you, either. We've been walking a razor edge far too long. In the beginning, all I wanted was to find the Implants' source, and seal it off. I figured... no more Implants, no more Trackers." He sighed, his gaze wandering to the surgical lamps suspended from the ceiling. "Things are more complicated than I expected. It never occurred to me that we'd be partnering with *Hoarders*, or having to deal with their alien allies. I didn't set out to recruit this team, but here they are, anyway. But, like I always say—"

"You play the cards you've been dealt." Doc nodded, finishing for him. "Well, Colonel Scott, I hate to admit it, but I think we're both delaying the inevitable. You should be on your way, and I need to make myself scarce."

She opened the door. Enrico, lounging against the opposite wall, roused himself.

Garr stepped into the corridor and handed him the second pack. "Take care of our doctor, Rico. We'll contact you when it's safe to return."

Enrico shouldered the backpack with a nod and a smile. "You have my word, Colonel. She'll be safe with me."

"Ha—more like the other way around." Doc extinguished the lights in the infirmary, gazing into the darkened room for a long moment before focusing on Garr.

"Take care of yourself, Colonel," she said, her voice cracking. "Bring them home, safe and sound. All of them."

Garr snapped to attention and sketched her a full salute—something he'd not done in years.

No words were spoken, but Doc recognized the implied promise. She gave him what she hoped was a reassuring smile and patted him on the shoulder.

They parted ways and she joined Enrico on their long trek out of the subterranean labyrinth.

FORTY-TWO

"Nothing's changed," Amos said as they finished restocking their packs with field rations. "It doesn't make any difference if Mateo reappears or not. I know the location of his 'secret' door. I can find it again."

Don held up his combat knife, admiring the razor-sharp edge he'd taken such great care to hone. He brandished it this way and that, examining it from all angles. Lantern light created dancing reflections along the blade.

"I'm not worried about your sense of direction." He squinted down the length of the blade at Amos. "My concern is whether or not Mateo's told anyone *else* about his secret entrance. Garr splitting us into teams makes sense, but the last thing we need is to run into some nasty surprises in the dark underbelly of Hoarderville."

"Getting past security won't be a picnic, either." Jane finished packing and sealed her pack. Like her companions, she'd added a combat knife to her supply of field rations. "I don't know what's more nerve-wracking—you guys sneaking in Mateo's secret door, or Garr trusting Darcy's man-servant to drive us through Gate Seven."

Amos shrugged, unconvinced. "The Hoarders managed to get us out of the Enclave with no problem. Darcy's name seems to have clout with Cascadia Security. Some of them could be his supporters, for all we know."

"Darcy Peterson, Cascadia's favorite psycho." Don stowed his knife, the wickedly sharp blade hidden by the scabbard. He added the ensemble in his pack, but the hilt protruded slightly under the flap. "That must've been surreal, sitting in his living room, discussing strategy over drinks."

"You'll get your turn soon enough." All heads turned as Garr entered the room, Megan close behind. "Keep your weapons stowed until we've made contact." He issued his orders crisply, looking at each Runner in turn. "Darcy's people will provide us with new outfits, so we'll be able to blend with the locals. This is *terra incognita.*"

"Hidden in plain sight, Hoarder-style." Don winced, shaking his head. "I'll wear the monkey suit if that's what it takes. I just hope some naive little brat doesn't ask me for directions to wherever it is Hoarders go for fun."

Who are you kidding? Amos's inner voice sprang to life, invading his thoughts for the first time in days. *A change of clothes won't be enough. You could betray yourself in a thousand ways, most likely the first time you open your mouth.*

Shut up, Gabriel. Amos took a cleansing breath, refusing to follow that line of thinking. *Rehearsing doomsday scenarios is a waste of time. Focus on solving problems, not imagining them.*

"I wouldn't worry about it," Megan said, dragging Amos's attention back to the mess hall. She pulled her hair into a ponytail, mimicking Sheila's no-nonsense approach. Her eyepatch, and the surrounding scar tissue, would be impossible to miss. "They'll be too busy staring at me."

Don glanced at her, fidgeting with his pack. He was, perhaps, recalling his former animosity for the "mindless killing machine," and wondering if Megan was aware of it.

"Is there anything you can tell us about the Enclave?" Don asked at last, his voice subdued. "You've got your speech back. Did any new memories come with it?"

"Nope." Megan eyed him coolly. "A few vague impressions, but nothing specific."

"Those Hoarders recognized you," Jane said. Her pointed words sounded like an accusation. "The blond kid called you by name. You must have *some* memory of them."

"We covered this during the debrief, Jane." There was no recrimination in Megan's voice, but Jane bristled nonetheless. Megan continued as if she hadn't noticed. "Garr says the boy's name is Connor. That may be true, but beyond that, his name means nothing to me."

"Doesn't it prove you used to be a Citizen?" Jane tried a different angle, still suspicious. "You saved Darcy's life once already. How do we know you won't do it again?"

"When did Darcy become our target?" Megan gave her a curious look, cocking her head to one side, eerily reminiscent of Mateo. "The Givers are the enemy. That's the whole point of the alliance."

Alliance. You sound like Mateo. Amos didn't find her answer at all reassuring. *I'm still trying to get used to you speaking.*

Megan turned to address the rest of the group. "This much I can tell you. I became a Tracker, against my will, but I have no memory of my life before that. For five years, I served as a bodyguard for the Givers, after which I was deployed on my first

Quest." She smiled ruefully, tracing the edge of her eyepatch with her fingertips, the gesture more human than Tracker. "You already know how that ended."

An awkward silence followed her unvarnished remarks. Garr cleared his throat. "Why would the Givers change your assignment? They must have had good reason to take a seasoned bodyguard and give her new orders."

Megan laughed bitterly. "There were never 'reasons,' only orders. Reasons were irrelevant. Trackers are obsessed with one thing—the Givers' approval. Once we're sent on a Quest, all that matters is the Harvest."

Amos swallowed with difficulty, picturing the murdered Runners they'd found, gutted for their Implants. The Givers had devised a brutally efficient counterattack to Darcy's strategy.

"I guess knowing they'll blow you up for failure is a good incentive, too," Don said dryly.

Megan didn't answer at once. "Fear is all we have," she said, staring off into the distance, not meeting anyone's gaze. "That, and the Quest."

Amos and Don exchanged glances, and Jane wisely dropped her thinly-veiled interrogation.

Megan addressed Garr, a haunted look in her eyes. "There's something else I need to tell you. Trackers don't compete with each other during a Quest. Only the Harvest matters." She swallowed hard, looking at the floor. "Yet I ... eliminated another Tracker that night. I was determined to complete the Quest, and he got in my way. Trackers don't function like that, not under normal operating conditions."

"You mean you were malfunctioning?" Jane managed to sound reasonable—barely. "After five years, your brain tech developed a glitch? And the Givers didn't notice?"

"I don't know." Megan glanced at her, but there was no animosity in her reply. "I'm only pointing out that I wasn't functioning like a typical Tracker."

"How does that intel help us?" Don directed his question to Garr. "I'm not trying to be flippant. I'm curious."

"I'm not sure." Garr rubbed his jaw, studying Megan closely. "At minimum, it might mean the Givers' control over Trackers isn't absolute. I can't think of any way we could turn that to our advantage, but every bit of intel helps, even if we can't see it right away."

Sheila and Aubrey entered the mess hall, each packed and ready to go. "We've said our goodbyes to Doc Simon," Sheila said. "When do we head out?"

"Now," Garr replied, rubbing his palms together. "The rendezvous is tomorrow morning, and Darcy said he'd have a vehicle waiting. I want to arrive before they do. No sense giving them the high ground, so to speak."

"Now you're talking." Don grinned, getting to his feet and hefting his pack in one meaty fist. "It's none of the Hoarders' business that we have Mateo's truck. Let them think we're on foot. We're better off if they underestimate us. As far as they're concerned, we're just mindless savages, after all. "

"I'm not sure the Hoarders would notice or care how we get to the rendezvous," Sheila replied with a wry smile. "Amos and Garr, I hope you packed those Hoarder outfits Darcy gave you. We'll need the camouflage soon enough."

Amos patted his pack. "Right here."

Garr paused at the door, turning to face them.

The air was charged with tension and adrenaline as they prepared for another foray into Hoarder territory. Amos felt it. He was certain his companions did, as well.

"Amos, you'll take Aubrey and Megan with you." Garr fell into the familiar role of leadership. "Once you've dropped us off at the rendezvous, I want you gone long before they arrive. The rest of you are with me."

Don slung his pack over his shoulder. "Aye, aye, Colonel."

Garr ignored his attempt at humor and swept his arm in wide arc to indicate the mess hall. "If we succeed, there won't be any need for Eastside Hub. And if we fail, none of us are coming back, anyway. I promised Doc I'd bring you back, safe and sound." His gaze wandered around the circle. "But let's be realistic—I've got no control over that. All I can promise is that I've got your back. Everyone needs to have each other's back. No exceptions."

Heads nodded solemnly. Amos took a deep breath. He had no real reaction to the idea they might never sit in the mess hall again. It was too far-off, too nebulous to consider seriously. All he saw in his mind's eye was the armament above Gate Seven, and Darcy's arrogant face.

"There's more than one way to skin a Hoarder," Don said in his thickest drawl. He sketched a grand gesture at the open door. "After you, Colonel."

Garr hitched his fingers into his shoulder straps and strode out of the room. His companions followed, one by one.

Amos and Sheila, out of long habit, extinguished the lanterns, plunging the mess hall into gloomy twilight. Amos felt an odd twinge in his gut. *I hope there's nothing symbolic about dousing the lights.*

Sheila waited by the door for him, and they jogged to catch up to the others.

FORTY-THREE

"I'm getting too old for this," Doc said when she and Enrico took a brief rest break. She bent over, hands on her knees, catching her breath. "Running through the tunnels is a game for the younger generation."

Enrico grinned, leaning against one of the rivet-studded pillars supporting the arched ceiling. "We've kept a decent pace, Doc, but I wouldn't call this *running*. Look on the bright side—at least we're following the subway, instead of the sewer. Aside from avoiding the stench, there's a challenging climb up a ladder in the ceiling ducts. Not for the faint of heart."

"Or the stiff of body." She straightened with a groan, pressing her hands against the small of her back. "Aubrey told me about the ceiling ducts during one of our PT sessions." She shrugged her shoulders, searching for a comfortable position for her pack. She couldn't find one.

Enrico watched her with sad eyes, but Doc pretended not to notice. He trudged a few yards further and halted before a nondescript door.

"We're almost there, Doc." He gestured to the door. "We've got two flights of stairs to climb, I'm sorry to say, but my truck's waiting at the top."

"Two flights—is that all? I thought you said this was going to be difficult." Doc took a deep breath, flashed him a weary grin, and nodded at the door. "And, just for the record, I'm not *that* old. After you, good sir."

Enrico nodded, leading the way up the concrete steps. Doc felt the ache in her knees as they climbed, accented by an insistent pain in the small of her back. *Almost there*, she told herself with each step.

The stairwell grew brighter as they ascended. Natural light leaked around the edges of a rusted door at the apex of the stairs. Enrico threw his shoulder against the door and, hinges whining, it swung grudgingly open. Doc followed him into an abandoned warehouse.

Sunlight filtered through a row of grimy windows set high in the wall, a welcome change after the gloomy tunnel. Enrico's treasured truck sat waiting in the middle of the empty space, and Doc felt her spirits lift.

Enrico halted abruptly, throwing out an arm to block her. Doc heard his sharp intake of breath a second before she spotted the problem. A young man, not much older than Amos, lounged beside the truck, one arm resting lazily on the hood. A glint of red showed around one eye.

"Ah, the mechanic," the Tracker said, as if anticipating their arrival. His gaze shifted to her, and he nodded, pleased. "And the physician."

Enrico cleared his throat. "You left the fake note in Eastside's dropbox." He sidled in front of Doc as he spoke, shielding her. She chose not to comment on his futile gesture.

The Tracker didn't deny Enrico's accusation. He scanned them from head to foot, his casual posture unchanged. The red circle faded, and he took three long strides to stand opposite them, his body a barrier between them and the truck.

Doc stepped in front of Enrico to confront the Tracker. "You used to be one of us. A free man, until the Hoarders kidnapped you and turned you over to the Givers."

"You're wasting your time, Doc," Enrico said bitterly. "It's a killing machine. Trackers think whatever the Givers tell them to think. You can't reason with it."

"Is that true?" Doc's mouth felt like it was full of cotton. "The Givers sent you to kill us?"

The Tracker cocked his head to one side, his expression neutral. "Your termination would serve no purpose," he said in an odd monotone. "Mateo has another use for you."

FORTY-FOUR

"You're sure this is the rendezvous they agreed to?" Connor couldn't resist the jibe.

Tony shot him a dirty look. "I know where I dropped the savages off. If they aren't here, that's not on me."

Connor shrugged and settled into his seat to wait. Their windshield was filthy, thanks to a hasty trip through the muddy roads of Parasite City. He smirked to himself. The shantytown's disparaging nickname was poetically apt.

Tony decided to park in the middle of a deserted intersection. The empty streets and abandoned buildings, in varying stages of disrepair and decay, were a stunning counterpoint to Cascadia's thriving economy.

The savages were late. Connor found the delay more troubling than he wanted to admit. The Council Chamber bombing, coupled with the heavy-handed tactics of the Peace Wardens at the protest, left his nerves frayed. The Infomedia's pro-Anodyne propaganda wasn't helping, either.

He'd anticipated a smooth rendezvous with the savages,

followed by a strategic retreat past Gate Seven. Their new "allies," it appeared, had other ideas.

We're sitting ducks. He cursed the savages under his breath. *If Darcy didn't need you as drones, I'd leave you behind.*

Darcy had decided to stay behind, strategizing new ways of dealing with the unexpected complications of the past few days. Connor knew his foster father was engaged in covert consultations with his allies and informants, probing for useful intel.

We'll play the role of shocked and grieving Citizens. Darcy was insistent, pointing out that any other public reaction could attract unwanted scrutiny. *Keep a low profile until I learn who's behind these attacks.*

Tony had suggested their identity was obvious—the Givers. Connor smirked at the memory of a livid Darcy putting the over-eager chauffeur in his place. *Of course, it was the Givers. But* which *collaborators acted on their orders?*

Beside him, Tony mumbled something under his breath. Connor glanced at him, annoyed, noting his restless mannerisms. The strain affected them all, but Tony seemed to be caving in. He drummed on the steering wheel, which was a slight improvement from whistling tunelessly between his teeth.

Connor felt a stab of irritation. Waiting for the savages in the Old City was bad enough. Sitting beside Darcy's pet killer was worse. Connor's mood darkened further. He'd never forgive Tony for Madison's murder.

"Maybe they're not coming." Tony shifted in the driver's seat. He sounded hopeful. "Maybe they figured out that Darcy plans to Implant them."

Connor rolled his eyes. "You give the savages too much credit. They don't have the brains to figure that out. They're animals, Tony, nothing more."

Tony had the nerve to laugh in his face. "Try listening to yourself sometime, Connor. Do you have any idea how *stupid* you sound, mindlessly repeating Darcy's talking points? You're worse than a trained parrot."

Connor's cheeks burned and he bolted upright. "Talking points? You don't know savages like we do ..." An image of Megan's disfigured face flashed across his mind. He faltered, unable to continue.

"I can't believe how gullible you are." Tony laughed, obviously enjoying the reaction he'd provoked. "You're half-right about the savages. They're primitive, filthy, and only fit for jobs on the maintenance level." He leaned over the console, his eyes narrowed in contempt. "But don't be an idiot. They may be animals, but they're *cunning* little beasts. When you underestimate them, you put everyone at risk."

Connor stared, stunned by his erratic mood swings, and noticed something at odds with his cocky bravado. The bleak look around his eyes, the fine sheen of perspiration on his face, the slight quaver in his voice—the combination betrayed Tony's true state of mind.

Fear. Tony was consumed by it. He was in way over his head, and the cracks were beginning to show.

Connor felt no pity. Tony was Madison's executioner, Darcy's spineless lackey who did his bidding without question or conscience.

"Don't be ridiculous." Connor lanced the strained silence, not breaking eye contact. "I know what the savages are capable of. I saw what they did to my sister." He turned away, glaring out the muddy windshield. "But they're still animals. Cannon fodder, nothing more."

His hand sought his sternum, feeling for the locket under

his shirt. It helped center him, gave him focus. "Once the Givers are gone, the savages will answer for what they've done."

Tony resumed his arrhythmic drumming.

For several long minutes, neither of them spoke.

FORTY-FIVE ◉

"ANYONE CARE TO PLACE a friendly wager on how much chaos there is inside Hoarderville?" Don gestured beyond their temporary hiding spot to the Enclave.

They'd chosen to wait on the flat rooftop of an abandoned apartment building a few blocks east of the agreed-upon rendezvous. The view was not expansive. The building was only three floors high, small enough that it didn't have an elevator. The monolithic walls of Cascadia were visible to the west.

Garr knelt by the parapet, sweeping the intersection with his binoculars. His position gave him a clear view of the waiting Hoarders without betraying their presence.

"It's been five days," Sheila said, keeping an eye on the truck in the intersection below. "I wonder how many Citizens have already lined up for their nodes?"

"Like mindless lemmings," Jane said, chewing on field rations as they waited. "Too bad we can't reprogram Trackers to go after nodes instead of Implants."

Garr sensed the tension eating at his companions. He heard

in their voices, despite their light-hearted banter. "I doubt the Givers would share their tech," he replied to Jane's half-joking suggestion. His lenses moved across the scene in a slow arc. "But I wouldn't put it past them to use Trackers to deal with any hold-outs among the Citizens."

"How long are you planning to make the Hoarders wait?" Sheila aimed a mischievous grin at him. "I'll bet the suspense is driving them crazy."

"Fine by me," Jane replied around a mouthful of dried fruit. "Let the Hoarders sweat."

Garr lowered the binoculars and rubbed his eyes. "We need to give Amos and his team enough time to get into position." He gestured at the Enclave, wreathed in the low clouds of an impending storm. "There's a lot of unknown variables—as Shei-la said, it's been five days. We have no idea what's happened in the meantime."

Don gave an evil chuckle, wringing his hands in a parody of the proverbial mad scientist. "And if it happens to fray the nerves of our waiting Hoarders, so much the better."

Jane held her hand out, and Garr handed the binoculars to her. She knelt beside him, poking her head over the edge for a clear look at the vehicle and its impatient occupants. "It's just the kid, Connor, and the old guy. No sign of everyone's favorite psycho."

Garr knew better than to take her bravado at face value. Jane was as anxious as anyone about the prospect of confront-ing Darcy again. *Like dancing with a scorpion*, he'd told Doc the previous evening. It felt like a long time ago.

He and Sheila wore the Hoarder outfits Darcy had given them during their first foray into Cascadia. Don and Jane took their jackets off and stowed them into their packs. Their shirts

weren't quite up to Hoarder standards, but were less conspicuous than their jackets. Jane shivered every now and then in the
autumn air. Don didn't seem to notice the chill.

"There's not enough seats," Jane said, studying the truck
through Garr's binoculars. "One of us is going to have to ride
in the back, like a piece of luggage."

"I nominate Don," Garr replied. "The less suspicion we
arouse, the better. Security will focus on the driver. Keep your
head down, Don, and try to look non-threatening."

"Like a daisy in the summer sun," Don drawled.

"We've given Amos's team enough time." Garr collected his
binoculars from Jane and stowed them in his pack. "Let's rendezvous with our new allies."

Jane got to her feet, shivering again. Garr knew better than
to ask. Sheila brushed dust from her hands, not looking at the
truck waiting below.

"Next stop, the friendly gates of Hoarderville," Don said
to no one in particular, and they descended the dusty stairs.

FORTY-SIX

HEADLIGHTS PIERCED the predawn darkness, illuminating the little-used service road running parallel to Cascadia's perimeter. Clouds hovered low overhead, the threat of a storm adding to the gloomy atmosphere. Aubrey couldn't see the Enclave's outer walls, but she felt their oppressive presence.

It's better than risking one of the gates. She strained to see what lay beyond the headlights. No stars, no moon, only the humid reminder of the imminent storm.

Sneaking in the back door sounds less dangerous. She swallowed the lump in her throat. *Who am I kidding? It's still the Enclave, and Darcy-the-devil is waiting.*

The service road was little more than a narrow gravel track, rising and falling in concert with the uneven terrain. It ran parallel to the Enclave, at a consistent distance of just over a quarter mile. Amos drove with cautious haste over the winding, long-neglected road.

Little had been said after dropping Garr's team off in the Old City. Amos focused on driving. Aubrey sat with her knees drawn up, gazing at the murky gloom, and Megan lay curled up in the rear seat. Aubrey couldn't tell if she was asleep or not. She envied the former Tracker's ability to block out the anxiety that plagued her and Amos.

They crested a steep incline, jolted over a ridge, and began an abrupt descent down the opposite side. Aubrey held her breath, clinging to the panic strap above the passenger door as the truck slalomed down the embankment. A muffled cry sounded behind her, and she felt the impact as Megan caught herself against the back of Aubrey's chair.

"Sorry about that." Amos down-shifted, braking cautiously. The instrument panel gave his face a strange greenish glow. "We've got to be there by sunrise. The window of time between low tide and the day shift is pretty tight."

"I was at the briefing." Aubrey braced one foot against the dashboard for good measure. She regretted her comment as soon as she'd said it. *Sarcasm isn't helpful, Aubs.*

Megan poked her head between the seats, her wavy hair a disheveled cloud around her head. "Don would probably say something funny to relieve the tension." She sighed, brushing her hair back with one hand. "But I'm not him, and I can't think of anything."

The dashboard lights painted her face with the same otherworldly glow, but to Aubrey it seemed somehow more alien. *She's still a blank canvas. Now that she can talk, it's like I have to get to know her all over again.*

Megan glanced at her, and Aubrey averted her eyes. She stared out the windshield and noticed that the sky was changing color. She stole a look in the side mirror, and the sullen storm clouds appeared lighter in the east.

"Should I thank you, Aubrey, or forgive you?" Megan leaned

further forward, her good eye fixed on Aubrey. "Which would you prefer?"

Aubrey twisted in her seat to face the former Tracker, too close for comfort in the truck's cramped interior. "I'm not sure what you mean."

Megan placed her elbow on the console, leaning her weight on it as she edged further into the front seat. "It's pretty simple, actually. Would you like me to thank you for freeing me from the Givers, or forgive you for blinding me with your prod?"

Aubrey recoiled from her frank stare. "I wasn't expecting anything from you," she said, fumbling for the right words. *Uh-oh, that came out wrong.* "What I mean is ... you don't owe me anything."

Megan didn't budge. "So, which is it?"

Aubrey forced herself to not flinch away as she tried to marshal her arguments, her justifications, her rationale. After a brief internal battle, she gave up. "Megan, I don't know what to say. What do you want from me?"

Megan gestured at Aubrey's arm, hidden in the folds of her hoodie. "Roll up your sleeve."

She obeyed without hesitation. Megan studied the scars running up her arm with a distant, clinical expression.

Aubrey was aware, in a peripheral way, of the rocky terrain, but for the moment, Megan held her full and undivided attention. She waited, spellbound.

Amos was abnormally quiet. He appeared content to allow the drama to unfold in the seat beside him.

Megan pointed at Aubrey's scars with her chin. "You weren't yourself when you got those. Am I right?"

It was a rhetorical question—Aubrey caught her point.

"No, I wasn't," she replied anyway. "Any more than you ..."

She hesitated, at a loss for the right words, and finished lamely, "when we first met."

The Implant turned me into one of Darcy's assassins. The Givers turned Megan into a Tracker. We were both forced to do another's bidding against our will. Aubrey was shaken. She'd never noticed the parallels before.

Megan nodded, not breaking eye contact. "Then will you *please* just relax?" She gestured at Aubrey's arm, and then traced a fingertip over the upper rim of her eyepatch. "Guilt is a distraction. We can't afford it once we're inside the Enclave."

"You sound like Mateo." Amos broke his self-imposed silence. "But you're not wrong. We've got to function as a team, no second-guessing. We need to have each other's backs."

"And you sound like Colonel Scott." Megan laughed, sliding back into the rear seat. Aubrey saw Amos smile slighly, but he said nothing.

The road remained little more than a wide stretch of packed earth, barely wide enough for two vehicles to pass. Trees towered on either side, masking Cascadia's massive walls. Amos rolled his window down, and Aubrey caught a salty whiff of ocean air. The lowering clouds were dark gray, and the distant rumble of thunder provided an aura of angry menace.

Aubrey opened her window, invigorated by the chill breeze. *Keep that overactive imagination in check, Aubs. The weather is the least of our worries.*

Amos slowed as they rounded another curve, angling the truck off the road to halt behind a copse of thick underbrush.

"End of the road," he said, climbing out of the truck. Aubrey and Megan followed. Aubrey pulled her jacket tighter in the damp air. She couldn't see the ocean, but she heard the unmistakable sound of waves breaking on the shore.

Amos shrugged into his pack, eyeing the threatening storm clouds. "Let's move. We've got a half hour of hiking ahead of us, and the tide won't wait."

FORTY-SEVEN

Dawn arrived, but in name only. The skies remained gray and threatening but, aside from an occasional sprinkle, the rain appeared to be biding its time. Storm clouds gathered just offshore, and a stiff breeze preceded the storm inland.

Wind lashed against them, carrying the unmistakable tang of sea salt. Amos's voice grew hoarse as he urged, encouraged, and cajoled them to keep moving.

A stronger gust hit Aubrey, pushing her off-balance. *Low tide won't wait. It's like the Givers arranged for a storm at just the right time.* She shook her head, banishing the thought. *Keep a rein on your imagination, remember?*

"How much further?" Megan raised her voice against the howling wind. Like Aubrey, she'd corralled her hair inside her hooded sweatshirt, knotting the drawstring under her chin. "I hear waves breaking on the shore."

"Almost there," Amos replied, pausing to take shelter behind another of an endless series of rocky outcroppings. "Just around this next corner."

"You've said that three times, already." Aubrey huddled on the leeward side of the outcropping. "How far are we from the Enclave?" The wind snatched her words and reduced them to shreds. Her voice sounded thin and fragile in her ears.

"Just over there." Amos waved one hand to the north. "We can't see over the edge of this escarpment, but it's about fifty yards from where we're standing."

"That's all?" Aubrey shivered, and not entirely from the cold. *Steady, Aubs. You are not the weak link.*

Amos pulled her with him as he rounded the corner. They left the relative shelter of the outcropping to face the full force of the wind. They'd taken no more than four or five steps when Amos halted without warning. Aubrey collided with him, scraping her cheek on the rough fabric of his pack.

"Good welcome, Amos." Mateo's voice was distorted by the wind, muffled by the pounding surf, but he sounded genuinely pleased. "I've been waiting. I see you've brought young Aubrey with you, and Megan. Excellent."

"Where have you been?" There was nothing warm about Amos's response. A low rumble of thunder offshore seemed to echo his belligerent challenge. "Your disappearing act is starting to get old."

Mateo squared his shoulders, his expression one of mild consternation. "Dr. Simon ordered me to vacate the infirmary. I took her suggestion to heart—in my own way. It was only a matter of time until you brought a team to my 'secret' door. It was logical to wait here." He stepped closer, ducking his head so they could hear him above the wind and waves. "We *did* discuss this during the briefing."

"I heard Garr's strategy," Aubrey interrupted, unwilling to be a mere spectator to his verbal sparring with Amos. "You made pretty good time getting here. We're a long way from the Mission district."

Mateo raised an eyebrow, as if the answer to her implied question was obvious. "I am a Tracker."

"His enhancements work—that means he's fast," Megan said. She pushed to the forefront. "Your blood transfusion worked—I can speak. Now, let's get out of this storm and into the Enclave. That's why we're here, isn't it?"

Mateo nodded and led the way, scrambling over the sea-drenched stones, taking care to avoid the slick green vegetation uncovered by the receding tide. The Runners hastened to follow, driven by the threat of the storm.

Mateo splashed ankle-deep into the ocean and ducked under a seaweed-draped shelf. Amos shucked off his pack and, holding it before him with both hands, awkwardly followed in Mateo's wake.

Aubrey stepped tentatively into the cold water, clutching her pack to her chest. She bent as low as she could and shuffled into a narrow passageway. She raised a cautious hand over her head and flinched away from sharp edges that stung her fingertips. So warned, she studiously avoided contact with the underside of the rock shelf.

For once, it's good to be short.

The air was heavy with the reek of sea-borne flotsam, but the wind's howl was muted. Even the pounding surf seemed lessened. *Don't kid yourself, Aubs. The tide's already coming in. The ocean is not your friend.*

Mateo handed Amos a battered lantern. Amos ignited it, and a warm glow partially dispelled the foreboding gloom in the confined space.

Megan splashed past Aubrey but halted abruptly beside

Amos. She looked troubled in the lantern's meager glow. "Something's wrong," she said under her breath, nodding at Mateo.

He stood with his back to them, unmoving, before a barnacle-encrusted wall. Aubrey could make out an oblong shape in the shadows beyond him. A circular handle, with four spokes, was set in the center of the hatch.

Amos raised the lantern, and its flickering light cast the portal into sharp relief. The outer rim was discolored, blackened as if scorched by fire. The surface was puckered in places, bubbles of molten metal now hardened into a solid mass.

Mateo tried the handle. It shifted slightly, perhaps an inch or two, but no more.

"It's been welded shut," he said bleakly, retreating to his instructor's voice.

Aubrey felt her throat constrict. *I've never seen that look on his face before.*

"We've been cut off." Amos stared at the portal in disbelief. "They knew we were coming."

FORTY-EIGHT ◎

"THERE'S SOMETHING seriously wrong with this coffee," Jane said, wrinkling her nose in disgust. "You'd think the high-and-mighty Citizens would know how to brew a decent cup. Oh well, at least it's hot."

Connor paused as he sipped his latte, fighting the instinctive urge to reply. *Don't let her bait you. By this time tomorrow, she'll be just another weapon in Darcy's arsenal.*

Tony lurched forward in his chair, glowering at Jane, spoiling for a fight. "Cascadian coffee is ground from high-quality imported beans."

Jane paused, cup in mid-air, a perplexed look on her face. She glanced across the table at Sheila and Garr, mouthing a single word. *Beans?*

"Don't worry, Jane." Sheila patted her on the arm, trying to hide a smile. "I guess the Citizens haven't discovered the benefits of chicory root yet."

Connor glared at them, irritated and making no effort to hide it. "In case you forgot, video surveillance is *everywhere.*

I chose this table because it's farthest from the cameras. That doesn't mean we haven't been catalogued already."

Don tugged at the sleeves of his new apparel, annoyed by the unfamiliar fabric. "And yet, it was *your* idea to sit out here, on display, for all of Hoarderville to see. We're lucky no one likes sitting in the rain, or we'd be surrounded by Hoarders."

"Hidden in plain sight, Don," Garr said amiably. He leaned back in his chair, glancing over the railing behind him at the mad dash of traffic on the level below. "And it's not raining yet. We couldn't afford to stay in the parking garage indefinitely, waiting for Darcy to contact us. *That* would look more suspicious than having coffee."

"Darcy will contact us when it's safe." Connor shielded the lower half of his face behind his latte. "After the Givers took out the Council Chamber, we're skating on a thin ice. We've got to act like normal Citizens, shocked and appalled by the 'tragic events'—as the Infomedia calls it—and watch our step more than ever."

Tony glowered at him, speaking as if the Runners were invisible. "You talk too much, Connor. They don't need to know all this."

"We've been over this before, Tony," Connor replied with equal heat. "Darcy told us to share information with our new allies. What kind of allies would we be if we didn't trust each other?"

Wow, listen to me. Almost as smooth as Darcy. And with a straight face, no less. His feeling of triumph was short-lived. The leader of the savages, the so-called "Colonel," was watching him. *He's clever, that one. Just sits back and observes. Very cagey.*

"I'm just relieved we made past Gate Seven without getting shot." Sheila pulled her jacket closer, warding off the chill breeze. She was speaking too quickly—clearly an attempt to distract. "Once we were inside, there weren't many places to run if things went sideways."

"We're not amateurs." Tony bristled at her remark, taking offense where none was intended. "It's going to get harder, once the Initiative's complete. The Peace Wardens will nail you on the spot—if you don't have a node."

No node, no Citizenship. Connor detested the Infomedia's propaganda, mindlessly parroted by the gullible masses.

"The Initiative hasn't been implemented yet?" Garr raised his eyebrows in surprise. Connor couldn't tell whether he was feigning his reaction or not. "I was under the impression the Council considered it a top priority."

Connor licked his dry lips, feeling the blood drain from his face. He was sure the savages noticed, but he forced himself to answer candidly. A "dangerous amount of truth," Darcy had said. *Well, here goes.*

"We've got a day, maybe two, before we'll be required to get our nodes." A hollow sensation settled into his gut as he faced reality. He took a hasty gulp of his latte, hoping to disguise the sudden tremor in his hand, and scalded his tongue in the process. "Darcy's on the Council. How would it look, if he doesn't lead by example?"

"Surely, a cruel twist of fate." Jane sipped her coffee, her eyes mocking him over the rim of her cup. "Or is it poetic justice?"

Connor ignored her. He knew his bitterness was showing, but he didn't care. "The collaborators will be watching for any hesitation among their fellow Council members. If the bombing didn't motivate every surviving councilor to get their node, it would raise questions." He closed his eyes, cradling his latte against his cheek, careful to mask his face behind it. "They're watching all of us, family members included."

Sheila rested an elbow on the table, cradling her chin in one hand. "Can you tell us more about these 'collaborators'? That's the second time you've mentioned them."

Tony jumped in, eager to assert his own importance. "They're Council members who've been cozying up to the Givers for years. They're always looking for ways to ingratiate themselves. Proximity means power."

You'd know all about that, wouldn't you? Connor kept his expression neutral and eyed the chauffeur with a new level of contempt. *Get over yourself, Tony. You'd jump off the Enclave wall if Darcy told you to.*

"The Givers use them to control Cascadia," Connor said, addressing Garr and ignoring Tony. "Not the whole Council, but a significant number of them. I wouldn't be surprised if they were behind the bombing."

"Weeding out anyone who doesn't play their game?" Don sounded suspicious, his low growl barely audible. "Or have they figured out what you and Darcy are up to?"

"Darcy should lead the Council," Tony interrupted, his face darkening. "We'd be better off with him in charge."

"King Darcy." Jane smirked, rolling her eyes. "Wouldn't that be peachy?"

Connor glared at her, but a beep from his wrist com cut off his hot retort. Tony bolted forward, rigid and pale. A five second pause, followed by a second beep. Connor glanced down and, with bated breath, eyed the miniature screen. He nodded at Tony.

"Darcy's made contact?" Garr asked. The Runners tensed visibly, watching Connor for his reaction.

He nodded, getting to his feet with a nonchalant air, and drained the rest of his latte, ignoring his scalded tongue. "Darcy won't risk saying anything over an open com. Our villa in Oceanview is secure. He'll fill us in once we get there. For now, just act like everything's normal."

"For the next day or two, anyway." Jane winked at him. "Until it's family node time."

Connor set his cup down with more self-control than he realized he possessed. He locked eyes with the obnoxious Jane, feeling far older than his seventeen years. "In the next day or two," he said as mildly as possible, "we could all be dead."

* * *

"How many survivors?"

Ethan Jacobs, his lab coat unfailingly spotless, consulted his clipboard. The digital tablet displayed a list of names, many of which were grayed out, leaving a much smaller sampling highlighted in color.

"It appears there are eight, Councilor." He kept his voice carefully neutral, clinical, as he scanned the list a second time, verifying his count. Councilor Sterne had zero tolerance for sloppiness. "All others have been accounted for."

"Eight." Sterne stood before the polarized window, hands clasped behind his back. Lightning flashed purple in the distance. Storm clouds reduced the mid-afternoon sky to near dusk, but he appeared not to notice.

Ethan knew the folly of interrupting his employer. He dialed up a new screen, anticipating.

Sterne turned from the window. "We'll proclaim tomorrow an official day of mourning." He watched as Ethan dutifully entered the information, efficient and precise. "We'll also call for an emergency Council session tomorrow evening. Assistants will need to be promoted, responsibilities shuffled in light of our losses—that sort of thing."

"If I may, sir?" Ethan looked up from his clipboard. "The Council Chamber—or what's left of it—is still an active crime scene. Where shall I tell them this meeting will take place?"

"Here, in the Citadel," he replied without hesitation. "The symmetry is perfect. This is where everything began, after all."

Ethan scribbled a note. "And Mateo?"

"Has been apprised." Sterne cut him off. He'd lost interest in the conversation. "He'll be here." He gestured at the device in Ethan's hand. "Have that printed on official letterhead, and send it out right away." He returned to his post by the window, his back turned to his underling.

Meeting adjourned.

Ethan tucked the clipboard under his arm. "As you wish, Councilor."

FORTY-NINE

CONNOR BREATHED a sigh of relief when the villa door opened. He spotted Darcy on the balcony, gazing into the falling rain. He knew what his foster father was doing: analyzing their situation from every possible angle. Darcy's ability to strategize—long-range or in the heat of the moment—was a rare gift, one Connor envied.

"Ah, Colonel Scott, and Sheila." Darcy stepped inside, closing the balcony door. He approached, extending his arms as if greeting long-lost friends. "I see you've brought some of your colleagues. Good welcome to you, as well."

Tony fidgeted beside Connor, looking uncomfortable.

Take it easy, Tony. Connor fumed at his lack of professionalism. *You'll make the savages suspicious.*

Garr led the way into the middle of the room, flanked by his companions. Unlike his host's feigned enthusiasm, he seemed detached and wary.

"Good welcome, Darcy," he said evenly, meeting his gaze as if they were equals. "Allow me to introduce you to my team."

"Don Benoit." The big man tugged at the sleeves of the garment they'd provided for him. He offered no handshake, standing aloof and defiant beside the colonel. Connor hid a smirk, aware of the burly savage's future.

Jane shoved forward, sticking out her hand. "Jane Avery," she said with a wide and insincere smile. Connor seethed anew. "But you can call me Snake Lady."

"Charming," Darcy replied dryly, ignoring her out-thrust hand. He averted his eyes, looking over her head to Garr. "If this delinquent child is the best you can offer, Colonel, we'll do our best to work with her."

Jane's mouth dropped open and her hands balled into fists. Sheila caught her arm with a firm hand. "Remember who the real enemy is," she stage-whispered, dragging Jane away.

Don shifted position, his feet set shoulder-width apart. The subtle movement did not go unnoticed.

Darcy eyed him with frank appraisal. "Colonel, as Sheila just reminded us, we have a common enemy." His eyes never left Don. "The Givers have taken some bold steps, and our window of opportunity is closing faster than expected."

"So Connor tells us," Garr replied, warning Jane with a stern look. "The last time we spoke, Councilor, none of you were part of the Anodyne Initiative. Connor says that particular window is about to close, as well."

"Tomorrow morning," Darcy replied. His expression didn't change. He might have been commenting on the weather. "As a respected Council member, I'll lead my fellow Citizens by example, giving the Anodyne Initiative my full endorsement by my participation."

"Who's holding a gun to your head?" Don's baritone drawl dripped with sarcasm. He eyed Darcy with a mixture of suspicion and doubt. "You expect us to believe you're doing this for the greater good of Hoarderville?"

Connor held his tongue by sheer willpower, comforted by the thought that the arrogant behemoth would soon be Implanted. *You won't be so mouthy then.*

Darcy regarded Don with a dispassionate stare, allowing the tension to supersaturate before he deigned to reply.

"There are very few things I *wouldn't* do for Cascadia," he said at last, his voice rich with scorn. "I have no desire to allow the Givers to track my every move, but to protect our alliance, I will. For the good of the Enclave."

The savages stood in a tight cluster in the middle of the room. Connor couldn't tell whether they took Darcy's speech at face value or not. He stepped between Darcy and the savages, acting as if they weren't there. He hoped they noticed.

"I've already explained how it would look if we didn't show up. They understand the collaborators will be watching for any hold-outs."

He took a deep breath, relieved it didn't sound too shaky. "Where, and what time, tomorrow?"

Darcy shook his head before Connor finished the question. "You won't be accompanying me. It's important that you're able to move under the Givers' radar for as long as possible. I alone will volunteer tomorrow."

Connor opened his mouth to protest, but Darcy stopped him with a frosty look. "You're a dedicated university student, who can't afford time away from class. Of course, as the son of a prominent councilor, you'll gladly accept your node." He allowed himself a cold smile. "But not yet."

Connor ducked his head in a quick nod, recognizing the alibi he'd just been handed. "Understood, sir."

Darcy looked past him to the silent knot of savages. "Where are my manners?" He gestured to the dining table with great enthusiasm. "You must be famished after your long journey through the sewers. The least I can do is offer you some proper nourishment."

No one moved. Connor tensed, very aware that the savages outnumbered them.

Darcy appealed to Garr and Sheila. "Remember how well we fed you during your first visit to Cascadia." He beamed like an exuberant *restaurateur*. "Join us, *s'il vous plaît*."

Connor wondered if they'd balk at his invitation, but there was no need to worry. Garr took a seat at the table, and the others followed suit.

Tony coughed, muffling the sound behind his hand. He gave Darcy an imploring look, gesturing at the closed door.

"Yes, of course," Darcy answered his unspoken question. His impatience suggested he'd forgotten Tony's presence. "I'll send for you later."

Tony nodded with obsequious gratitude, slipping out before Darcy finished speaking.

"Tony has a wife and children. He's a good father," Darcy said, speaking to the savages as if they were old friends. "It's a pity he can't join us, but one must admire his priorities."

Darcy seated himself with a flourish at the head of the table, gesturing for Connor to sit at the opposite end. He obliged, astounded at the lengths Darcy was going to in order to woo the savages. The feast was extravagant, overloading the table with steaming platters of choice cuisine.

Connor repressed a smile.

He's pulling out all the stops. Personally, I wouldn't have wasted our best food on them.

The savages picked at their food at first, but the enticing aromas won them over in little time. Even Jane wolfed her food down as if she hadn't eaten in years.

Connor smirked as he ate. *We're all eating from the same menu. That should put them at ease.* He caught himself humming an old tune, and realized his mood was improving.

Two additional drones by morning. That, all by itself, was worth celebrating.

FIFTY ◎

CONNOR LOADED THE LAST of the dishes into the sanitizer, stifling a yawn as he activated the appropriate cleaning cycle. The humming machine reminded him of many evenings from his childhood—a full meal, the ritual cleanup, and the familiar sound of the sanitizer purging microbes from their dishes.

This evening was different, on several jarring levels. The presence of the savages, the lack of genuine camaraderie and conversation around the table, and the incessant gnawing of an uncertain future—a marked departure from his childhood memories.

He touched the metal lump under his shirt, caressing the locket's outline. His mind wandered beyond their mission to rid Cascadia of the Givers. He was going to rescue Megan from the savages, no matter what.

He yawned again, and when he opened his eyes, Darcy was there, standing in the kitchen's arched entryway. Connor waved a weary hand at him. He felt hazy and fuzzy, and all he wanted was to lie down.

"Here, you'd better take these." Darcy held out his hand, dropping two red tablets into Connor's open palm. "They'll counteract the sedatives."

Connor mumbled his thanks and popped the pills into his mouth, stumbling across the kitchen to help himself to a drink from the cooler.

"Where'd you hide them?" He propped himself against the counter as he waited for the medication to take effect. "In the meat, or the potatoes?" He snapped his fingers, trying to focus on his hand and failing. "Dessert. That's it, right? You put the sedatives in the dessert."

Darcy leaned against the counter opposite him, casting a wary eye on the gathering room. The savages were crammed into the guest room for the night—*you'll need your energy for tomorrow*—but Darcy was too smart to drop his guard. Or allow his voice to be overheard.

"All of the above." A sly grin creased his face. "There's too much at stake *not* to lace the entire meal with sedatives." He took a generous sip of his whisky. "Sheila and Garr will enjoy the deepest sleep they've had since … well, since the night they received their Implants. They won't even realize we've taken Don and—what did she call herself—Snake Lady?" He chuckled. "After tonight, she'll be more poisonous than she could ever imagine."

Connor managed to focus on Darcy's face. "You're going to go through with it—the node, I mean." He admired Darcy's unflinching commitment to the cause. "That wasn't a speech just for savages' benefit, was it?"

Darcy sighed, looking pensive. "We—*I* don't have a choice. It's a strategic risk, Connor. Yes, I'll have a node, and that will limit what I can do and where I can go. But it will also deflect suspicion away from us." He took another gulp of his drink, swallowing mightily. "The Council's called for an emergency session tomorrow evening. I'll have a node by then, and they'll track my whereabouts if I don't show up. But by the end of the meeting, I'll know which Councilors survived the bombing. We'll match our new drones to them."

Something was off. Connor's mind moved sluggishly. *Are the sedatives still affecting me?* He massaged his temples, hoping to clear his thoughts. "You meant to say the collaborators. Not the entire Council."

"*All of them,*" Darcy hissed between his teeth. He put a hand on Connor's shoulder, his eyes glittering, alive with malicious fire. "None of them can be trusted. We'll rid ourselves of the aliens *and* the blind fools who conspired with them. The Cascadia Enclave will be human-only again."

Connor nodded, anticipating their next move. "And then we'll reverse the Anodyne Initiative."

"No, no," Darcy replied, digging his fingers into Connor's shoulder. "I've realized what a mistake that would be. Don't you see? The Givers have given *us* a gift—the ability to keep tabs on Cascadia's entire population. Just *think* of what we could do for the good of the Enclave."

He released his grip and staggered into the gathering room. Connor stared after him, shaken. *He doesn't mean that. He's drunk, that's all.*

But the more he thought about it, the more Darcy's plan made sense. Even the parts that made him uncomfortable.

It's for the good of the Enclave.

* * *

"I'LL PICK YOU UP LATER," Tony said, hovering near the door. They were in one of the faceless financial high-rises near the center of Cascadia. It was late, well after business hours, and the office towers were dark and empty.

Except for one basement unit. Darcy's anonymous clinic, staffed by equally anonymous medical personnel.

"Three hours, no more." Connor tried to put the crack of an order in his words. "Darcy expects us back long before daybreak."

"I know the routine." Tony glared at him through bloodshot eyes. He'd developed a nervous tic. "I've never been late."

"Okay, sure, see you then." Connor dismissed him, too tired to waste time arguing. *He hates being told what to do by someone half his age.*

Tony muttered something under his breath, and then he was gone. Connor heard the exterior door open and shut.

A few more hours with the wife and kids. They're already sound asleep, Tony. What difference will it make?

It hadn't been easy, manhandling Don's bulk down the hallway and into the elevator. In the end, Tony and Connor threw one of his arms across each of their shoulders, and half-carried, half-dragged him. They threw in a few calculated remarks about having too much to drink, for the sake of any surveillance cameras.

Darcy followed, carrying Jane's limp body in his arms. He was sober enough to perform the task without falling over. If anything, his erratic gate and slurred speech would lend credibility to their cover story.

"It's two-thirty in the morning. Would you like to get some sleep, sir?" It took Connor a moment to realize the orderly was speaking to him. *I'm not used to people calling me "sir."*

"That sounds like a good idea," he replied, stifling a yawn. "Big day tomorrow."

"You mean today." The orderly grinned, pointing to a clock on the wall. "There's a bed in the next examining room. We'll wake you once the Implant procedure is complete."

Connor thanked him and wandered into the adjacent room. He extinguished the light and stretched out on the cot with a grateful sigh. He spied the orderly peering around the edge of the door, keeping a watchful eye on him. Connor smiled, grateful for the added security.

Being Darcy's foster son has its perks.

He rolled onto his side and dozed off almost immediately, dreaming of a Giver-free Enclave.

FIFTY-ONE ◉

MATEO LAUNCHED himself at the sealed hatch, wrenching at the circular handle. He didn't attempt to rotate it, opting instead to pry it outward. A metallic shriek rent the air, and he staggered back as the handle tore free.

The hatch was designed to open outward, in deference to the water pressure at high tide, and the hinges were mounted on the exterior. Mateo focused his attention first on the top hinge. Cracks appeared under his frenzied assault, spreading outward in a metallic spider-web pattern.

Amos motioned for his companions to give Mateo a wide berth. They retreated as far as the small cavern would allow. Seawater sloshed around Amos's ankles. The tide was returning.

Mateo redoubled his efforts. He pried the upper corner of the hatch free and, grasping it with bloody hands, wrenched and twisted the stubborn metal.

The scorched welds cracked, and the hatch came abruptly loose. Mateo fell heavily, and the mangled hatch landed on him. Amos stared, paralyzed by shock.

Mateo groaned and the spell was broken. Amos dropped to his knees and hoisted one end of the hatch. Aubrey and Megan hurried to assist, and together they lifted the weight off Mateo. He levered himself into a sitting position, breathing heavily. A multitude of bloody lacerations crisscrossed his forearms, and his hands trembled from exertion.

Aubrey caught her breath. "I don't believe it."

Amos felt the same way, but he'd seen it, too. Mateo's injuries were healing. The flow of blood had slowed, halted, and the rips in his arms were closing.

"The subroutines," Megan said softly. She placed a gentle hand on Mateo's shoulder. "They're still functioning."

The Tracker nodded without looking up. "Staying here is unwise. The tide rises."

Aubrey sloshed to the open bulkhead. She extended a hand, but stopped short of touching the sharpened edges.

"I'll be right behind you," Mateo said. His voice sounded stronger, and he flexed his hands as they regenerated. The lacerations had closed, and he was no longer losing blood. Amos wondered if his scars would fade equally well.

Mateo seized one corner of the hatch and shoved Amos with his other hand. "Get moving. This setback has cost us valuable time." He retreated toward the shoreline, dragging the hatch behind him.

A gout of seawater surged over the bulkhead threshold, galvanizing Amos into action. He beckoned to Aubrey and Megan, and led them into the narrow crevice, scrambling over the water-drenched surface and into the maintenance level.

He crouched on the catwalk to get his bearings. The lighting array was dormant, and he breathed a sigh of relief. Despite their unexpected delay, they'd managed to arrive before the day shift began. Megan assisted Aubrey as her feet landed on the catwalk. Seawater trickled from the crevice, a warning of what was to come.

Aubrey pulled herself up, grasping the rail for support. Her mouth fell open at the sight of the vast array of machines below. She glanced at the trickle of seawater. "The temporary workers ... they're *our* people. Won't they get hurt?"

"I wouldn't worry." Amos raised his voice to be heard as the machines groaned and popped into grating life. He gestured at the growing rivulet of seawater. "It won't take them long to figure out what's happening."

Mateo emerged from the crevice. He was a wild sight, disheveled and bloody. His clothing, rain and sea-soaked, clung to his body as he strove to catch his breath. Behind him, the water trickle began to flow with greater insistence. The salty brine pulsed through the catwalk's mesh floor and sprinkled the machines below.

Megan eyed him. "Where is it?"

Mateo gulped another breath, wiping moisture from his face. "I pitched it into the ocean, where it promptly sank to the bottom."

Megan frowned. "What for? It's not in any condition to be reinstalled."

"Perhaps not." Mateo cocked his head to one side, a faint hint of a smile showing. "My action may not be logical, but I found it psychologically satisfying." He gestured to the steady stream of water. "We should take advantage of our unintentional distraction."

"Nothing like a leak in the dam to create a diversion," Amos said, savoring the taste of their improvised solution. "I'll bet Darcy never anticipated anything like this for his secret door."

Seawater surged behind them, and the trickle became a growing stream as the tide continued its inexorable return. Without the hatch to hold the ocean at bay, the stream would become a raging torrent, flooding the maintenance level and wreaking havoc on the machinery.

"You're sure the workers aren't in danger?" Aubrey grasped the railing with both hands, leaning over to take in the dizzying view. "They'll escape before it's too late?"

"The Enclave will dispatch emergency crews." Megan laid a hand on her shoulder. "They won't want their repairs slowed by floating corpses."

Amos winced at Aubrey's stricken look. *Nice try, Megan. I guess tact and diplomacy weren't part of your programming.*

Mateo came to Aubrey's rescue. "The Citizens won't waste assets. Workers are a valuable resource. The machines, however, were never designed for immersion in seawater."

"I don't want their deaths on my conscience," Aubrey said. She glanced at the volume of water cascading from the crevice. "How long will it last?"

"The tide will peak in six hours before it recedes again," Mateo replied promptly, back to his instructor role. "The higher the tide, the greater the water pressure behind it." He turned abruptly and began jogging along the catwalk. "We're wasting valuable time."

Aubrey ran with one hand poised above the handrail, as if she might need to steady herself at any moment. She avoided looking down as she ran, keeping her eyes fixed on Mateo's back.

Amos glanced through the mesh flooring and guessed the source of her unease. *Vertigo. There's no hiding how high the catwalk is.*

He was out of breath by the time they reached the first ascending staircase. Aubrey and Megan appeared equally winded. Mateo was the exception. He appeared invigorated by the exercise, and quickly began to climb.

Megan grasped the handrails for support but halted without warning on the first step. Amos almost collided with her. Beside him, Aubrey gasped, her scarred hand rising to cover her mouth.

Amos whirled, expecting to face attack.

FIFTY-TWO ◉

THE TRICKLE OF SEAWATER GREW into a driving waterfall, cascading over and through the catwalk to crash against a very different shore. The rising tide was nowhere near its peak, but the effects were already spectacular.

Amos leaned over the handrail, noticing the feverish activity below for the first time. Uniformed supervisors ran up and down the aisles, waving their arms and shouting at the workers. Their words were lost in the droning bedlam of the engines. As Amos watched, several machines below his position went dark as their frenzied operators shut them down.

Never designed for immersion in seawater. He recalled Mateo's earlier statement with a shiver. Electricity began to arc between the machines. Artificial lightning bolts cast wild reflections in the waterfall they'd inadvertently created. Thunder boomed, drowning out the mechanical cacophony. It was accompanied, more than followed, by a blinding flare of purple lightning. Amos blinked hard to clear his eyes.

The artificial lighting array, suspended in racks above the

maintenance level, went dark below the waterfall, obscuring his view of the electrical explosion's aftermath.

That wasn't a natural lightning strike. Amos's mouth went dry and he squeezed his eyes shut, the purplish afterimage still visible. *Water conducts electricity.*

He pushed the idea out of his mind. Megan resumed her climb, forcing Aubrey to ascend the stairs ahead of her. Mateo hadn't paused, and was near the apex of the staircase. If Megan had arrived at the same grim conclusion, she made no mention of it. *I won't lie to Aubrey. But if she doesn't ask, I'm not going to say anything.*

A wild chorus of raised voices wafted up from below, loud enough to eclipse the ringing in his ears. Amos clung to the handrail, pivoting to look down at the maintenance level. The smell of ozone hung heavy in the air.

It took him a moment to locate the reason for the uproar. Numerous agitated workers gestured overhead, pointing.

Pointing *at him.*

Amos scrambled up the stairs and lunged past Mateo into a locker room. The door slid shut, muffling the cacophony of machinery, shouting, and the rushing waterfall. Mateo locked the door and smashed the digital controls.

Aubrey and Megan huddled close together, catching their breath. The contrast between the antiseptic locker room and the grimy maintenance level was jarring. Mateo rummaged through the nearest bank of lockers, pulling out Hoarder clothing and sorting it. He tossed most of the items on the floor, but a few pieces caught his eye.

"Put these on, both of you." He handed the stolen garments to Aubrey and Megan. "Amos, I trust you brought along the clothing Darcy gave you?"

Amos nodded and trailed Mateo into an adjoining room. Aubrey gave him a relieved look before shutting the door, her new outfit clutched in her other hand.

Amos squatted, opening his pack and removing the fashionable but impractical garb Darcy had provided. "If we want to make up for lost time, we should 'commandeer' another truck." He peeled his sodden clothing off and shrugged into the Hoarder outfit. "The subway will slow us down."

"Public transit isn't an option," Mateo replied, sounding distracted. "Too much surveillance, too many Citizens who may ask the wrong question about the Initiative. Public paranoia is at an all-time high. I've arranged a vehicle for our use."

He stepped aside as the door opened, admitting Aubrey and Megan. Mateo nodded with approval at their new attire, but Amos was less convinced. Aubrey's long-sleeved guise effectively concealed her scarred arm, but Megan's eyepatch and facial scarring would be a beacon of imperfection in Cascadia's pristine society.

"We'll need to keep a low profile." Mateo's unblinking gaze settled on Megan, but his expression betrayed nothing. "I know the perfect hiding place. For a few hours, at least."

FIFTY-THREE

JANE WAITED until the guest room door closed before speaking. "If any of them says 'for the good of the Enclave'—just one more time—I'm going to puke on Darcy's fake fireplace."

Don feigned dismay. "I told the Hoarders you were house-broken. Are you trying to make a liar out of me?"

Darcy had departed earlier that morning, like a practiced martyr, en route to receive his node. Connor became sullen and uncommunicative after his foster father left. The Runners elected to stay out of the young Hoarder's way, taking shelter in their spacious and overindulgent guest room.

"You don't have to *like* Darcy," Don said, smoothing the silky fabric of his shirt with a look of distaste. "But try to fake it, okay? For the good of the team."

Jane shook an accusing finger at him, fighting back a grin. "I thought you were going to say 'the good of the Enclave,' just to see what I'd do."

"If we were *too* friendly, we'd look suspicious," Garr said, grinning. He seemed to enjoy their verbal jousting. "There's no love lost here—for any of us. I can't wait to leave Cascadia for the last time, never to return."

"As we all live 'happily ever after' in a Giver-free world." Sheila laughed as she gathered their empty breakfast plates. "One thing I'll say for our hosts, though—it's been a long time since I've eaten so well."

"Only because you have yet to experience *my* cooking," Don said, adopting a snobbish air. "All else will pale by comparison, I promise. You know, I *did* sleep well last night, although I'm not sure I want to give the Hoarders credit."

The door opened, revealing the taciturn Connor.

"Darcy wants us to meet him downtown." He spoke only to Garr, pivoted on his heel, and left. The door closed behind him with a soft *click*.

Don raised his eyebrows. "Someone got up on the wrong side of the Enclave this morning."

Garr shrugged in response. "You heard him. Darcy's expecting us."

* * *

THE INFOMEDIA FLICKERED on the flatscreen over the hearth—picture only, volume muted. Connor stood facing it, but his attention was devoted to removing his wrist com.

Once upon a time, this was the only way the collaborators could trace our location. He tossed the com on the coffee table, aware of the stark symbolism. *The next time I see Darcy, he'll have a node. And my turn's coming.*

"What's on the Infomedia?" Sheila asked as the savages filtered into the gathering room. "More node propaganda?"

Connor shook his head. He'd been preoccupied with morbid visions of the collaborators forcing Darcy to accept a node against his will. "They're having some problems in the power plant. One of the temporary workers screwed up and caused a power outage. Must be a slow news day."

He pointed a remote at the flatscreen, and the image blinked out with an audible *pop*.

"So, you've heard from Darcy." Colonel Scott's expression was hard to read. "He's now a card-carrying member of the Anodyne Initiative?"

Connor refused to be baited. "Tony made the call. Darcy has to watch his step, now that he's got a node." He unzipped his jacket, patting an inner pocket. "But he gave me all of his codes for the Citadel, just in case."

Do you hear me, savages? Darcy left me in charge.

He gestured to the door. "Tony's downstairs in the parking garage. Let's not keep Darcy waiting."

The savages hesitated, looking to their leader. Garr didn't disappoint. He opened the door without question and led his motley crew out of the villa.

Connor smirked as he followed, pausing to lock the door. *Darcy took the Implant tablet with him. It's time to start earning your keep, savages.*

FIFTY-FOUR

THE INTERIOR of the truck was cramped and uncomfortable. They'd exceeded the seating capacity, but had no other choice. Connor tried to calm his nerves. He'd ordered Don to ride in the cargo area, and was secretly relieved when the big man complied. He wanted the thuggish savage isolated in the confined space. Still, having four savages seated behind him—even if they all had Implants—was unsettling.

No matter. Connor steeled himself to show no concern. *Darcy's counting on me. I won't let him down.*

Tony looked terrible. His eyes were puffy, his face pale and sweaty, and his habit of drumming on the steering wheel— badly—was more irritating than ever. *Lot of good those extra couple hours of sleep did, huh, Tony?*

Tony shifted into gear, whistling tunelessly as he edged toward the vehicle lift. It was close to midday, but there was no line-up. Connor gazed out the side window, distracted by thoughts of Darcy, taking revenge on the savages, and his own impending node.

The engine stalled, jarring him out of his preoccupation. Tony yanked the keys out of the ignition, bolting out of their vehicle as if his life depended on it.

The savages protested, but Connor stared dumbly, frozen in place by Tony's gloating expression. The chauffeur backed out of the lift as the overhead lights flickered on. The gates began to close—the lift was about to engage. Tony twirled the keyring on one finger and tossed it over his shoulder with exaggerated nonchalance.

Connor scrambled awkwardly over the console, thrusting his head and shoulders out of the open window. "What's the matter with you? Darcy's waiting for us."

The words were barely out of his mouth when he spotted a dark figure approaching. The newcomer half-ran in an odd crouch, cradling the latest weapon from the Givers. His face was hidden behind the black visor of a Peace Warden in full riot gear. He took a sentry position behind Tony, waiting.

The barred grate descended from the ceiling, meeting its solid counterpart rising from below. They were trapped. Tony leered between the bars, in obvious triumph, and Connor finally caught on.

"*Traitor.*" His fists clenched in impotent rage. *How did I not see this coming?*

"You're so naive." Tony laughed, self-assured on the opposite side of the gate. "Darcy's brainwashed protégé, ready to give it all for the good of the Enclave."

Connor clawed at the door handle. The door popped open, spilling him on the unforgiving metal floor. He ignored the pain and threw himself at the gate. The savages scrambled out of the truck, knotted together in a tight circle of alarm.

Connor lunged, one arm stretching between the metal

bars, but the cocky chauffeur retreated, just out of reach. The Warden stood a pace or two behind him. Watching, waiting.

"Darcy's not a martyr for getting a node," Tony sneered at Connor with undisguised contempt. "He's just taking himself out of harm's way. Darcy's gift to himself—complete deniability. You've heard his speech about cannon fodder. What makes you think either of us are exempt?"

"*Liar*," Connor snarled at him, not believing a word of it.

"Last night at the clinic—I'll bet you couldn't keep your eyes open." The lift shuddered, beginning its ascent. Tony threw Connor a mock salute. "Darcy may have given you the codes, but he kept the tablet, didn't he?"

The Warden fired his weapon. Tony collapsed.

"Our mole, revealed at last." Jane's caustic voice broke the heavy silence. She spat at the gate where Tony stood moments earlier. "Looks good on him."

Garr didn't relax. "Something's off. Why would the Peace Warden shoot him?"

Don snorted. "My guess? Moles are expendable once they've done their dirty work."

Sheila paced back and forth across the vibrating lift. "Then he would've shot Tony immediately, and maybe us too. It's like he was waiting until ..." She halted, eyes widening. "He was gathering intel."

Connor hung his head, staring at his feet. His heartbeat thundered in his ears, and he found it hard to breathe.

My hands are shaking. He tried to control the tremors, keep his wits sharp, and failed. *I'm trapped in a lift with mindless savages. We're all going to die, and they're debating why Tony got shot.*

"Anyone have an inspirational idea?" Don's baritone drawl

echoed as the lift passed another parking level. "Our mole tossed the keys. I guess I could try hot-wiring this thing."

Connor exploded in fury. "There's no time." He rounded on his useless allies, jabbing a finger at the far side of the lift. "Our next stop is street level, and the Wardens will be waiting. In about thirty seconds, we're dead."

Colonel Scott took charge. "Behind the truck, everyone," he said, leading the way. "It's not much of a strategy, I know. I'm open to suggestions."

"It beats lining up for a firing squad," Sheila said dryly. She crouched beside him, forcing a weak smile. "It's been an honor serving with you, Colonel."

Don reached inside the truck, yanking a combat knife out of his pack. He unsheathed it, gazing wistfully at the serrated blade. "I was hoping to use this on a Giver. Once we reach street level, it's going to be like shooting fish in a barrel." He dropped to one knee beside Jane. "It's not as much fun when you're one of the fish."

Daylight filtered through the metal grate, eclipsing the artificial lights. The lift clanked to a halt and, after an eternity's pause, the gates retracted. Connor squeezed his eyes shut, his hand instinctively seeking the talisman around his neck.

The guttural hissing of Hoaeder weapons greeted them. The sound seemed to be amplified inside the lift, followed by an eerie silence. Connor forced his eyes open, looking over his shoulder at his equally mystified companions. Garr edged past him, craning his neck for a guarded peek. His jaw dropped and he sat back on his heels, presenting a clear target.

"Now, I've seen everything." Garr got to his feet and circled the truck, heading for the gate. His companions scrambled to follow, emerging to stare in shock at the improbable scene.

Connor counted four Peace Wardens. Three sprawled in awkward heaps on the ground, dead. The fourth stood at ease, his weapon aimed harmlessly at the ceiling. He flipped his visor up, revealing a red circle of light around his left eye.

"I know you." Jane's voice was hoarse. "In the Old City, a couple of days ago. You were so close, I could've touched you."

The Tracker removed his helmet with his free hand and tossed it on the pavement. "Yes, I remember. You were with Amos at the time." He strode to the truck and opened the door. "When these Wardens fail to report in, the Givers will dispatch more. We can't stay here."

Don climbed into the driver's seat, reaching beneath the dashboard. "And go where, if you don't mind my asking?"

Connor was as unnerved as the savages by the Tracker's casual answer.

"Wherever Mateo decides."

FIFTY-FIVE ◉

RAINDROPS DRUMMED on the roof of the truck in a relentless, unbroken rhythm. The wipers lanced back and forth in a valiant effort to improve visibility. On all sides, the traffic level was crammed with a wide assortment of competing vehicles, all undeterred by the relentless downpour.

Aubrey huddled in the front seat, knees drawn up under her chin. Her eyes were wide, and she looked overwhelmed.

Amos felt some sympathy for her, recalling his first foray into Hoarderville. "It's a different world, isn't it?"

Aubrey leaned forward, peering through the storm-lashed windshield. The rain obscured any view of the upper levels. "Right now, I feel like an epitome of the wide-eyed country girl. I'm gawking like a tourist." She heaved a sigh, settling into her seat. "This must be what a rollercoaster feels like."

"Almost there." Mateo cut their conversation short as he merged into a new lane. He caught Amos's eye in the rearview mirror. "Remember your role. Hidden in plain sight, as your Hub network likes to say."

Amos nodded, more uneasy than he cared to admit. He understood the rationale behind Mateo's plan—the Enclave's parking garages were a potential trap. Instead, the former Tracker's audacious proposal was to park in plain sight, outside the Cascadia Security Monitoring Division's rear entrance.

Amos's task was simple: shield Megan from the camera's eye until they were safely inside CSMD. *Simple or not, this is going to be awkward.*

Mateo accelerated as they exited the traffic level. A steep tunnel curved up and to the right, depositing them into a busy outdoor parking complex. Mateo showed no sign of concern as he navigated between rows of empty vehicles. In a final brazen flourish, he chose a parking space designated "Emergency Vehicles Only." The rain beat a staccato refrain on the roof as he shut the engine off.

Aubrey took a deep breath and opened her door, ducking her head against the heavy rain. Mateo rounded the front of the vehicle, ignoring the foul weather, and they jogged up a short flight of steps.

Amos held the rear door open. Megan slid across the seat to join him. She tugged her hooded sweatshirt forward, but her eyepatch remained visible. As per Mateo's suggestion, she curled one arm around Amos's waist, burying the side of her face into his jacket. He threw an awkward arm around her shoulders and they hurried to catch up to Mateo and Aubrey.

Megan's foot slipped on the rain-slicked curb. Amos gasped as she tightened her arm around his waist, digging her fingers into the tender scar tissue just under his ribs.

How's that for irony? He gritted his teeth. *A former Tracker finds the scar from my former Implant.*

He was well-aware that surveillance cameras tracked their

every move. They kept up their diversionary façade, splashing through puddles on the sidewalk until they ducked into the foyer inside the rear entrance.

Mateo led them with unerring aim to Tara Lindholm's office, pausing only to enter a code in the wall-mounted keypad. The door slid open, and without waiting for an invitation, they barged inside.

"Well, well, well," Tara swiveled her chair to face them, leaning back for a good look at her visitors, "if it isn't Cascadia's most notorious saboteurs. The Division is honored."

"Why are your screens blank?" Amos ignored her acerbic greeting. He crossed her office, the pain in his side forgotten. "I thought it was your job to keep an eye on things."

"I must concur with my colleague." Mateo loomed over her, his gaze shifting from screen to screen in short, sharp jerks. "It appears you've failed in your duties."

Tara leaned an elbow on the arm of her chair, a bemused look on her face. "Failed in my duties, huh? If that's the case, I have you to thank for it. Here, take a look." She rotated her chair, pointing to the only active screen, a live-feed from the Infomedia. "Your little stunt has been wreaking havoc on our electrical grid. Over a third of Cascadia is without power. Naturally, first priority has been given to the Infomedia. You're just in time—they're running your story again."

She turned the volume up. The screen showed a rain-soaked reporter, huddled outdoors against a backdrop of high-rise buildings. Every window was dark, as were the traffic lights in a nearby intersection. "Early reports indicate that temporary workers failed to observe standard safety precautions in Cascadia's power plant. The result was a chain reaction in the electrical grid, plunging much of Cascadia into chaos..."

"Don't you just love the Infomedia?" Tara laughed. "They never miss a chance for propaganda. Stoke the fears just right, and now people are complaining the Initiative's taking too long. Ah, here's the part you'll find interesting."

The news report switched to a much darker, grainy set of images. *That's the power plant.* Amos caught his breath, watching in fascination as frantic supervisors splashed through the water between the machines. Several workers shouted emphatically as they pointed at something overhead.

The reporter's voice-over continued. "Shocking footage of the terrorists responsible for the sabotage ..."

A burly figure rose in front of the security camera, wrenching at it with frantic hands. The picture shook as the camera was twisted out of its mooring, now aimed at an unnatural angle above the malfunctioning machinery. A slab of featureless wall appeared, bisected horizontally by a metal catwalk. The autofocus spun, blurring the footage for a moment, and then the camera zoomed in.

The video quality was poor, but clear enough to reveal three figures racing up the staircase, and a fourth waving them on from an open door at the top.

The scene shifted without pause to a recording with much higher resolution. The footage showed the Runners, in vivid detail, as they exited the room where they'd changed into Hoarder attire.

Tara jabbed a button on her console, freezing the image. Her chair creaked as she leaned back, gazing around the circle of astonished faces. "See what I mean? You're famous. All of Cascadia is looking for you." She pointed a finger at Megan. "Especially this one. She's hard to miss."

Amos's inner voice shrilled a paranoid warning. He tore

his eyes away from the incriminating footage. "Why are you showing this to us?"

Tara rolled her sleeve up to display a puffy red welt on the inside of her forearm.

"As dedicated CSDM employees, we were among the first to receive our nodes," she said dryly, studying the welt with distaste. "They say the swelling goes down in a day or so. Well, we'll see." She waved in the general direction of the door, dismissing them. "Make no mistake. I'm a loyal Citizen of the Enclave, but I hate the nodes as much as I hate the Givers. Do whatever it takes to help Darcy get rid of them."

Amos returned her gaze, unsure what to say.

Tara threw her head back with a bitter laugh. "Besides, if anyone sees your fugitive faces leaving my office, I'm as good as dead anyway."

FIFTY-SIX ◉

"CAN WE VERIFY anything Tony said?" Don kept his voice low. There was nothing to be gained by Connor overhearing their conversation.

The Runners sat in a semi-circle in the gathering room of a modest ground-level villa. The power cut out shortly after they arrived, leaving the room dark and gloomy.

Connor slouched in the corner of a covered outdoor patio, looking miserable. Heavy rain pelted down two or three feet beyond. The patio door was open, but it was unlikely the young Hoarder could hear their voices above the droning downpour.

Garr leaned back on the overstuffed couch, running his hands through his hair. "You mean what Tony said about Darcy leaving the dirty work to us? That makes no sense, even if he gave the codes to Connor. Bypassing security locks won't do us much good if we don't know where to go—or what to look for—once we're inside the Citadel."

"I'm not sure we can trust anything Tony said. He almost got us killed," Sheila said, slumping in a recliner opposite Garr.

"I'll bet he gave our location away before the Tracker ambush. Mateo warned us before—he said there was more than one set of Hoarders hunting us."

"I trust Mateo less than I trust Hoarders," Jane replied, sitting cross-legged on the floor beside the coffee table. She glanced around the room with an exaggerated shudder. "It's creepy, waiting in some dead Hoarder's apartment."

Don shrugged, not disturbed in the least by the fate of their unknown host. "When the Tracker who just saved your life says 'wait here,' I'm inclined to give him the benefit of the doubt. Besides, what choice did we have? He took our truck."

Garr shook his head, adjusting his position on the couch. "Darcy's truck is a liability. Our young Tracker friend is doing us a favor by getting rid of it."

"His name is Logan Johns." Mateo's voice wafted out of the darkened kitchen, startling everyone. He stepped over the threshold to join them. "Although the name holds neither memory nor identity for him."

Don jumped to his feet. "It's considered polite to knock first. Or didn't they teach you that in Tracker school?"

Mateo cocked his head to one side. "The kitchen window was open, and a far more discreet entry point than the front lobby. Our friend from CSMD is correct. As criminals, we're quite notorious at the moment."

"So the Infomedia told us, just before the power went out," Jane said irritably. She took a deep breath, placing her hands palm-down on the coffee table. "Welcome to Cascadia's 'most-wanted' club."

FIFTY-SEVEN

CONNOR HEARD the savages' voices inside the deserted villa, but couldn't make out what they were saying. He preferred it that way. He needed to sort things out, and none of them could possibly understand the full impact of Tony's betrayal.

He welcomed the cold, damp air and the rain's soothing patter. It helped him focus.

They'd always known the collaborators would come after them, if and when they knew whom to look for. The threat of exposure was always there, lurking in the back of their minds. But the risk was worth it, for the promise of restoring a human-only Cascadia.

There was also the possibility that one of their colleagues might crack under pressure and betray the cause. Connor had little difficulty acknowledging that danger, in theory.

But more than Tony's betrayal was troubling him. *Complete deniability.* Those had been his exact words. *Cannon fodder.*

Tony's parting words left Connor shaken. He was loyal to Darcy, devoted to their shared cause, but there was a ring of authenticity to Tony's outlandish accusation. *Darcy ordered Madison's execution.* Connor tried to reason objectively. *And he threatened me—there's no other word for it—told me I was expendable if I jeopardized the cause.*

His thoughts strayed to the savages. They'd all received Implants, as planned. *Animals. That's all you're good for.*

For the first time, the words lacked conviction. The recurring theme was Darcy's ruthless obsession with his cause.

He wouldn't sacrifice me along with the savages. Connor couldn't accept the implications of Tony's accusation. *Taking a node so he'd have an excuse to not join us when we go after the Givers? No—Tony's a liar.*

A thunderclap startled him, vibrating through the patio stones. He glanced through the patio door, and was surprised to see Mateo. Connor jumped to his feet and slipped inside. Don was speaking as he entered.

"Your young associate—Logan, is it?—told us to stay put." The big man sheathed his combat knife, but kept a casual grip on the hilt. "I think 'wait here' were his exact words."

Mateo studied him with a benign expression, undeterred. "Those were my instructions, yes. You were to remain in this villa until I arrived. Now that I'm here, we must move without delay. The rest of the team is waiting for us."

"Maybe you haven't heard." Don crossed his arms over his barrel chest. "We're on Cascadia's most-wanted list, and the Peace Wardens are looking for us. Logan said the owner of this villa died in the Council Chamber bombing. This is as good a hidey-hole as any."

Garr interrupted their tense standoff. "Darcy and I haven't finalized our plans yet. We can't confront the Givers without a proper strategy. We need to lay low until we hear from him."

Mateo cocked his head to one side. The fiery red glow of his scanner flashed into brilliant life. "A number of the Peace Wardens searching for you are Trackers," he said, indicating his glowing eye.

"What—is that supposed to be some kind of a threat?" Jane snorted, not looking at him. "Trackers can scan until their eyes fall out. We aren't packing high-tech weapons. There's nothing for them to scan"

Sheila bolted forward in her seat. "There's something else. Something you're not telling us." Her accusation hung in the air between them.

Keep your mouth shut, Tracker. Connor balled his hands into fists, desperately trying to catch Mateo's eye. *Don't give away Darcy's strategy.*

Mateo paused, his mouth open, looking from Sheila to Garr and back. "Sheila, I regret there's no better way to inform you," he said at last. "You and Colonel Scott were Implanted during your first visit to Cascadia."

The savages' collective gasp covered Connor's sharp intake of breath. Sheila, her face ashen, was the first to find her voice. "How long have you known?"

"You *knew*?" Don unsheathed his knife. "When were you planning on telling us, or were you?"

"Our infirmary at Eastside." Garr's quiet voice was a stark contrast to Don's outrage. "I saw the look on your face, but it never occurred to me..."

"The information wasn't relevant at the time," Mateo said in his calm instructor's tone. "There was no strategic value in alerting you. The knowledge would've been a distraction."

"What do you mean—not *relevant*?" Don brandished his weapon, a bull about to charge.

The red circle around Mateo's eye was a malevolent beacon in the shadowy room. He gazed at each Runner in turn. "I regret I must further compound the bad news. Since last we spoke, Don and Jane have also been Implanted." He lowered his voice, locking eyes with Garr. "Darcy's strategy against the Givers should be obvious by now."

Traitor! Connor raged, beside himself with fury. *I knew you couldn't be trusted.*

Then he realized, with a stab of panic, that the savages were eyeing him. Jane looked as though she was about to vomit. Sheila's eyes were wide in her pale face. Garr's expression was dark and threatening, second only to Don's growl of menace as he hefted his combat knife.

Mateo stepped in front of Connor, shielding him. "Don't be too harsh on our young colleague." He glanced over his shoulder, the glowing scanner obscuring half of his face. "I'm detecting an additional Implant."

Connor felt the blood drain from his face, and he couldn't breathe. Tony's final taunt echoed in his mind. *Darcy kept the tablet, didn't he?*

His hands began to shake, the tremors running through his body as the implications of Mateo's and Tony's words coalesced into horrific, crystal-clear focus.

Darcy kept the tablet.

Connor slumped to his knees, no longer caring about the knife in Don's hand. His world shrank to the carpeted floor. Thunder rumbled, and in that sound, he heard the harbinger of his impending execution.

FIFTY-EIGHT ◉

A PAIR OF BOOTS ENTERED Connor's circle of vision. He looked up, expecting to confront Don and his blade, and was surprised to find Garr. The colonel stared at him for what seemed an eternity, and crouched to look Connor in the eye.

"Is there anything else you'd like to tell us?" Garr's voice was measured, but Connor recognized the fire in his eyes. *He'll accept nothing less than a straight answer.* He gulped, his hand unconsciously seeking the locket around his neck.

Darcy kept the tablet. Cannon fodder.

Connor made his decision.

"There's an emergency meeting of the Council, or what's left of it, in a few hours." The words tumbled out faster as he spoke. "They aren't sure who they can trust, but Darcy's proven his loyalty by getting a node. He'll see who shows up for the meeting, compile a list ..."

The words caught in his throat. He heard someone retching in the kitchen, and felt like he might be next.

Garr steadied him, placing a surprisingly gentle hand on

his shoulder. "Darcy's going to program our Implants with specific targets after tonight's meeting." It was not a question.

Connor nodded, gulping another breath. He stared at the carpet.

"We can't stay here." Mateo repeated his earlier warning. "Darcy's objectives have become clear, and therefore, so have our own."

Garr stood, pulling Connor to his feet. "Whatever we're going to do, it has to be tonight, before Darcy figures out who his next targets are." He directed his last question to Connor. "Where's this meeting supposed to take place?"

Connor paused, taking a deep breath. *I'm committed now.* "The Citadel. It's not far from the Council Chamber. Darcy gave me the codes to bypass the security locks."

Don sheathed his knife. "Darcy may have been planning to activate Connor's Implant last, once we were all past the Citadel's security. There's no way to know."

"Darcy's timing is irrelevant." Mateo's scanner faded, and the room returned to its former dusky atmosphere. "What *is* significant, however, is that the meeting will take place inside the Citadel."

Don eyed him with unconcealed suspicion. "Why would that make any difference?"

Connor found his voice again. "The Givers are there. They never leave. The Citadel's their fortress."

Don burst into incredulous laughter. "The news just keeps getting better. We're supposed to break into this Citadel before Darcy pushes the button on our Implants—oh, and by the way, the Givers might pop by for drinks and dessert."

Mateo nodded in the semi-darkness. "The Citadel is also where Trackers are created."

"Darcy was ordered to go there for the Council meeting," Connor said, addressing Garr. "It wasn't his idea."

Sheila reentered the gathering room. "A new vehicle just pulled up to the curb."

Jane followed on her heels, wiping her mouth on the back of her hand. "Looks like Logan managed to find us an alternate means of transportation."

"Those were his instructions," Mateo said succinctly, stalking to the door. "We've wasted too much time already. We must rendezvous with the others."

Garr nodded, joining him by the exit. "First, the Citadel, and then the Givers." He paused. "Too bad Megan's enhancements don't work like they used to."

Connor stopped dead in his tracks. The hollow sensation in his stomach threatened to engulf him. "What did you say?"

Don answered, looking surprised. "Megan's enhancements —you know, from when she was a bodyguard for the Givers." He turned away, shaking his head. "I never thought I'd hear myself say this, but right about now, we could really use her Tracker abilities."

Connor's inner world crumbled. Megan—a Tracker? Impossible! The Givers wouldn't dare. Darcy told me what the savages...

He stumbled after the colonel, numb.

Cannon fodder.

* * *

AUBREY FOUND JANE slumped in the corner of a small examining room, sitting motionless on the floor. One hand covered her face, while the other fidgeted with a strap on the pack beside her. She didn't look up as Aubrey entered.

Aubrey flicked on the overhead lights, bathing the room

in a sterile fluorescent glow. She lingered just inside the door, leaning on the frame.

"I have no memory of this place." Jane's voice was muffled behind her hand. "But I must've been here last night. This is the hellhole where they do the Implants, isn't it?"

Aubrey glanced around the utilitarian room. A chair, a folding cot, a wall-mounted sink, and a faint but distinct odor she couldn't identify. A shiver ran down her spine.

"That's what Mateo says," she replied. "I don't remember being here, either, but this must be where everything began for me. I guess Mateo's right—it's the last place Darcy would think to look for us."

Jane dropped her hand and stared at the ceiling, shaking her head in a slow arc. "Darcy..." She snarled, baring her teeth. "I wish you'd shot him when you had the chance."

Aubrey stared at the floor, unsure how to respond. A distant echo of Doc Simon's voice stole across her mind. *You're not a murderer.*

Jane opened the flap of her pack and rummaged through its contents. Aubrey tensed as she pulled out her Glock, cradling it in both hands. Jane stood and approached her, holding the blue-gray handgun out, handle-first.

"Take it." She shoved the weapon into Aubrey's reluctant hands. "Keep it with you, at all times. No exceptions."

Aubrey's hand shook. She stared at the Glock with horrid fascination. "Jane, I can't. I hate what Darcy did to us, everything he stands for, but—"

"It's not for Darcy," Jane interrupted, temper flaring. She took a shaky breath, controlling herself with visible effort. "It's your turn, Country Girl. If you see me start to change, if my Implant takes over..." She gestured at the Glock, her voice filled with loathing. "I won't be one of Darcy's brainwashed assassins. Promise me, if you see it starting, you'll use this."

"Jane, no." Aubrey tried to push the Glock back into her hands. "Doc can remove the Implants, remember?"

Jane laughed bitterly. "Doc's a long way from here." She lifted her hands, palm out, refusing to accept the weapon.

"You couldn't shoot me." Aubrey looked up from the Glock, eyes pleading. "When my Implant activated, you had the chance, but you couldn't go through with it."

Jane shrugged, dropping her hands as she backed away. "Then you'll have to be stronger than I was, Aubrey."

FIFTY-NINE ◉

"THIS SHUTDOWN IS unnecessary and insulting. How long do they expect us to postpone the surgeries?" Campbell knew she was treading in a political minefield with her relentless inquiries. Tension inside the Citadel's medical facility had worsened of late, especially after the Council Chamber bombing.

Ethan didn't answer, opting instead to frown intently at his digital clipboard as if he hadn't heard. His feigned absorption was doubtlessly, in Campbell's opinion, influenced by the nearby presence of Councilor Sterne.

She sighed in frustration at Ethan's obsequious subservience. He seemed perfectly incapable, or unwilling, to say or do anything without Sterne's permission. *Maybe I should turn you into a Tracker. At least you'd finally have a spine.*

Sterne overheard her insolent tone, as she'd intended. He left his vantage point by the floor-to-ceiling windows overlooking the storm-wracked downtown. Dusk had arrived early under gray skies and heavy rain, and at least a third of Cascadia was still without electrical power.

"Are you worried the Givers will have no further need of your services?" Sterne strode across the polished floor to stand on the opposite side of the operating table. "Or, more to the point, that they may have lost patience with your unreliable production in recent weeks?"

A tremor of anxiety shot through the doctor. She glanced involuntarily at the dull black wall of the Givers' private chamber—a citadel within the Citadel. It was rare for the aliens to leave their inner sanctum, and, although she'd never admit it publicly, Campbell preferred it that way.

"Have you forgotten about my ninety-seven percent success rate?" She camouflaged her trepidation behind a façade of professional indignation. She was the best in her highly-specialized field of expertise, and she knew it. But Sterne's whims could be unpredictable, and the Givers were just so ... *alien*.

"And the remaining three percent have been *extraordinary* failures," Sterne replied with a condescending smirk. Campbell wished she could wipe the sneer from his smug face. "Never, in the recorded history of Cascadia, has it been necessary to dispatch Trackers to hunt down malfunctioning units. You've changed that."

Campbell leaned on the operating table, her posture deliberately nonchalant. "Your memory's a little selective, Councilor." The surgical lights gave her countenance an odd glow. "I'm also responsible for creating the *successful* units that tracked them down."

Ethan coughed politely into his hand, interrupting their dance of mutual dislike. "Sir, if I may? The other Council members will be arriving shortly. Perhaps we should adjourn to the conference room to prepare."

Adjourn? Campbell rolled her eyes at his pretentiousness.

Are you trying to impress the boss? Your groveling is pathetic and obvious.

Sterne nodded. "After our tragic loses in the Chamber disaster, this evening's gathering will be a delicate matter. Navigating the changes will require some finesse." He smirked across the surgical table, clearly relishing the opportunity to remind the doctor of her lesser role. She knew his methods. "You may finish sterilizing your operating theater, Maggie, and then you may leave. The Givers have no pressing need for your presence this evening."

He spun on his heel and departed through the heavy door that separated the medical facility from the conference room. Ethan tucked his clipboard under one arm and trotted dutifully in his wake. Neither looked back as the door closed.

Dr. Campbell was left alone in her medical domain, fuming at Sterne's patronizing use of her given name.

"As you wish, *Councilor,*" she muttered under her breath, despising them both.

SIXTY ◉

THE DOOR TO DARCY'S unregistered clinic opened, admitting Garr and his companions. Megan turned at the sound, and was immediately drawn to the haggard face of a young Hoarder. She recognized him. Connor—Darcy's protégé. He stared at her, mouth agape, his fingers clasping a locket on a silver chain around his neck.

"Megan..." He took an awkward step forward, his eyes searching her face. "They told me you were dead."

She waited to hear more before realizing he expected a reply. She hoped her smile was reassuring. "Well, you can't believe everything you hear." She saw his confused expression, and regretted her tactic. *Don's the comedian, not me.* She cocked her head to one side and tried a different approach. "You seem to assume I should know you. Why is that?"

"You're my sister." His face flushed red, eyes brimming with tears. He hastened to unclasp the silver chain, fingers fumbling in his eagerness to open the locket.

Megan sensed the palpable shock from the Runners, felt

their eyes boomerang from her to the young Hoarder. Garr recovered first, and covertly herded his companions into the next room. Megan caught Sheila's troubled look out of the corner of her eye as Garr eased the door shut.

Connor succeeded in prying the locket open, holding it toward her in cupped hands. Megan bent to inspect the tiny image, astonished to see a younger version of herself. She studied the picture from several angles, but it failed to elicit either memories or emotion.

She looked up to meet Connor's gaze, and recognized the anguish in his eyes. "I believe you," she said, touched by his obvious distress. "I can visually confirm our genetic resemblance."

She handed the locket back to him. He eased it shut with obvious disappointment.

"But you don't remember me." He sighed deeply and fastened the chain around his neck when she shook her head. "Do you remember anything at all? Hunting trips, our villa ..." His voice caught and he swallowed hard. "Mom and Dad?"

Megan wished there was something she could say. *This isn't the time.* "My memories began on the day I became a Tracker." She gave him the unvarnished truth. "For five years, I served as a bodyguard for the Givers. Everything before that is a blank." She paused, choosing her words with care. "You know my name, and you have a picture of me. You say I'm your sister, and I believe you. But I have no memory of it."

"Five years ..." He looked stricken, as if she'd slapped him when he expected a warm embrace. "So much has changed." He laughed nervously, his voice cracking. "You used to be taller than me."

Megan placed a hand on his sternum, feeling the hard lump of the locket beneath her palm. "Connor, somewhere inside you, you have an Implant. Darcy will activate it, tonight, if we don't act quickly. Stopping him, and the Givers, must be our first priority. Anything else is a distraction."

Connor flinched when she mentioned his Implant. He gulped a quick breath and nodded. "I know. I'm just in shock. I mean, they told me you died, and then, less than a month ago —out of nowhere—I saw you. Ever since, I've been trying to imagine ..." His voice trailed off under her steady gaze. "You're right." He nodded, straightening his shoulders. "We'll have time later. No distractions."

Megan dropped her hand. He crossed the room and opened the door. She heard Sheila's voice, and Garr's quiet response, although she couldn't make out their exact words. Connor held the door ajar, waving her in.

Megan nodded solemnly and ducked past him. She found herself hoping he would survive the night. He seemed like he'd make a good brother.

She banished the thought before it could take root. Nothing could permitted to interfere with her new Quest.

SIXTY-ONE ◉

"ACCORDING TO MATEO'S INTEL, the Citadel's basic layout looks like this." Garr sketched a diagram on a scrap of paper. "It's four floors high, hexagonal in design, with a central core running from ground level to the top of the structure."

"*Hexagon* means it's got six sides." Amos poked Don in the ribs. "And a hole in the middle. Like a doughnut."

"I know what a hexagon is." Don nodded at Garr's sketch. "And it's not a *hole*, it's a structure within the structure." He caught Amos's quizzical look. "Connor told me about it on the way over. As Darcy's adopted son, he's got the inside scoop."

"Lucky for us," Jane muttered under her breath. She and Aubrey hadn't said much since rejoining the group, each appearing lost in her own thoughts.

Amos stole a glance at her, a twinge of uneasiness gnawing at his gut. *There's no good way to find out you've got an Implant. I just about lost my mind.*

Garr scribbled, shading the circle at the center of the hexagon and adding lines from the center to the outside.

The diagram resembled the spokes of a wagon wheel. He used his pencil as a pointer, indicating each section between the spokes.

"Everything connected to the Givers and their advanced tech is stored inside this building." His pencil tapped from section to section. "There are meeting rooms, like any other office complex, and, depending which floor you're on, there's also facilities for weapons manufacturing, an armory, and research and development labs for adapting the aliens' tech to mesh with Cascadian." He paused, his expression grim. "And, on the uppermost floor, a surgical facility where the condemned are remade as Trackers. As an added bonus, it's also where the Givers have their personal bunker."

A pensive silence followed. If Megan had any reaction to Garr's blunt recitation, she gave no indication.

"What about the nodes?" Sheila asked, her brow furrowed. "Are we assuming they're manufactured and monitored from the Citadel?"

Connor spoke for the first time. "They're monitored by another department at the CSMD. But the main signal will be broadcast from the Citadel. And the nodes are manufactured there, as well."

"The Givers are pretty tight-fisted with their toys." Don peered over Amos's shoulder at the diagram. "Let's hope alien paranoia works in our favor."

Garr leaned his full weight on the table. "Don raises an important point. The Givers are, first and foremost, *aliens*. We know nothing about how they think, what they feel, or why they do what they do. We don't dare assume anything about their objectives, or try to second-guess what they may or may not do." He paused for emphasis, looking around the cramped clinic. "We have two objectives. Stop Darcy from activating our Implants, and put an end to the Givers' ability to use their tech against us."

Amos leaned forward, jabbing a finger at Garr's drawing. "We take out the Citadel, and no more Trackers. We take out Darcy, and no more Implants. It's that simple."

Amos saw Connor's stunned reaction out of the corner of his eye, but he didn't care. *Do the math, kid. Your father doesn't care who he Implants. You should know that by now.*

"Once we arrive at the Citadel, we'll split into teams." Garr took charge. Amos recognized the subtle shift in his voice and demeanor. "Connor has the Citadel's security codes, so getting inside will be relatively easy. Darcy will be focused on his strategy, but he has no idea we're on to him. He won't be expecting us." He jotted notes, point-form, outlining their game plan. "Most of the staff will have left by the time we arrive. The only people present should be a skeleton crew and what's left of the Council. And the Givers, of course."

"Mateo's gone ahead," Sheila said. "He took Logan with him. They're Trackers—they'll get there faster on foot than we will in vehicles."

Don raised his hand. "What about weapons? Combat knives aren't much against the kind of firepower Hoarders have."

"You can't bring weapons," Megan interrupted from the opposite end of the table. "The doors are equipped with built-in scanners." Her warning silenced everyone. "Any advanced weaponry will activate the security alarms."

Connor jumped in on the heels of her sobering comment. "But once we're *inside* the Citadel, we'll have access to any weapons we need." He patted his jacket pocket for emphasis. "I can get us past the locks on the armory. Codes are codes."

"What did I tell you?" Don nudged Amos, grinning wickedly. "There's more than one way to skin a Hoarder." Connor winced but said nothing.

Garr tossed his pencil on the table. The simple gesture spoke volumes. "Okay, everyone. Let's get this over with."

Next stop, the alien heart of Hoarderville. Amos took a deep breath as that sunk in.

For once, his inner voice could suggest nothing worse.

SIXTY-TWO ◉

DR. CAMPBELL PAUSED, one hand poised over the security keypad. She ran through her mental checklist one last time before exiting the Citadel for the evening.

She knew Sterne would like nothing better than to replace her with his own hand-picked physician. She doubted he'd be able to find one as efficient as her, but she suspected he'd try.

And she wouldn't put it past the bootlicking Ethan to pull some stunt to make her appear vulnerable.

Politicians and their petty machinations. The Givers need my expertise.

She jabbed an angry finger at the keypad. The door opened, and she raised her umbrella as protection against the rain. Power outages painted the surrounding area with an odd patchwork palette—lights burning bright in a few buildings, while the majority remained cloaked in darkness.

Campbell expected the early-evening commute would be more sparse than usual. Severe weather would make the average Citizen think twice about venturing out. The power outages added another depressing layer to a general sense of malaise in Cascadia after the twin bombings.

No thanks to the Infomedia. She pursed her lips in silent disapproval. *Their fear-mongering may have bolstered the Anodyne Initiative, but they don't know when to quit.*

She shivered as she crossed the lawn to the parking lot. A cold wind was partially responsible, but she found the haphazard blackout the most disconcerting.

Campbell put it out of her mind and fumbled with her keys. She managed to open the car door and ducked inside, muttering curses as she wrestled with her dripping umbrella.

The surviving Council members were arriving for their precious meeting. She'd made use of a different staircase for her exit, having no desire to see their sanctimonious faces. *If you've met one politician, you've met them all.*

Her engine roared to life and she glanced up at the featureless Citadel. The conference room's floor-to-ceiling windows were ablaze with welcoming light, in stark contrast to the darkened floors below.

She threw her vehicle into gear. Gouts of water fountained from her tires as she sped out of the parking lot.

For a brief moment, she thought she detected movement in her rearview mirror, a slight stirring in the decorative bushes on either side of the front entrance. She set her windshield wipers to *high* and concentrated on her driving.

* * *

THE RUNNERS WAITED outside the Citadel, wet and miserable, until Garr was satisfied the last of the Council members had arrived. They crept within a few feet of the door, camouflaging themselves behind the decorative shrubs. Garr stretched up a hand to enter the access codes.

The door burst open without warning. Aubrey ducked low to the ground, heart pounding.

A middle-aged woman stalked imperiously out of the Citadel. Aubrey sensed her companions holding their collective breath until the woman drove out of the parking lot.

Garr tried the codes a second time. The door hissed open and Aubrey breathed a relieved sigh. One by one, they scuttled into the Citadel. *We made it over the first hurdle. The codes worked. We're inside.*

Darkness shrouded the interior of the Citadel, broken here and there by miniature rectangles of light. The tiny beads of luminescence were scattered across the floor in no discernible pattern, and also served as outlines around doorframes, blinking in random sequence—blue, white, red, green.

Just like an active Implant. Aubrey immediately recognized the similarity, and a shiver ran down her spine.

The dark floor was polished to an obsidian sheen that reflected the pulsating lights, diffusing their colors to a fuzzy glow around the doorframes. Phosphorescent trails crisscrossed the floor, some outlining various pathways leading away from the entrance, and others appearing to be random swirls with no practical function. It reminded Aubrey of an enormous spiderweb, which did nothing to steady her nerves.

They lingered just inside the entrance until their eyes adjusted. Aubrey stiffened as a puff of humid air caressed her face. Garr glanced over his shoulder, his face dimly lit by the ghostly lines in the floor. He signaled to Don—*go left*—and led his unit in the opposite direction.

Aubrey rose to a half-crouch, following Don along one of the spidery threads of light. Connor slipped past her, scampering on silent feet to catch up to Don. He tapped the big man on the shoulder, indicating a door nearest the outer wall. Don cracked the door open, and after a quick moment's reconnaissance, darted up the stairs on the other side of the portal.

Connor followed, then Aubrey, with Megan bringing up the rear, easing the door shut behind her.

Connor moved with confidence as he guided them through a convoluted maze of corridors, pausing at last in front of a sealed door. He consulted his list of codes, and his fingers danced over a circular keypad that wrapped around the door handle. His efforts were rewarded by a soft click, and the door swung open.

Connor ducked inside. Don and Aubrey crowded in behind him and Megan, as planned, assumed sentry duty in the corridor. Inside, a bewildering array of viewscreens confronted them. Tiny beads of light crawled across a majority of the displays, moving in intricate patterns from screen to screen. Connor glanced at them with the first genuine smile Aubrey had seen on his face.

"All the data from the Anodyne Initiative is processed here," he whispered, indicating the winking lights. "Any Citizen with a node can be identified and traced in real time. CSMD has a *lot* of monitoring stations, but this is the nerve center. The mainframe. Everything flows through here."

Don seated himself before the largest console. "So, all we need to do is short-circuit this heinous monstrosity, and none of the nodes can be tracked. Does that give us free access, anywhere in the Enclave?"

Connor shook his head, his earlier enthusiasm fading. "Nodes are keyed to individual Citizens, but every vehicle's been outfitted with geolocation tech as well. Cascadia Security can track any vehicle inside the Enclave, but they can't identify drivers or passengers. But anonymous occupants in a registered vehicle would be a dead giveaway. The Peace Wardens would spot the anomaly in a second."

"Then this had better work," Aubrey said, relieved that her voice sounded calm. "We'll need a quick escape route."

Don pulled out a packet of tools and ducked beneath the console to pry it open. After a moment's fiddling, the panel popped loose, and the big man crawled inside.

"We're lucky there's so many the power outages," he said, his voice muffled inside the console. "Pulling the plug won't set off alarms, literally or figuratively. That should buy us enough time to escape."

Connor knelt and squeezed in beside him. It took the two of them less than a minute to find the correct circuit board. Aubrey smiled to herself when she heard their triumphant—if muted—celebration. She crouched for a peek, but couldn't see past them in the cramped space.

Connor unfolded a paper schematic, referring to it as he directed their strategic vandalism. Don clipped a few wires at seemingly random locations, muddling their trail of sabotage. There was a flicker of light inside the console, and Aubrey heard their satisfied exclamations.

She climbed to her feet, anxiously scanning the multiple screens on the console. Nothing had changed. She opened her mouth, about to sound a warning, when the screens froze. A myriad of light specks flickered in unison—once, twice—and flared to high intensity before fading to black.

Don backed awkwardly out of the console and rose to his knees. "Mission accomplished. Everything's off the grid, but that won't last long." Connor flashed him a thumbs-up, and they quickly reinstalled the console panel.

Light from a quartet of active viewscreens drew Aubrey's

attention to a secondary console. The screens, arranged two-by-two in a square formation, appeared to be dedicated to exterior surveillance. The images switched to a second set of viewpoints as she watched, then a third.

"Rotating vantage points, covering the perimeter," Aubrey muttered under her breath. Her eyes widened as she realized what she was looking at. "Getting out of here just got a little more complicated." She managed to keep her voice level. "You'd better take a look at this, Don."

Don scrambled to join her, seating himself before the console. Connor hovered over his shoulder, his face oddly lit by the glowing screens. Aubrey pointed without speaking.

In each camera view, a line of Peace Wardens in full riot gear stood at rigid attention, weapons held ready. They kept a watchful vigil, encircling the Citadel, none stationed more than twenty feet from the outer walls. Darkness and pouring rain did little to conceal the red glow behind each visor.

"Trackers." Don shook his head in disbelief. "They let us waltz right in, then closed the gap behind us. It's a classic strategy—we're surrounded." He glanced at Aubrey, then over his shoulder at Connor. "They knew we were coming."

An invisible band tightened around Aubrey's chest, and breathing became difficult. She recognized the symptoms. *Panic attack. Easy, Aubs, take slow, deep breaths. This is no time to become the weak link.*

Connor's unexpected outburst startled her. "Where's Megan?" He bolted out of the door and into the corridor. Aubrey and Don followed, spreading out, searching for any sign, any clue. Their efforts were short-lived and futile.

Megan was gone.

SIXTY-THREE ◉

GARR EASED the door open and peered into the corridor. Sheila and Jane pressed themselves against the wall behind him, making as small a target as possible. Amos kept a wary eye on the stairs they'd just climbed. Garr gave the all-clear signal and stepped into the waiting corridor.

The armory. Amos had zero interest in the Research and Development Department or any of the other subsections on the second floor of the Citadel. Once they'd armed themselves with Hoarder weapons, he would gladly return to wreak havoc on R&D.

The second floor was as dimly-lit as the first, adorned with the same trails of spidery phosphorescence on floor, wall, and ceiling. Tiny rectangles of light framed doorways and decorated the corridor walls, blinking on and off—blue, white, red, green —at unpredictable intervals. Where the ground floor had been open and expansive, the second was a claustrophobic maze of corridors and intersections.

Sheila pulled out a pencil-thin flashlight she'd stolen from the clinic and consulted a hand-drawn schematic. The tiny penlight was blinding by comparison, and she cupped her fist around it to minimize the glow.

"Left at the next intersection," she whispered. The penlight snapped off, and Amos blinked at the blue-white afterimage. "There's a set of double doors just past the intersection, and the next door on the right is the armory."

"Double doors, next right," Garr replied in a stage whisper. His silhouette nodded once and he resumed his slow and stealthy advance. The obsidian floor, replete with luminous spiderwebs, was hard and unyielding. They modified their tread, as close to silent as possible.

They paused at the intersection and Garr edged cautiously around the corner. The double doors were a further twenty feet down the new corridor. They gathered around Garr as he cracked the door ajar. The slight *click* of the latch felt obscenely loud in the unnatural stillness.

Amos's hand strayed instinctively to the hilt of his knife, and he grimaced in silent disgust when his fingers met with nothing. *Combat knives won't be much use in here, anyway.*

The corridor on the other side of the double doors was circular in shape, following the segmented curve of the Citadel's hexagonal architecture. The rectangular lights and glowing spiderwebs were joined by a series of serpentine strands, made of the same phosphorescent material and roughly the thickness of Amos's thumb. The strands lined the corridor in sets of three, roughly six feet apart.

"Like a ribcage," Amos muttered, more to himself than any of his companions. The comparison didn't sit well, but at least the corridor wasn't quite as dark as the stairwell.

Jane overheard his observation. "Yeah, it feels like we're

crawling through the inside of a snake," she whispered, glancing at him over her shoulder. "Not my favorite place to play hide-and-seek."

They rounded a bend in the corridor and located the armory. The door was recessed into the curving wall, creating a small alcove. Garr and Sheila ducked into the cramped space. The penlight's muted glow showed in Sheila's fist as Garr consulted the codes Connor had written down for them.

The armory door was wide, with an elaborate doorknob and locking mechanism set dead-center. The digital keypad was hexagonal, with the doorknob in the middle, and glowed faintly. The mechanism reminded Amos of the clandestine hatch into the maintenance level, but more sophisticated.

Garr's fingers danced over the keys, and the keypad blinked twice in response. He grasped the doorknob and gave it a slow, cautious twist. The locking mechanism held firm. Amos heard his frustrated expulsion of breath as he tried again, firmer this time. And again.

The keypad changed color, from pale blue to emerald green.

Sheila's penlight showed again. She abandoned any attempt to shield it. "Do we dare try again?"

The keypad seemed to be mocking them. The lights around the doorway continued their random dance—blue, white, red, green—indifferent to their plight.

"No other choice," Garr replied, *sotto voce*. Amos could hear the tension in his voice. "Time's running out."

A lifetime supply of Hoarder weapons, almost in reach. Amos clenched his fists, mortally aware of their precarious situation. He felt small and useless. *But we can't get past the gate.*

Garr repeated the coding sequence, painstakingly slow.

Sheila extinguished the penlight and stuffed it into one of

her pockets. The keypad flashed twice, as before, and emerald morphed into a menacing amber.

"Connor gave us the wrong codes," Jane whispered harshly.

Garr took a deep breath. "Or someone changed them." He wrapped his hand around the doorknob. The amber light pulsed in a steady rhythm, accenting his taut fingers.

Sheila laid a hand on his shoulder. "What about Don's team? Their codes may have been changed, too."

Garr shook his head and tightened his grip. Perspiration trickled past his temple, reflecting amber. He glanced at Sheila and quickly away. "No choice—we can't back away now."

He twisted the doorknob, slowly at first, and then more firmly. Amos head the *click* over Jane's sharp inhalation, and realized he was holding his breath.

The lock held. The keypad flashed—deep crimson.

Garr dropped his grip and retreated a step into the corridor. The keypad glowed brightly, the color eerily reminiscent of a Tracker's scanning eye. The lights surrounding the door continued their random pattern—blue, white, red, green.

The keypad went abruptly dark, then flashed brilliant scarlet. A split second later, the door lights froze, winked out, only to resume their endless pattern. The sequence repeated, keypad first, followed by door lights. And a third time.

Everything went black—keypad, door lights, spiderwebs, ribcage—snuffed out like candles in a gale-force wind. Amos gasped, struggling to keep his balance without external points of reference. The darkness was absolute. He couldn't see his hand in front of his face.

The cliché fits, Gabriel said solemnly.

"Get a grip, everyone," Garr said tersely, a commander giving orders to his troops. He didn't raise his voice, but he deliberately invoked Colonel Scott. Several seconds passed before he spoke again. "First things, first. Sheila, check whether or not your flashlight still works."

Amos heard a slight rustle of fabric to his right. He could almost picture Sheila digging frantically into her pocket.

Jane hissed sharply, and Amos felt his skin crawl. She stumbled against him and grabbed his arm, whispering hoarsely, "We're not alone."

Amos was about to reassure her, but a sixth sense stole his confidence. There was something in the air—a wrongness, an alien vibration—and his heart began pounding.

Twin beams flared red, blinding after the oppressive darkness. Trackers—a pair of them—stationed barely ten feet away, their glowing scanners giving them the ghostly appearance of disembodied heads, floating in mid-air.

The optical illusion was short-lived. As if a signal had been given, the corridor was suddenly awash in light. Ceiling tubes added stark clarity to the glowing spiderwebs and ribcage. The armory keypad reverted to a calm, pale blue.

The taller Tracker stepped forward, hefting his rifle into firing position. He cocked his head to one side, eyeing them dispassionately. Behind and to his left, his companion trained his weapon on them.

"Good welcome, Colonel," Mateo said, his greeting terse, emotionless. "And to your colleagues, the same. The Givers have been expecting you."

Logan Johns advanced to stand beside him, his stoic expression all the more ominous in the eerie light. He flexed his grip on the Hoarder weapon, his eyes cold and remote.

Amos's emotions ran the gamut from shock to anger, and coalesced into fiery defiance. "If you're expecting us to beg for mercy, think again." He heard Jane's slow, steady breathing beside him. He knew her well enough to know she was about to explode. His heart skipped a beat, expecting the worst.

"I've got a working theory about who changed the codes," Garr said mildly, ignoring Mateo's welcome.

"On your feet," Logan said, his voice cold, distant, almost robotic. "They're waiting."

Amos refused to comply, waiting for Garr's lead. Sheila and Jane did the same. *It's your move, Colonel.*

Mateo lowered his weapon a fraction. "Colonel Scott, a good commanding officer knows when to advise their troops against any ill-conceived gestures of final defiance. Consider the facts. You are unarmed. Our weapons are the finest the Givers can offer. In addition, twenty 'Peace Warden' Trackers now surround the Citadel."

Logan stood motionless, his expression unreadable. His weapon spoke volumes. The Runners held their positions. Garr matched the Trackers' gaze, stare for stare, unflinching.

Mateo broke the stalemate. "Logan and I, Trackers in full control of our enhancements, are more than a match for the four of you. The logical choice is to do as we say." He aimed his weapon at Garr's head. "I will not ask a second time."

SIXTY-FOUR ◎

HARLAN STERNE CASUALLY RECLINED in his high-backed leather chair, watching with heady anticipation as his fellow Council members took their places around the conference table. Eight colleagues, men and women he'd known for years, with whom he'd debated—vehemently at times—and also formed temporary coalitions, when it suited his purposes.

After this evening, none of them would be necessary. In any capacity.

He beckoned to Ethan, and his assistant bent down to listen. The murmur of small talk among the other councilors masked what he said. "Everyone is present and accounted for. Bring the Peace Wardens inside the Citadel, and post them at every exit. *No one* leaves, unless I give the word."

Ethan nodded, tucking his clipboard under one arm, and left to carry out his assignment. Sterne paused before calling the meeting to order, savoring the moment.

An oval table, its mahogany surface buffed to a satin sheen, was situated in the epicenter of the conference room. Behind him, polarized floor-to-ceiling windows showcased Cascadia Enclave in all of its grandeur.

Sterne had chosen the placement of his chair for maximum effect. The thunderstorm was an unexpected bonus. Darkness and flashes of lightning added extra drama to his evening of triumph.

A polite beep sounded from the console in front of him. He glanced down to see a flashing pinpoint of light, confirming the signal he'd been waiting for. Sterne rose to his feet, reveling in the perfect symmetry of the moment.

Ethan returned through the door to his left and, at the opposite end of the room, a set of double doors opened to admit his special guests.

The patter of small talk faded into stunned silence.

Mateo Reyes herded his prisoners into the conference room at gunpoint. The fugitives entered with hands on their heads, sullen defiance etched on their faces. Mateo ordered them to kneel and, under the threat of his weapon, the savages had no choice but to comply.

Flawless. Sterne clasped his hands behind his back. *The stage has been set.*

SIXTY-FIVE ◉

"Where do you think you're going?" Don seized Connor by the arm, restraining him. "Our orders were to disable the node-tracking system and rendezvous with Garr's team on the top floor." Connor's face contorted, but Don overrode his protest. "We don't know where Megan's gone. We can't waste time searching blindly and trusting to dumb luck to find her."

Aubrey put a hand on Connor's arm, hoping to calm him. "Megan's a survivor," she said, not going into the details. *I almost killed her—but it's probably better if I don't mention that just now.* "She can handle herself."

"There's also twenty Trackers waiting outside the Citadel," Don said. He dropped his grip but used his body as a barrier. "I promise we won't leave without her, Connor, but we've got to be smart about this. Did she mention *anything* about what she's up to?"

Connor took a deep breath, running a nervous hand through his hair. His initial panic had dissipated. "We haven't had much time to talk, and when we did, it was mostly about how she doesn't remember anything before..." His voice trailed off, and his eyes widened. "Megan used to be a bodyguard for the Givers." He looked at his companions with growing excitement. "She said her first memories began as a Tracker—the medical facility is on the top floor. I'll bet that's where she went."

Don said nothing. Aubrey knew he was turning over the variables in his mind.

"Colonel Scott's expecting us to rendezvous with his team," she said, hesitant to interrupt. "They're hitting the armory first, and then the conference room."

Don glanced at her, nodding. "And they'll have no choice but to storm the castle, with or without our help." He turned to Connor. "Garr's counting on us. Sorry, kid, but we're going to stick with his plan. If all goes well, we'll find your sister later. You have my word on that."

Connor shook his head, the emphatic gesture tempered by his wide grin. "The medical facility is beside to the conference room. There's a door between the two—we can sneak through one to get to the other."

Don glanced at Aubrey, thinking hard, and poked a thick finger into Connor's chest. "The Givers, and then Darcy. That's the order of our priorities. If we run into Megan along the way, fine. But if not, we stick to Garr's strategy. Got it?"

"Got it." Connor pointed confidently down the corridor to their right. "The stairway to the medical facility is that way. It's not far."

Aubrey glanced through the open door behind her. The viewscreens were unchanged—lightning, rain, Peace Wardens encircling the Citadel. "Assuming this works, what about all those Trackers downstairs?"

"One impossible thing at a time," Don replied, motioning

for Connor to lead the way. "Let's hope Garr's team is waiting upstairs. I don't like the idea of facing the Givers with nothing but my bare hands."

Connor jogged to the stairwell, stepping lightly to mask his footsteps. The ghostly spiderwebs gave Aubrey a queasy feeling, and she was relieved when she set foot on the spiral staircase.

A heavy lump in her jacket smacked against her thigh as she ascended. She cupped one hand over her pocket, securing the Glock before it gave her a nasty bruise.

SIXTY-SIX ◉

MEGAN HALTED in a small foyer on the fourth floor. As a former bodyguard for the Givers, the Citadel's layout should have been familiar, almost automatic. She felt a twinge of unease. Her memories were less complete than she'd hoped.

She scanned—back and forth, up and down, side to side to side—a predator on the hunt.

Was this her first visit to the medical facility since the day she'd awakened as a Tracker? She concentrated, but couldn't seem to locate the missing puzzle pieces.

The ghostly spiderwebs had provided enough illumination to get her this far, but they diverged at the top of the stairwell, leading in opposite directions to identical doors. Rectangular lights outlined each portal, winking in random patterns as if taunting her—blue, white, red, green.

She ignored the lights, imposing calm on her frayed nerves, and allowed her mind to float in free association. Instinct guided her decision—the door on her right. She held her breath and entered the codes.

The pale blue keypad blinked once before morphing to a deep ocean-blue as the locking mechanism disengaged. Megan smiled to herself. Memorizing the codes when Connor read them aloud to Garr had been simple.

They still underestimate me, even Colonel Scott.

She pushed the door cautiously open, peeking around the edge before entering. Apprehension sent a shiver down her spine as she stepped inside. She closed the door behind her, carefully, silently.

I have no memory of this place. The medical facility, where she'd been recreated as a Tracker. *Why not?*

The lighting was subdued. Logical—the staff had gone home for the evening. No glowing spiderwebs on the floor. Indirect lighting fixtures lined the walls instead, just below the vaulted ceiling. The lights had been dimmed after-hours, providing the bare minimum to offset the missing spiderwebs.

The brightest light source drew her eyes to an enormous screen, centered above a complicated computer workstation. A memory fragment clicked, and she recognized its significance—the link between the Givers and the mental processors embedded in every Tracker's skull.

A solitary figure hunched over the keyboard, and Megan crouched instinctively, terrified by the prospect of betraying her presence. She was tempted to turn and bolt out of the facility, but held her place.

Analyze. Adapt. Enact?

The white-coated tech didn't pause, furiously typing lines of code into the computer, too engrossed in his task to notice her. She breathed a sigh of relief and scrambled to take shelter behind a large wardrobe of sorts.

Surgical attire and laundry, she guessed.

With a dramatic flourish, the tech tapped a final keystroke, rising from his chair to assess the onscreen changes. Satisfied, he smoothed the front of his spotless lab coat and tucked a digital clipboard under his arm. His gait was confident as he strode to a door on the opposite side of the room. He paused to enter a code into the keypad, and exited the facility.

Megan rose from her hiding place and tiptoed across the floor. The medical facility was large, but home to only a single operating table, located fifteen feet in front and to the right of the computer workstation.

Midway between her hiding place and the workstation was a living/dining area, complete with kitchen appliances and a set of expensive-looking couches around a glass-topped coffee table. The arrangement resembled an open-concept apartment. Curious—she detected no sterile barriers separating the living quarters from the operating theater.

The remaining space was dedicated to a number of laboratory stations, glass-doored refrigerators, and storage units, all shrouded in after-hours twilight. A scrupulously-tidy office area completed the interior.

Megan found no hint of sanitizers or cleaning solutions, yet the medical facility exuded the aura of an antiseptic desert. She sniffed to be sure, alert. Even the air itself seemed unnaturally, artificially sterile.

She darted behind one of the overstuffed couches, her near run-in with the departed tech looming large in her imagination. She crept around the couch on her hands and knees, every sense alert. The door the tech had used remained firmly shut, framed by the omnipresent rectangular lights. The keypad remained a benign gray-blue color.

Sentry mode, a ragged fragment of memory suggested.

She scurried in a half-crouch to take shelter behind a bulky medical refrigerator. The metal was cool to the touch, and she flinched from thinking about what might be stored inside. A sixth sense—or maybe a subroutine fragment—sounded a warning. She made herself small, biding her time.

I'm not alone.

She didn't have long to wait. A stealthy figure emerged from the shadows behind the workstation, skirting around the console to confront the central screen.

Megan's breath caught in her throat. *He was at the clinic, with Mateo. What is Logan Johns doing here?*

Logan didn't seat himself, as the first tech had done. He extracted a small object from an inside pocket—an external hard drive, judging by the size—and connected it to the computer. He bent over the keyboard and, a few keystrokes later, his task was complete.

A new set of icons appeared on the screen, shifting in complex patterns across the vertical and horizontal axes. The icons appeared to be reorganizing, deleting, and overwriting the existing onscreen files.

Logan noted their progress, nodding to himself as if pleased, and disconnected the external drive. He retreated a step, pocketing the drive almost as an afterthought, and pivoted without warning. Megan froze, afraid she'd been discovered, but he ran quickly past her and through the stairwell exit, bolting down the steps two at a time.

The door swung shut, muting his reckless descent.

Megan rose from her hiding place and padded silently to the workstation. She leaned over the edge of the console, captivated by the aggressive icons. Her lips moving silently as she tried to decipher their meaning.

The animated sequence accelerated, and her eyes widened as she realized what Logan had done. She retreated instinctively. Analyze. Adapt. Enact.

I've got to warn everyone!

She backed awkwardly away from the workstation, eyes fixed on the ominous display, and collided with an obstacle behind her. She spun about, heart in her throat, to confront the operating table. Time slowed to a suspended crawl as she stared down at it, paralyzed by fear.

This wasn't just any operating table. It was *the* operating table. Trackers were created on its soulless, antiseptic surface.

Megan stretched out a tentative hand, all thoughts of Logan erased. The table's surface was cold—ice-cold—bone-dry and yet somehow damp, and gave off multitudinous pinpricks of static electricity.

She jerked her hand away, wondering absurdly if the discharge might adversely affect her partially-restored subroutines.

She leaned over the table, twisting her spine in order to view the ring of surgical lamps overhead. They were dark and sedentary, a circle of grim sentinels awaiting the next procedure. She gazed into their unseeing eyes, trying to imagine them activated, brilliant, pinning innocent victims to the table beneath their merciless glare.

Her attention returned to the surgical table, and she flattened her palms over the brushed-metal surface, close but not actually touching it. Her fingers tingled and she vividly recalled the restraints that had lashed her down, against her will, but saw no evidence of them.

No. Inaccurate. The restraints were very real, even if invisible to the naked eye.

Her questing fingers discovered a control panel under the

table's edge. She crouched to examine it, and her past and present momentarily clicked. Her body shook in a visceral—almost primal—reaction to the terrifying memories.

She was a prisoner, shackled by bonds she couldn't see and surrounded by strangers who'd sold their souls many years ago. She heard a distant echo of her own voice, shrill with shock and betrayal. *Why are you doing this to me?*

The nightmarish vision of the hand surged to the surface, and her stomach heaved. Paired processors, shiny and pristine, prepped and ready for installation inside a Tracker's skull—*her* skull. She was trapped, pinned to the operating table, powerless to resist and unable to defend herself.

Please, don't turn me into one of Them!

Megan fell to her knees, dazed and nauseous. She slid down to the polished floor, propping herself against the base of the table for support. The throbbing in her head subsided, and her mind gradually cleared.

She'd come to the Citadel seeking answers, any clue to unlock her past. She'd managed to locate the medical facility where her life had been irreparably changed, but all she had to show for her trouble was the same recurring nightmare.

She wanted to scream.

The door opened behind her, and she froze, heart pounding anew. Someone entered the facility, their footsteps beating a staccato trail to the opposite side of the operating table.

The white-coated tech? Does he know about Logan?

The footsteps stopped abruptly, and she heard a voice. A man's voice, reciting names between clenched teeth, spitting out each one with venomous loathing.

SIXTY-SEVEN

AMOS KNELT ON THE plush carpet, hands clasped on top of his head. He felt the stares from the Hoarders seated around the ornately carved table. Their gaping mouths and hushed comments among themselves confirmed that the Runners hadn't been expected. Even Darcy, seated at the far end of the conference table, appeared blindsided by their arrival.

Amos wondered if Darcy was only pretending. He wouldn't be surprised to learn that Mateo had been in cahoots with the Hoarder sociopath all along.

One glaring exception caught his eye. He nudged Jane, elbow to elbow, and nodded to indicate the smirking Hoarder at the head of the table. He was the only one standing, arm resting casually on a high-backed leather chair, his back to the storm-lashed windows. The Hoarder's self-satisfied expression set him apart from his counterparts.

He knew we were coming. Amos glared as the implications sank in. The smug Hoarder was the obvious liaison between Mateo and the Givers. *He's the puppet master.*

Mateo stood over Amos, cradling a Hoarder weapon in his arms. The smug councilor inclined his head slightly, acknowledging his presence, and Mateo basked in his approval like a rattlesnake on a warm rock. Amos's contempt sharpened into razor-tipped fury. He couldn't even look at the Tracker.

Gabriel was quick to jump into the fray. *And yet, once upon a time, you trusted Mateo. If only Trey could see you now—he'd be so proud.*

Amos ground his teeth, berating himself for letting his older brother down. Again.

"My fellow Council members," the Hoarder said, breaking the uneasy silence. His mellifluous voice reeked of Cascadian arrogance. "This is truly an auspicious occasion. We, the surviving remnant of the Council, are about to inaugurate a new era of peace and security for Cascadia."

A few councilors eyed him with suspicion. Others continued to stare, with a mixture of curiosity and repugnance, at the prisoners kneeling on the carpet. Little wonder—Amos tasted a bitter tang at the thought—their faces had been featured on the Infomedia, in an infinite loop, for the entire day.

Cascadia's most-wanted savages.

The councilor left his chosen post, circling the table to stand before the Runners, hands clasped behind his back, clearly enjoying himself. He inspected each of them with equal contempt, one by one, and turned to address Mateo.

"Just like you promised, Mr. Reyes." He smiled, a gracious despot commending an underling for a job well done. "You've earned your place in the Citadel. The Givers will be pleased."

"It was and is my privilege, Councilor Sterne." Mateo bowed his head slightly. "The Givers are as wise as they are generous."

Jane returned Amos's elbow nudge. He glanced her way,

and she pointed with her chin at the rest of the Council. The mere mention of the Givers produced a noticeable effect on the Hoarders seated around the table. Several exchanged uneasy looks, and a few rose to their feet—half-eager, half-wary. The spike in tension was unmistakable.

Darcy lurched to his feet at the first mention of the aliens. Unlike his fellow Hoarders' obvious trepidation, his face contorted with a madman's wrath.

Amos chafed at his powerlessness. The Hoarders clearly didn't trust each other, and he could only guess at the layers of intrigue and subterfuge lurking below the surface. A virtual cabal of raw ego and lust for power.

And we have Mateo to thank for betraying us to them.

A door opened behind him. Logan entered the room, taking up a position beside Garr. Councilor Sterne paid him scant attention beyond a curt nod and took a step back, sweeping his arm out in a magnanimous gesture to Mateo. "Come, my friend. Step forward and be recognized."

Sterne retreated to the center of the conference room to face a featureless black wall. Its surface was seamless, as if cast from a single slab of black granite, rough-textured and impenetrable. Lightning flashed outside the windows, but Sterne didn't seem to notice. He appeared to be waiting, his attention fixated on the granite wall. His colleagues got to their feet, their apprehension clear.

Mateo glanced at his kneeling prisoners, cocking his head to one side. "I bid you all a good journey."

Amos spat at him.

* * *

A LOW, MECHANICAL GRINDING filled the conference room, like the gears of a long-neglected drawbridge, and the striations in the granite wall came alive with the same phosphorescence as the ubiquitous spiderwebs.

A crack appeared, running in an unnaturally straight line from floor to ceiling. The gap expanded incrementally, and a sickly, green-tinged glow emanated from the Givers' inner sanctum, bathing Councilor Sterne in an eerie glow.

Sterne relished the swirling emotions of his fellow Citizens —anticipation and curiosity, anxiety and fear.

Fear was the strongest.

Out of the corner of his eye, he spied one of his colleagues steal away, slinking into the medical facility. He took note of the coward's identity. Darcy Peterson, the smooth-talking hothead. Sterne scoffed silently. Darcy's xenophobia blinded him to the opportunities afforded by aligning with the aliens.

He won't get far. Peace Wardens are stationed at every exit. Sterne banished him from his thoughts. Ethan, his loyal aide, came to stand beside him. Sterne smiled, reveling in his young assistant's adulation.

At the far end of the room, the savages watched in stunned silence, spellbound. Logan Johns, Mateo's young protégé, stood guard over them. He took a restless step forward, his face alight with eager anticipation.

The mechanical grinding grew louder, and the floor rumbled beneath their feet. The thin crack grew inexorably wider, morphing into a gaping crevice as the granite slab gradually split into two halves, rotating outward.

A droning vibration filled the air. Sterne felt static electricity tingling on his skin. He squinted, resisting the urge to shield his eyes. Green-tinged light, crackling with spidery bolts of energy, cast a sickly pallor over the room.

The Givers were on their way.

SIXTY-EIGHT ◉

CONNOR CLEARED THE LAST STEP to the foyer at the top of the fourth-floor stairs. He braced one hand against the door—palm flattened—and feverishly entered the codes. The keypad blinked ocean-blue in response, and the door opened. Connor stepped aside, allowing Don to enter first.

Aubrey edged past Connor, and he followed, crowding in behind her. The door swung shut with a soft *whoosh*, and she almost collided with Don. The big man's outflung arm barred her advance. She heard Connor's sharp intake of breath a split second before he bumped into her.

A complex computer array and a high-tech surgical station dominated one portion of the facility. And hovering next to the operating table ... Aubrey's world shrank to a single, sanity-threatening detail. *I'm not ready to face him again.*

Darcy Peterson whirled to face them. His eyes widened, betraying his shock at their rapid and unexpected arrival. Time seemed to freeze. Aubrey saw every detail, every nuance, with pristine clarity. The operating table, the surgical lamps poised above it like grimly expectant vultures, the digital tablet clutched in Darcy's hand—all passed before her eyes with excruciating slowness. Her pulse throbbed in her ears, equally lethargic and obscenely loud.

Darcy's face contorted from shock to rage to mania, and his pale eyes appeared more feral than human. He raised the tablet, fingers stabbing at it with manic precision.

"The tablet!" Connor's hoarse voice jarred Aubrey out of her paralysis. "He's programming our Implants..."

Crack!

A dark object struck Darcy full in the face. Blood erupted in a glistening fountain of red. He staggered, clawing blindly at his eyes. His other hand tightened on the tablet, clutching it to his chest.

The object clattered to the floor, bouncing once and landing at Darcy's feet. Jane's Glock. Aubrey gasped, belatedly realizing what she'd done. Don rushed forward, diving for the weapon.

Darcy pounced, snatching the Glock away from the big man's grasping fingers. He took two quick steps back, brought up short by the operating table, and took aim at his would-be assailant. Don rose to his hands and knees, meeting Darcy's malignant gaze eye-to-eye, defiant to the end.

A gloating smile creased Darcy's face. His eyes were wild. Blood streamed from his shattered cheekbone, flowing freely over his wide sneer. He stood over Don, Glock in one hand and tablet in the other.

Megan vaulted over the operating table, driving her shoulder into Darcy's spine. He stumbled forward, recovered, and spun to retaliate, swinging the Glock into firing position. Aubrey couldn't see his face, but he seemed to freeze for a split second at the sight of Megan.

She slammed against him, her face contorted with calculated menace, knocking him off-balance and locking her hands around his wrist. She wrenched the Glock up and back, twisting savagely. Darcy yelped in pain, dropping the tablet in a frantic attempt to regain control of the handgun.

Don got his feet under him and dove at Darcy, driving a massive shoulder into his midsection. Darcy's eyes bulged, and he gulped desperately for air. Don clasped his arms around the Hoarder in a crushing bear hug, and they ricocheted off the operating table before crashing heavily to the floor.

Megan managed to twist away, tearing the Glock out of Darcy's grip. Connor lunged forward to join the fray, scooping up the tablet. Megan tossed the Glock out of reach and scrambled back to the operating table. Aubrey skidded to her knees on the floor, retrieving the Glock and scurrying out of reach.

Megan circled the table, intent on a small control panel. "Bring him here, Don."

Don dragged the Hoarder to his feet. Darcy's blood-streaked face was a gory mask, and his ragged breathing sounded wet. With Connor's help, Don manhandled him to the operating table and flung him on it. Darcy struggled, but Don held him in place, one hand at his throat.

Megan gave Don a quick nod, fingers poised over the controls. Don whipped his hand away and she jabbed at the panel. A thin bead of light came to life around the edge of the table. Darcy strained against invisible restraints, to no avail, functionally paralyzed from the neck down.

An uncanny stillness settled over the facility. Aubrey joined her fellow Runners—and Connor—around the operating table to look at the monster responsible for the Implants.

Megan leaned on the edge of the table, supporting herself

on both hands as she studied Darcy's bloody countenance. His pale eyes lost their icy confidence as she hovered over him, expressionless. It was plain to see—he recognized her.

Megan slid the eyepatch aside, slow and methodical, revealing her ruined eye socket. "Do you remember what you said to me that day, *Councilor*? The last human words I heard before the Givers turned me into a Tracker?"

Darcy gasped raggedly and said nothing, but his terrified expression spoke volumes. Aubrey felt neither pity nor satisfaction. She was numb.

Megan leaned in close, until their faces were a mere handbreadth apart. "You said, 'Will someone *please* shut her up.' *Remember*?" Her scathing challenge became an accusation. She straightened, easing the eyepatch back into place. Her voice was low and laced with revulsion. "The Givers may be aliens, but that doesn't make you human."

She backed away. Connor stepped forward, staring at his foster father as if seeing the face of a stranger. He held the tablet aloft, where Darcy could get a good look at it. Without a word, he smashed it against one corner of the table, near Darcy's head. The tablet splintered on the unyielding surface, and stray bits of glass and plastic shrapnel peppered Darcy's face. Connor dropped what remained of the tablet on the floor and stomped it repeatedly under the heel of his boot.

Don appeared at Aubrey's elbow. He gestured at the Glock, his voice muted. "Throwing your weapon at the enemy? They didn't teach us that in basic training. Lucky for me, you've got good aim." He glanced at her when she didn't respond. "Darcy *was* about to shoot me, you know."

Aubrey pocketed the Glock, not looking at him. "It wasn't loaded. I didn't . . ." She shrugged. "Forget it. I'll explain later."

A concussive roar reverberated through the medical facility, and the floor shuddered underfoot. Aubrey caught at Don's arm to steady herself. *Was that an earthquake?*

Megan pivoted to face the computer array, scanning the shifting icons. She nodded as if she'd been expecting this. "It's begun," she said cryptically. "We're out of time."

Without waiting for a reply, she strode briskly to the conference room door. Don took one look at the computer display —icons now accelerating in dizzying swirls of color—and seized Aubrey by the arm.

"What's happening?" Aubrey made no attempt to hide her ignorance.

"You think I know?" Don replied, hustling her to the door. "I'm just following Megan."

Megan entered a code into the keypad. The pale blue glow darkened to emerald green, blinked twice, and shot immediately to an angry amber. Aubrey's pulse raced at Megan's alarmed expression. *The codes don't work anymore.*

Don pressed his ear to the door. He clenched his fist and pounded on the stubborn portal in impotent rage. "I hear Hoarder weapons. Garr..."

Megan spun to face the operating table, every muscle taut. "Connor—the codes have been altered!"

Connor kicked the shattered tablet aside and hurried to join them. His fingers flew over the keypad, and the amber glow retreated to its former emerald hue. Megan shot him a sharp look. He shrugged, looking sheepish. "I didn't think anyone would need Darcy's personal override." His fingers danced over the keys a second time. "This should do it."

The keypad blinked three times in quick succession, and emerald green cross-faded to ocean blue.

The locking mechanism meekly disengaged.

Don seized the handle, taking a deep breath and shooting his companions a warning glance. "Ready or not ..."

"*Connor.*" Darcy's desperate howl drew their attention back to the operating table. His pale eyes were wild and pleading, his face gaunt and bloody. "You can't just leave me here!"

"Oh yes, I can," Connor replied, in a voice that sent a chill down Aubrey's spine. "For the good of the Enclave."

SIXTY-NINE ◉

THE GIVERS WERE A NIGHTMARE unlike anything Amos could have imagined. Megan's crude sketch—so many months ago— couldn't begin to compare with reality. He wrestled with an on-slaught of vertigo when he tried to focus on the aliens.

That's the problem. A headache erupted behind his eyes. *It's impossible to get a good look at them.*

The Givers—*are there three of them, or more?*—entered the conference room in perfect formation, their every move mir-rored in precise, flowing fluidity with their counterparts. The aliens appeared solid at times, and then partially translucent, flowing back and forth into each other.

Or is that an optical illusion?

Flickering bolts of green light left burning afterimages in Amos's eyes, and the inner sanctum exhaled a pungent cloud of sickly-sweet sulfur.

The Council members, rising to greet the aliens, seemed to be experiencing the same queasiness. Several collapsed into their chairs, hands clamped over their mouths.

"I can't even look at them," Jane whispered harshly, lowering her arms. Logan didn't seem to notice. She wrinkled her nose. "Ugh. What a stench."

Amos dropped his arms as well, massaging his wrists to restore circulation. "Garr was more right than he knew. Everything about them is totally … alien."

The grinding noise faded, but crackling energy bolts lashed the carpet just beyond the edge of the inner sanctum. A swarm of pallid creatures scuttled back and forth just inside the opening, roughly the size of Amos's hand, but with far too many legs to be spiders.

Councilor Sterne, flanked by his assistant and Mateo, stood before the Givers without flinching. Amos heard nothing but crackling energy, but Sterne smiled and nodded as if the aliens were communicating with him. He placed a hand on Mateo's shoulder, giving every appearance of introducing him.

Mateo ducked his head in a slight bow, and glanced over his shoulder in Amos's direction. The greenish light gave his face an inhuman tinge, offset by the unexpected activation of his scanning eye.

He cocked his head, his expression indecipherable, and nodded to Logan. "Proceed."

Amos whipped his head around to stare at the other Tracker. Logan pulled a small device from inside his jacket, using his thumb to depress a short plunger on one end.

The floor shook violently in response, and the muffled roar of a devastating explosion—or multiple explosions—rumbled beneath their feet. Red-tinged smoke roiled up the outer walls of the Citadel, obscuring the windows.

Pandemonium broke loose before the echoing shockwaves died down. The overhead lights flickered, and Logan fired his

weapon repeatedly. Council members dove to the floor, screaming in terror. Mateo whirled about, his weapon held ready
as he shielded the Givers with his body. He gestured for the
Councilor and his aide to take cover behind him.

The alien cluster shrieked, a piercing ululation that echoed
painfully in the confined space. They pivoted with chaotic synchronicity and escaped into their inner sanctum in a nausea-
inducing swirl of color and liquefied motion.

The guttural hiss of Hoarder weapons was constant. Mateo
took careful aim around the conference room, covering the
aliens' retreat. The cathedral windows fractured and collapsed
in the crossfire, and the howling storm drove clouds of noxious
smoke into the conference room. The air reeked of scorched
metal and an unidentifiable organic stench.

The Citadel was burning.

The remaining Council members rushed for the nearest
door—the medical facility—only to discover it was locked from
the other side. Terror drove the panic-stricken Citizens over
the edge. They pivoted *en masse* and charged in a frantic stampede for the opposite end of the room, almost trampling the
Runners in their crazed exit.

Jane coughed convulsively as acrid smoke filled the room,
and Amos pawed at his watering eyes. Wind gusted through
the shattered windows, driving the rain before it. The swirling
smoke cleared for an instant, and he spied Councilor Sterne
staggering into the inner sanctum, his assistant clinging desperately to his arm.

Mateo crouched in a defensive stance, his back to the green-
lit portal and weapon held ready. The blood-red glow around
his left eye accentuated his gaunt face.

The granite slab began to close, and the conference room

darkened as the green light was cut off. Mateo held his position, weapon trained outward, although he had ceased firing.

Logan darted forward, halting a few paces from Mateo and lowering the muzzle of his weapon. The Trackers eyed each other silently, as if sharing some form of unspoken communication in defiance of the cacophony surrounding them.

Mateo straightened, relaxing his defensive crouch. He gazed at his weapon for an extended moment, an odd expression on his face, and allowed it to slip from his fingers. The Hoarder weapon landed heavily at his feet. His red-rimmed gaze shifted from Logan to include the Runners.

"This is where it began," he said, his voice barely audible over the thunderstorm. "This is where it ends."

He pivoted without warning and flung himself into the maw of the inner sanctum, clearing the gap just before the granite slab snapped shut. The green light was extinguished, plunging the conference room into a murky twilight, held partially at bay by the glowing striations.

The door to the medical facility burst open, and Don's team scrambled into the smoky room. The big man kicked one of the heavy chairs aside, eyes wary as he tried to make sense of the chaotic scene. The rest of his team crowded in behind him, fanning out on either side. They looked relieved and perplexed to find no trace of the Givers.

Amos scrambled over the up-ended chairs to snatch Mateo's discarded weapon. He trained it on the featureless slab, searching in vain for any sign of the vertical seam.

Nothing. Not even a hint.

He aimed a frustrated kick at the barrier, screaming at the utter futility of it all. The spiderwebs faded, and the monolithic slab mocked him in wordless defiance, solid and unmoving.

He raised the Hoarder weapon, about to fire indiscriminately, but couldn't bring himself to pull the trigger. It was pointless. He lowered the rifle, pivoting to face Colonel Scott.

"Our mission was to stop the Givers." His voice cracked, the bitterness of defeat gnawing at him. He pointed helplessly at the impenetrable wall. "But they're out of reach *and* under Mateo's protection."

Some sixth sense warned him of Logan John's approach. Amos whirled to confront him, weapon poised to fire.

Logan froze momentarily and then, comprehension dawning, upended his weapon and—with exaggerated care—laid it on the conference table. He turned to face Amos, empty hands raised in a gesture of surrender.

"Didn't you hear what Mateo said?" Logan kept a respectful distance, raising his voice over the storm. "He's not protecting the Givers—he's preventing their escape. We don't have time to argue about it. We need to abandon the Citadel, *now*."

Garr laid a hand on the barrel of Amos's weapon, forcing it down. "What are you saying, Logan?"

Sheila and Jane clustered around, and Don's team joined them, presenting a united front opposite the young Tracker.

Garr crossed his arms, studying Logan with a critical eye. "Mateo surrendered his weapon," he said evenly, watching for his reaction. "He's no threat to anyone in there."

Logan shook his head. "Mateo is a Dissident." Lightning flared outside, accented a split second later by a thunderous boom, as if underscoring his words. "The Givers can't control him. He—*we*—are in full command of our enhancements."

He stepped closer to Garr, clearly frustrated by the Colonel's inability to connect the dots.

Amos raised his weapon a fraction higher.

Logan ignored him. "*All* of our enhancements," he said, eyes fixed on the colonel. "Including the self-destruct."

"He's going to self-detonate," Garr said bluntly.

Logan nodded bleakly. A look of pain flitted across his face. "We have to get out of here while we still can."

Amos lowered his weapon, stunned. Jane shoved past Logan, scooping up his discarded rifle. "We've got at least twenty Trackers between us and the exits." She hefted the weapon, defying anyone to take it away.

Logan dug into his pocket, extracting the small device he'd activated earlier. He held it aloft in one hand, as if about to explain, but never got the chance. The Citadel shook again, more violently than before.

The granite slab bulged outward, as if rammed with great force from within. Spiderwebs blazed into unnatural life across the textured surface, and winked out almost as quickly. Cracks appeared, and pinpoints of sickly greenish light pierced the gloom. A hideous wail erupted—shrill and outraged—assaulting their ears.

"*Run!*" Logan bolted for the open door and the stairwell beyond. His frantic departure goaded the Runners into action, and they pelted down the stairs in his wake. Acrid smoke stung their eyes and lungs, and desperation drove them to reckless, breakneck speed.

The unearthly wail—an adversary defying rational description—chased them down the circular staircase.

SEVENTY ◉

A SECOND EXPLOSION rocked the Citadel. Aubrey stumbled on the staircase, clutching the handrail for support, her other arm shielding her head from falling debris. The lights flickered and dimmed, turning the stairwell into an artificial cavern. She choked on dust and smoke, and even Logan's reckless descent faltered to an abrupt halt.

Aubrey clung to the railing, the labored breathing of her companions filling her ears. She sensed their close proximity, but couldn't see anyone.

Artificial light abruptly returned, fluctuating on and off in a rapid, disjointed fashion. A hideous shriek snaked down the stairwell, rising in pitch, volume, and fury. Aubrey glanced over her shoulder, half-expecting to spy one of the aliens slithering after them.

They bolted down the stairs in spite of the light's stroboscopic effect. Nausea threatened Aubrey's equilibrium as she was forced to all but guess where to place her feet.

A war zone awaited them on the ground floor. The walls

in the Citadel's lobby hung in tattered shards between skeletal support pillars, allowing the storm-driven deluge easy access. The front entrance had been obliterated, leaving nothing behind but a ragged, gaping hole where the doors had been.

Darkness mercifully obscured the full extent of the devastation, but flashes of lightning exposed the charred evidence of multiple explosions. Blast craters pockmarked the floor, and there was no sign of the rectangular lights or glowing spiderwebs. Peace Wardens/Trackers—or what little remained of them —lay scattered about the lobby as well as on the scorched lawn outside the missing walls.

Logan dodged through a jagged hole near the foot of the stairs and into the storm, sprinting across the manicured lawn until he reached the parking lot. Garr guided the rest of the Runners out of the Citadel, picking their way over the grisly debris with feverish haste.

Aubrey wished she could filter out a charred smell she didn't want to think about. She tripped on something that rolled under her foot and barely stifled an outcry. A searing burst of lightning confirmed her worst fear—a human leg, complete with booted foot. Darkness and rain obscured any additional remains. Megan caught her out-flung arm, dragging her along.

She fought her heaving insides. *Don't look down.*

They gathered in a compact huddle near the center of the empty parking lot. Aubrey sank to her knees on the wet pavement, hardly daring to believe their escape. The thunderstorm lashed at them, cold and remorseless, and the keening wail escalated in an ear-splitting crescendo.

A greenish haze wrapped itself around the Citadel's uppermost floor—an enraged phantasm of crackling, vindictive energy. As they watched, the Citadel began collapsing inward, top to bottom, imploding degree by tortuous degree. Metal pillars and girders groaned in protest, accompanied by a cascading series of internal explosions and flame-lit black smoke.

The unearthly howl intensified, and the green haze darted to and fro like a malevolent entity. The Citadel's disintegration accelerated, until all that remained was a jumbled mound of scorched and smoking debris.

The screeching howl faded into merciful silence. The green phantasm seeped and swirled over the rubble, like a dispossessed spirit seeking a new host to inhabit.

Failing that, it dissipated, the last tendrils scattered by the storm-driven wind.

Rain lashed the Runners, relentless and uncaring.

SEVENTY-ONE ⊙

"IT'S ALMOST THREE o'clock in the morning." Enrico hovered in the doorway to an examination room, cradling a medium-sized box in his hands, clearly anxious to depart. "How much longer is this going to take?"

Logan sat just inside the door, keeping an eye on an unconscious figure on the room's single cot. Colonel Scott slept soundly, motionless, as the anesthetic worked its gradual way out of his system.

Logan leaned back in his chair, stretching his aching back. "Not as long as you might think. There were five Implants requiring extraction, and the procedure can only be done one at a time. Garr insisted on going last."

Enrico nodded, watching the slow rise and fall of Garr's ribcage. "That sounds like something the colonel would do. That's why people trust him."

Darcy's unregistered clinic, located a healthy distance from the smoking ruins of the Citadel, had, a few hours earlier, been the site of an exuberant reunion. The Runners, rain-soaked and exhausted, arrived just before midnight to discover Doc Simon waiting.

Doc put the clinic's high-tech medical equipment to good use. "This won't even leave a scar," she'd promised each candidate for surgery.

Logan smiled at the memory, and then noticed the box in the mechanic's hands. "Is that the last of it?"

Enrico hefted the open container and gave its contents a shake. "The last Implant was the colonel's, so yes, that's all of it. Dismantled, shredded, chopped in half, and whatever other damage I could inflict on them. Then, just for good measure, I melted everything down with a blowtorch. Good riddance to Implant technology."

"Amen to that," Logan replied enthusiastically. He gestured vaguely at the office area. "Mateo cooked up a malicious virus for the clinic servers. It's already uploaded, and I'll set it loose as soon as we're finished here." He glanced up at the mechanic. "It'll corrupt any and all files—upstream and down."

Enrico nodded before giving him a reproving frown. "You knew what Mateo was planning. You could've said something, or at least dropped a juicy hint or two."

"*No es mi culpa*, Señor Torres." Logan shrugged, flashing him a weary smile. "I was sworn to secrecy. Call it the 'Dissident's Code,' if you like. Mateo had his reasons."

* * *

TARA LINDHOLM UNLOCKED her office at CSMD, ready to begin her shift. She slid into her leather chair, taking a cautious sip of her steaming latte. More than a week had passed, and the majority of her viewscreens were still blank.

The restoration schedule was a hot mess. Bureaucrats, architectural contractors, and special interest groups had all but guaranteed a prolonged gridlock. First priority was reserved for the as-yet-unresolved damage on the subterranean maintenance level, and remediating the desolate husk that was once the Citadel.

The Anodyne Initiative had been placed on hold, pending the outcome of a fierce and protracted debate in the chambers of the recently appointed Council of Cascadia. The new Council members, it appeared, were eager to flex their muscles and test the limits of their political clout.

Truth be told, her shifts at the Division were much less complicated, thanks to a minimum of functioning surveillance cameras relaying data to her station. She hadn't seen or heard a word from Darcy, or any of his associates, since the night the Citadel was destroyed.

Tara had no complaints. The peace and quiet was a welcome change.

To alleviate the boredom, she kept one screen tuned to the Infomedia. It caught her attention now, displaying a dramatic aerial view of the Citadel's contorted wreckage. The scene shifted to a somber-faced reporter, microphone in hand, intoning his report for the masses.

"Oh, this oughta be good." Tara stretched, reaching over to increase the volume. She settled into her chair with a cynical smile, cradling her latte. "What new conspiracy theories are the authorities peddling today?"

It would be entertaining, of that much she was sure.

"People will believe just about anything," she murmured aloud, "if they see it on the Infomedia."

SEVENTY-TWO ◎

SHEILA SIPPED a cup of hot chicory, grateful for the familiar taste after enduring Cascadian coffee. "So, your working theory is that Mateo never had any intention of leaving the Citadel. His entire strategy, beginning to end, was a one-way trip."

Garr nodded from his usual chair at the mess hall table. "It makes the most sense, based on what Logan told me. I've been going over it in my head, analyzing it from every possible angle. After eight days, you know what I've realized?"

Don pulled out a chair, seating himself opposite the colonel. "That the only thing more remarkable than my rugged good looks is my legendary culinary skill?"

Garr laughed, wadding up a piece of paper and tossing it at him. "Save your bragging until *after* supper. Your kitchen wizardry remains a fairy tale until proven otherwise."

"Inform your taste buds they are about to enter paradise," Don replied, his drawl more pronounced than usual. "Our final meal in Eastside Hub will be a culinary masterpiece worthy of such an occasion."

Sheila took a seat beside him, bracing her elbows on the table and cradling her mug between her hands. "Getting back to Mateo ... what conclusion did you come to, Colonel?"

Garr paused, studying the table's scuffed surface. "That he's arguably the most brilliant strategist I've ever met. He played both sides so well that none of us, Runners or Hoarders, knew what to think. It didn't matter what we thought of him. He had one objective—the Givers."

Sheila finished her drink and went to pour herself a refill. She held an empty mug aloft. "Coffee?"

Garr held up a hand. "None for me, thanks."

Don affected a pained expression. "What about me?"

"You hate coffee, big guy." Sheila waved him away and sat down. "We always say 'this can't be about revenge.' Any guess as to Mateo's motivation?"

"Payback, plus justice," Don said, unsheathing his combat knife and admiring its gleaming edge. "If Mateo only wanted revenge on the Givers for turning him into a Tracker, he'd have gone after them all by his lonesome." He sighted along the blade to meet Garr's pensive gaze. "But he dragged us into it, as well, and helped us put an end to Darcy's Implants."

Garr nodded and got to his feet. "He was running a high-stakes poker game, doing whatever was necessary to get access to the Givers. He knew nothing would change otherwise. He had it all planned, right down to the last detail."

"Including his self-detonation," Sheila said somberly, stirring a spoonful of raw sugar into her mug. "Mateo fooled us all. More to the point, he fooled the Givers."

A solemn hush settled over the mess hall.

Garr beckoned to Don. "Let's get started. I promised everyone a celebration when this was over, and I meant it."

SEVENTY-THREE

THE WARM AFTERNOON SUN offset a cool autumn breeze. Connor and Megan ambled along a merchants' row of shops not far from Eastside Mission. They'd volunteered, at Don's request, to pick up a few items for his promised "culinary extravaganza."

Connor tried his best not to stare, but getting used to the Old City was a work-in-progress. Where he'd expected to find squalor and cutthroat competition, he found instead, with a few minor exceptions, a vibrant and cooperative community.

It's not perfect. He wasn't naïve enough to sugarcoat reality. *But it's not like what I was raised to believe, either.*

"Last crop, most likely." The shopkeeper's voice drew him back to the present. He handed Connor a bag of potatoes and escorted them to the door of his shop. "Won't be much more this season, what with winter just around the corner."

Megan smiled and thanked him, and they resumed their stroll along the street. Connor was content to let her do most of the talking, still unsure of how to act outside the Enclave.

Megan had brushed her long, wavy hair to minimize her

scars, but disguising the eyepatch was impossible. Connor said nothing, but worried how people might react. She was the eldest, and could obviously handle herself, but he felt protective.

Their shopping trip turned out to be a pleasant surprise. A few people crossed the street to avoid them, but for the most part, she was treated respectfully. A fresh start beyond Cascadia's walls might be possible, after all.

Megan nudged him with her elbow. "Something on your mind, Connor?"

He hesitated, caught off-guard. *Should I even ask?* He took a deep breath and decided to risk it. "Darcy was there when the Givers..." His voice trailed off.

Megan gave her head a firm shake. "You're about to ask if Darcy had anything to do with our parents' deaths." She glanced at him and then away. "I've told you everything I remember. He was present for my Tracker surgery, but beyond that, I don't know." She halted, putting out a hand to block him. "And I think it's dangerous to speculate. Obsessing over the past won't do either of us any good. Please, don't ask me again."

"You're right." Connor raised his hands, surrendering. "I get it, but not knowing's hard." He took a deep breath. "Never again. I promise."

She took his arm and they resumed walking.

Connor glanced at her. "They've given you space after what happened at the Citadel, but it's only a matter of time before Garr—I mean, Colonel Scott—wants to debrief you."

"That's what I figured. Don't worry, I plan on telling him the truth." She sighed heavily, not looking at him. "That Connor Sinclair, my little brother, wet the bed until he was seven years old."

He pivoted to face her. "I did *not*."

She doubled over, laughing. Connor stared, dumbstruck, and then caught on. He lapsed into an embarrassed grin, shaking his head. "You know, that's more how I remember you. Less like a Tracker, and more like … you."

Her laughter faded as she considered his comment. "I'll always be a bit of both," she said, abruptly serious. She tucked her hands into her pockets. "And, let's face it, my memories aren't likely to return. We *both* need to accept that."

Connor broke eye contact, making no effort to hide his disappointment. "You make it sound so final. To tell you the truth, I hope you're dead wrong."

"Your locket." Megan stopped and held her hand out, palm up. "Give it to me."

Connor halted, surprised by her demand. He slipped the chain over his head and handed the locket to her.

Megan pried the casing open to reveal her photo. "For you, this picture conjures up hundreds of memories, maybe thousands." She lifted the locket between them. "But when I look at it, I see only two things. First, I recognize myself, or how I looked when I was eighteen."

"And second?" Connor prompted when she paused.

Megan tried, and failed, to repress a facetious grin. "I'll bet people didn't stare as much when I had two eyes." She cocked her head to one side and her hair obscured the eyepatch. "I'm free of the Givers and their mind control. At first, that was enough, but I'm not satisfied with that. Not anymore."

Connor waited, curious.

Megan pushed her hair back, revealing the scars encircling her eyepatch. "Everything I knew as a child was stolen from me. And—if I could—I'd gladly lobotomize myself to erase the memories of what the Givers forced me to do." She took a deep breath, allowing her hair to fall into place. "Cascadia Enclave wasn't *all* bad. I want to hear about the good times. I need you to tell me about my past, my family—*our* family. Those are the stories I want to focus on."

Connor nodded, zipping his jacket against the breeze. "I'll do my best. We've got a lot of catching up to do."

She grinned, handing the locket back. "And, in exchange, I'll teach my over-serious little brother how to buy food in the marketplace like a normal person."

Connor refastened the silver chain and tucked the locket inside his shirt. "Sounds like a fair deal."

She punched him playfully on the arm. "Let's head back to Eastside. We don't want to keep Chef Benoit waiting."

SEVENTY-FOUR

"IT'S LIKE A GHOST TOWN," Aubrey said, taking stock of the gutted infirmary. The gurney had been removed already, and shelving units and cupboards were stripped of their contents. She marveled at the few remaining packs lined up atop the worktable. Even Doc's favorite stool was nowhere in sight.

"I prefer to think of it as a chrysalis after the butterfly has emerged," Doc replied cheerfully. "Cocoons are necessary for a season, but only as a transitional stage."

"Nice metaphor." Aubrey squeezed the rubber ball they'd discovered while packing up. The faded gray orb had been her constant companion during rehab. She bounced it once on the floor, catching it between her scarred fingers. "Scientific *and* poetic."

So many defining moments happened here. She pocketed the ball, a keepsake she intended to take with her. *This is as much Eastside's nerve center as the mess hall.*

Doc finished packing her antique microscope, the same model she'd used since her earliest days as a medic. Aubrey hid a smile. Dr. Emily Simon, former armed forces medic, would never allow anyone else to lay a hand on her prized possession.

"What are your plans after the big feast tonight, Aubrey? Heading back to your hometown, perhaps?"

"That's a good question, Doc." Aubrey took an extra moment to ponder her answer before speaking. "I don't know, to be honest. My grandparents would be thrilled to have me back on the farm, but I have a hard time imagining myself settling into small-town life like nothing's happened. Feels like I'd be starting over from scratch."

Doc watched her closely, nodding sympathetically.

Aubrey glanced around the infirmary, gripping the ball in her pocket. An image of the Coopers' farmhouse, engulfed in flames, flickered and was gone. "I'm not the same Aubrey Carter who showed up in the Old City last spring. I'm not sure I *can* go back." She laughed, feeling self-conscious. "Sorry, Doc, I didn't mean to dump all that on you. Just thinking out loud. What about you? What new adventures are you off to?"

"Nonsense." Doc waved a hand at her. "You're not 'dumping' anything on me. I'm your doctor. But at my age, I'm not in the market for new adventures. Peace and quiet appeals to me." She paused. "On the other hand, Logan sneaking Enrico and I into the Enclave—right under the Hoarders' noses—was the most terrifying and exhilarating rollercoaster ride of my life! I wouldn't have missed that for *anything*."

Her laughter was contagious. Aubrey couldn't help but join in.

Doc fiddled with a strap on the nearest pack, a faraway look on her face. "I've decided to relocate topside. Eastside Mission could use a trained medic, and the Mission district has grown on me. Plus, fresh air appeals to me more than the fragrance down here." She pinched her nose for effect. "I could use a medical assistant, Aubrey, if you'd be open to a different kind of adventure."

"Are you serious?" Aubrey raised her eyebrows, surprised and intrigued by the offer. "I don't know what to say, Doc. You caught me off-guard. Wow…" She chewed on her lower lip, turning the idea over. "Can I have some time to think about it? I'd be a pretty raw recruit."

Doc scoffed. "I'll whip you into shape in no time."

Aubrey pulled the ball from her pocket, holding it up between them. "Another rehab challenge, Dr. Simon?"

"I'll be honest." Her light-hearted smile faded. "You've all been through hell and back, each in your own way. Psychologically, that's going to leave a mark. I wouldn't be much of a doctor if I wasn't just a little concerned."

"Thanks for caring, Doc." Aubrey squeezed the ball between her fingers. Grip, relax, grip, relax. "I hope that's not the *only* reason you're inviting me to stay."

"Not all at." Her smile flashed again. "I could use the help, frankly, and I think you'd be good at it."

Don's voice bellowed down the corridor, his words indecipherable but delivered in a commanding tone.

Doc nodded at the door. "Sounds like dinner is served."

Aubrey grinned and stepped into the corridor. She pivoted to toss the ball back into the infirmary. It ricocheted off the far wall, bouncing once on the floor before she snatched it out of midair. "I *will* think about it, Doc. I promise."

Doc Simon extinguished the infirmary lights. "My offer's open-ended, Aubrey. Take all the time you need."

SEVENTY-FIVE ◉

AN UNMISTAKABLE HINT OF WINTER'S APPROACH hung in the air, adding its frosty bite to Amos's breath. The forested heights outside the Old City would soon be cocooned, possibly within a few weeks, under a blanket of snow. But on this autumn afternoon, standing outside the mouth of the cave, Amos took comfort in the sun's warm rays.

Their final celebration as Eastside Hub was as memorable as Don promised. Amos could still smell the mouth-watering aroma of the big man's signature feast.

Turns out, the guy can *cook, after all.*

The feast and accompanying camaraderie, as much as he relished it, left Amos with a gnawing restlessness. He had unfinished business. Today's trek to the rocky hillside was the result.

He slipped out of his shoulder straps, dropped to one knee on a fresh layer of leaves and pine needles, and set his pack on the ground. The flap rustled as he opened it, stiff from the cold. The slight noise seemed too loud in the crisp air, a sacrilegious intrusion in nature's cathedral.

Amos retrieved his Implant and placed the despised piece of Hoarder tech on the stone slab above the mouth of the cave. Squirrel's Perch. He stared at the Implant for an indeterminate time, reliving the moment he'd first held it, glistening wet and red in his palm, freshly excised from beneath his ribs.

Today was different.

No tiny pinpricks of light—blue, white, red, green—danced over its metal surface. No microscopic filaments needled in and out of either end, bent on injecting homicidal poison into their unsuspecting host's bloodstream.

The Implant lay where he'd deposited it. Lifeless and inert.

He reached into the pack and seized the framing hammer he'd borrowed from Enrico. Its wooden handle, worn smooth by years of constant use, felt good in his hand. He hefted it, testing its weight and balance.

His inner voice scoffed disdainfully. *This is pointless. A complete waste of time.*

Amos raised the hammer and pounded the Implant against the unyielding stone. The handle quivered in his fist, and jarring vibrations raced up his wrist, elbow, and shoulder. He kept at it, striking repeatedly. The sharp blows rang in his ears, reverberating in concussive echoes across the silent forest.

Satisfied, he dropped the hammer into the open pack.

His inner voice scoffed disdainfully. *This changes nothing.*

Shut up. The frosty air chilled Amos's fingers as he brushed the pulverized remnants into his hand. He crouched and flung the debris into the cave, dusted off what little stuck to his palm, and stood upright. The moment was over.

You're dead to me, Gabriel.

"Feel better now?" The frosty cathedral muffled Jane's voice. It was an honest question, delivered without a hint of sarcasm.

"I'm not sure." Amos glanced into the cave's dark maw, but spied no trace of his Implant. "It's just something I knew I had to do. Closure, maybe."

Jane dropped to a knee beside him, pushing the hammer aside and digging her Glock19 out of his pack. The dull gray handgun stood out in sharp contrast to the autumn leaves scattered across the steep hillside.

Jane cradled the Glock in her hands, studying it wordlessly. With a half-hearted flip of her wrist, she tossed the weapon into the cave. The Glock bounced as it fell—once, twice—its sharp *ping* of descent less punishing than Amos's hammer.

Jane stood, staring into the cave, her expression difficult to pinpoint. Amos watched her closely, but she didn't return his gaze. He kept his mouth shut, waiting for what he hoped was a respectful amount of time.

"Okay … it's done." he said tentatively. "How do you feel?"

"Cold," she replied, gazing into the distance. She cupped her hands together, breathing on her fingers to warm them. "Maybe I was expecting too much. I'm not even sure what I hoped this would accomplish." She gestured half-heartedly at the cave. "None of this brings back the people we've lost. It's just a symbolic gesture. It doesn't mean anything."

Amos looked at his feet, then into the cave and, finally, down the steep slope to his brother's unmarked grave. It was blanketed under frost-tipped orange and yellow leaves, but he knew exactly where to find it.

He would always know where to find it.

"The Givers are gone," he said, quietly, urgently. "So are the Implants, and Trackers. Maybe that doesn't bring back the people we've lost, but it means it won't happen to anyone else, either." He scooped his pack from the ground and slung it over his shoulder. "And it means the future doesn't have to look like the past. We had a hand—all of us—in making that future possible. That's not symbolic, Jane. It's real."

Jane drew a deep lungful of cold air and exhaled in a white cloud of condensation. She glanced at him, the faintest hint of a smile toying at the corners of her mouth. "I like the way you said that. It was profound." She tried to repress the smile. "You surprise me sometimes, Amos Morgan."

Amos grinned, stamping his numbed feet. "Gee, thanks, Jane ... I think."

She laughed aloud, surprising him. It was a spontaneous, genuine sound.

When was the last time she enjoyed a good laugh? Amos couldn't recall, but hearing it gave him hope. "Maybe you're feeling better than you realize, Jane."

She faced him squarely, hands on her hips, head tilted to one side. "Call me Snake Lady."

Amos laughed and sketched her a mock salute.

Together, they turned their backs on the cave—and the grave —and began the long trek west to the Old City.

# # #

AFTERWORD

Sheila Murphy once joked with Amos and Don about "living happily ever after in a Giver-free world." She wasn't serious, of course, because life doesn't work that way.

Especially in a dystopian science fiction tale.

In a perfect, fairy-tale ending, the walls of Cascadia are torn down, and penitent Hoarders share their wealth in a burgeoning utopia. The Runners are no longer regarded as savages or terrorists, and one or two—Colonel Scott comes to mind—become respected members on the Council.

Any surviving collaborators are brought to justice, and/or admit the error of their ways and humbly seek to make amends. And finally, the Infomedia commits itself to objective journalistic standards, versus twisting facts to bolster their preferred narrative.

Of course, that wasn't the Runners' experience.

Any significant change always occurs *within* the characters. As Aubrey said to Doc Simon, she's no longer the "country girl" she once was. She's come a long way, from a patient under Doc's care, to becoming a medical assistant (assuming Aubrey accepts Doc's offer, which I think is likely).

The Sinclair siblings have a lot of baggage to sort through—Connor as the protégé of a sociopath and Megan as a disfigured former Tracker—but they have each other to lean on. I've got a good feeling about them.

Amos understands human nature better than he gives himself credit for. His final scene with Jane is honest and realistic. Society will go on much the way it always has, inside the Enclave and out, but that doesn't diminish the Runners' impact on history.

On a side note, a few readers have wondered if there's anything brewing between Amos and Jane after their last scene together. Honestly, it never occurred to me to ask, and neither of them are dropping any hints. I suspect it's wise to stay out of it—Jane's "Snake Lady" nickname is well-earned—and drop by in a year or two.

Much like the unsung heroes in grocery stores and essential services, Amos Morgan, Aubrey Carter, and Jane Avery will never be household names. Their exploits will forever be anonymous and, simultaneously, world-changing.

They'll adapt to their "new normal" without recognition or reward. Most of the people with whom they'll rub shoulders will never know how special they are.

They're okay with that.

The bizarre and unpredictable entity known as 2020 presents us with a similar opportunity. Next time you're in a grocery store or walk-in clinic, check the name tags. There may be an Amos, an Aubrey, a former Tracker, or—you never know—an unusual nickname like "Snake Lady" behind that Plexiglas shield.

If I could indulge myself, one last time, in Mateo Reyes' penchant for wise old sayings, "Not every hero wears a cape."

Until next time, drive friendly.
Deven

ABOUT THE AUTHOR

DEVEN KANE PLAYS a mean bass and loves to tell stories. He writes dystopian sci-fi thrillers and urban fantasy, which he describes as "supernatural thrillers set on another world."

"Speculative fiction allows me to explore human nature, interpersonal conflicts, the desire to rise above our circumstances, and the obstacles holding us back," he says.

"Settings can change—Earth's near future, the past, or an alien culture on another world—but the most engaging stories are about our personal interactions. The good, the bad, the ugly, and our need to transcend."

His novels include the dystopian *Tracker Trilogy*, the urban fantasy *Darkwood*, and the *Treehawke Saga*.

Deven and Wendy live in western Canada under the benevolent supervision of a bemused Husky named Dakota.

Visit Deven online @ devenkane.com.

TRACKER
BOOK 1

"An imaginative world, an array of
diverse, well-rounded characters, and
a pleasantly unpredictable plot."

FEAR THE HARVEST ⦿

Before the Trackers, survival was easy

A generation ago, Earth's wealthiest citizens—the Hoarders—seized control of the planet's resources, retreated into their fortified Enclaves, and left the rest of the population to fend for itself.

Now, the Hoarders have begun randomly Implanting people with a new kind of microtechnology, capable of converting their unsuspecting hosts into violent and deadly automatons. They also created Trackers, a stealth unit of mechanically and chemically enhanced creatures fanatically devoted to hunting down and killing anyone unlucky enough to have an Implant.

Amos Morgan and Aubrey Carter, together with a small band of fellow Runners, must unravel the mystery, racing against time before the Trackers discover them.

And before their own Implants change them into...
Something else.

DISSIDENT
TRACKER BOOK 2

"Deeper, darker, and even better
than the first one."

FEAR THE HARVEST

HELL HATH NO FURY LIKE A TRACKER LEFT FOR DEAD

The Cascadia Enclave is the ultimate symbol of the Hoarders' dominance. From behind its impenetrable walls, they escalate their campaign to Implant the innocent, while their subhuman Trackers hunt down and exterminate the unfortunate.

The only hope for Amos Morgan, Aubrey Carter, and their team of Runners is to infiltrate Cascadia and take the fight directly to the Hoarders. But they'll need help from *inside* the Enclave, and their only guide may be a double agent.

Then there's Tracy.

Hoarders stole her humanity, turned her into a Tracker, and left her for dead. The Runners took her in, but can she be trusted?

One thing is clear: she's on a mission.

NEW FROM DEVEN KANE

"*Darkwood* will certainly have a place in
my personal library beside the likes of
Dune and *The Way of Kings.*"
~ Whistler Independent Book Awards ~

What if there's more to climate change than just the weather?

The centuries-old warnings of the Forest Prophets have fallen on deaf ears. Caorran, the capital city, has turned its back on the Forest, refusing to acknowledge the environmental crisis.

Journalists R'chelle and Jacotan thought their documentary on climate change would be a routine assignment—until they stumble upon the Eve of Battle, an ancient warrior rune.

Caorran's hostility toward the Forest Prophets takes a turn for the worse with the arrival of Mar-Kryn, high priestess of the Forest, who harbors a secretive mission of her own.

A teenage runaway, hounded by the Desert Spirits, seeks asylum in the troubled capital. She could be the key to the Eve of Battle. Or a pawn of what lurks Below.

Darkwood
SOMETHING LURKS BELOW

Sneak Preview

What if there's more to climate
change than just the weather?

 I. Toxic Parley

TENSION GNAWED at Jacotan Beltrus. The alley was dark, the desert wind hot and burning on his skin. He dropped to one knee, fidgeting with his camera. The baleful wind snaked around him and he paused to adjust his sandshades. The last thing he needed tonight was razor-edged grit in his eyes.

"Are you ready, Jaco?" The whisper came from his left. R'chelle Darlos crouched beside him in the filthy alley, clutching a microphone in her diminutive fist. She flashed him a reassuring grin. "We've covered stories in sketchier locations than this."

"It's not the location that bothers me." Jaco took a steadying breath. "Have you ever confronted a Forest Prophet before?"

"Don't you mean a *back-alley* prophet?" R'chelle replied, using the unflattering nickname favored by most Caorranians. Her shoulders rose and fell in a casual shrug. "They're more annoying than dangerous. Nobody takes their doomsday theories seriously."

Jaco kept his opinion to himself. The back alleys of Caorran were familiar territory to him. He'd grown up in the tenements adjacent to the industrial Traig–Saogal District; she hadn't.

R'chelle craned her neck. "I hear footsteps."

Jaco rose to his feet, pasting his left eye to the camera view-finder. A solitary figure shuffled toward them under the silvery light of the twin moons.

R'chelle edged in front of him, eager for the surprise inter-view. He wished he could shield her behind his body, but he knew better. R'chelle Darlos was fearless, a feisty journalist who liked living on the edge.

A tall figure came into focus, muffled in the tawny robes of the Forest religion. His head was covered by the coarse-woven cowl traditionally worn by the Forest Prophets, oddly coupled with a pair of modern sandshades like the ones worn by Jaco and R'chelle.

The robed figure halted abruptly as he caught sight of them. He kept a wary distance, the fingers of one hand clenched around a long wooden staff.

Jaco took three long strides forward, and R'chelle darted in front of him, aiming her microphone at the cowled face.

"R'chelle Darlos, Channel Five News." Her voice raised a hollow echo in the alley's narrow confines. "I'd like to hear your thoughts on the new bylaw restricting back-alley prophets from the public square."

"Channel Five?" The prophet lifted the edge of his cowl and spat on the pavement. "The media are pawns of the Assembly —the howling dogs of your blind leaders. Traitors, all; you have forsaken the Forest."

Jaco kept filming, but placed a cautionary hand on her shoulder. "Easy, Chelle," he said *sotto voce*. "They call them-selves *faidh*, not back-alley prophets."

His words seemed to incense the faidh. "How dare you address her in such cavalier fashion? You are her Left Hand, nothing more. I forbid you to touch her again!"

R'chelle barked a humorless laugh. "Jaco's not my Left Hand. We're coworkers, equal partners. Your caste system's been dead and gone for over a decade. And good riddance."

The faidh leaped at her with an inarticulate cry, snatching the microphone from her hand. Jaco shoved between them, and the faidh brought his staff down on the camera with a sickening *crack*.

Jaco had expected such a tactic, and allowed the camera to slide from his shoulder, using its momentum to spin in a tight circle. His boot caught the faidh in his unprotected midriff.

The back-alley prophet collapsed to the pavement, trading his outraged howl for a series of wheezing gasps. His staff slipped from his fingers.

Jaco kicked it out of reach, whirling to face R'chelle. "He may not be alone. It's best if we go."

She grinned as if nothing had happened. "Did you get a good close-up? We got some great sound-bites."

Jaco shook his head, in equal parts worry and admiration. "You're incorrigible."

R'chelle winked as she retrieved her microphone from the grimy pavement. "All in a night's work." She wiped the microphone on her trousers and sauntered back the way they came.

Jaco scooped up his camera bag and snugged the camera inside. He stole one last glance at the fallen faidh—hunched on hands and knees as he emptied his stomach on the concrete—and hurried after R'chelle.

II. Spy for Hire

"DO YOU UNDERSTAND THE TERMS of your assignment?" Senator Adrán's haughty expression was the perfect match for his imperious tone.

Daenag "Daen" Sarko kept his expression carefully neutral. He was a career *glausadan b'haile*—a listener-in-secret—and well-versed in dealing with the arrogant attitudes of those who paid for his services.

"Yes, of course," he replied smoothly, with a carefully cultivated nod. Senators like Lor Adrán—the Assembly's Public Relations spokesperson—could be won over by subtle signs of deference. Hence his calculated nod. "It's a natural extension of this afternoon's exercise at the Alternative Energy Research Center."

Adrán watched him closely. "Ah, yes, you visited AERC today, didn't you?" The Senator's question was rhetorical and Daen knew better than to respond. "Do you have anything to add to Meyrad's report?"

Again, those watchful, calculating eyes.

"Nothing beyond what Meyrad's already told you," Daen replied, clasping his hands behind his back. He elected to focus on the bare facts. "The researchers on the second floor are compartmentalized; they have no idea or interest in what's being done with their work." He dared a casual shrug. "I've been there several times, and built connections with several of them. I haven't heard any suspicions about the project. No guarded inquiries. No whispers around the water cooler. As for the project itself..."

"Go on," Adrán said when he hesitated. "What do you think of the project?"

A nervous spasm shot up Daen's spine. *Be careful.* "The project remains unknown to me, sir." He caught the shrewd look Adrán shot his way and dared to confront the older man's suspicions. "I'm a seasoned glausadan, sir. You don't last long in this profession if you can't follow the rules."

Or keep a secret, he added silently.

Adrán's probing gaze was unchanged. "Are the warehouse workers as disengaged as the researchers?"

Daen was prepared for the question. "All proper non-disclosure protocols are consistently followed."

He hesitated again and Adrán was swift to pounce—just as Daen had hoped.

"But there's something else. What did you pick up on, Sarko? Disloyalty?"

"No, sir." Daen shook his head, exhaling slowly. "Fear." He left the word dangling between them for a deliberate moment. "The harnesses and safety protocols are strictly adhered to, but it appears to be common knowledge that some scientists will never return to their former jobs." He schooled himself to meet the Senator's gaze without flinching. "The project remains unknown to me," he repeated firmly. "But I can tell when people are scared."

The door to Adrán's office opened to admit Tehl Meyrad, the Senator's most recently-hired consultant. Daen considered himself an expert at finding connections with people—it came with the job—but something about Meyrad set his nerves on edge.

Also blatantly obvious: Meyrad had no use for him, either.

"It's time for the interview." Meyrad came straight to the point. "Channel Five is waiting in the office next to the press room. They sent their hotshot reporter, R'chelle Darlos, and her cameraman."

"Jacotan Beltrus," Daen said quietly. He caught Meyrad's irritated glance. "They're my assignment; learning their names is just common sense."

Senator Adrán cleared his throat. "Let's not keep Channel Five waiting."

Meyrad pivoted on his heel and left the office.

Adrán turned at the door to favor Daenag with an imperious glare. "R'chelle Darlos and her Left Hand are your most important assignment. Don't screw this up, Sarko."

Daen allowed himself a confident smile. "Don't worry, Senator. You've hired the best."

 III. Mar-Kryn of Dilleag-Lusán

"You seem troubled, Mar-Kryn." Árd-Shagar's gravelly voice interrupted her reverie. He peered at her with obsidian-dark eyes, one gnarled hand wrapped around his wooden staff.

Mar-Kryn lifted her head, gazing at him through half-lidded eyes. Among the Forest Prophets, she alone was tall enough to look the Árd in the eye.

"It was a memory, Shagar, of an era long past." Her fingers tightened in a painful spasm around her bonemask. "Before the Desert Spirits set their teeth against Leaf and Branch."

The wall-mounted torches lit the Árd's face in a flickering pattern of light and shadow. His head dipped in a solemn nod, and the lines in his weathered face seemed to deepen. "And what did the Forest reveal to you, Bearer of Memories?"

Mar-Kryn swallowed with difficulty, battered by a sudden desire to be in the Forest's central glade. Not in this accursed cellar. Not near the venomous black mist hovering just above the room's earthen floor.

"I stood upon the slopes above Caorran," she said, her

husky contralto raising a faint echo. She closed her eyes, recalling the vision's details. "Long before it became the capital city. Caorran, then only a small village on the shores of Saogal Bay." She inhaled deeply, scenting the malodorous rot emanating from the mist. "I heard a voice behind me. I was powerless to turn and see who spoke, but the words ..."

Árd-Shagar waited for a ponderous moment before speaking. "The words, Mar-Kryn? What manner of fell omen has stolen your breath?"

A tremor ran down her spine, like one of the quick-footed desert lizards. "It was the ancient war rune," she said hoarsely. "The Eve of Battle—proclaimed aloud for the first time." Her face hardened. It was all she could do to restrain herself from spitting at the malevolent mist. "The dark portal of What Lurks Below was there, as well. The ancient battle was won ..."

The words caught in her throat.

The Árd donned his bonemask, peering at her through the carved eye slits. "And yet the mist has reappeared." He clutched his staff, the veins in his hand standing out in sharp relief. "Caorran's contempt for the ways of the Forest has invited its return."

Mar-Kryn glared at the odious mist, resisting its hypnotic appeal, its attempt to lure her into its flesh-eating embrace. She spoke, her voice tinged with resolve and bitterness. "The Caorranians shrug and say it is 'only climate change.' The fools have no idea what they've unleashed."

She met Shagar's gaze and slipped her bonemask on. "I will not yield our Realm without a fight."

Árd-Shagar smiled grimly. "All of Dilleag-Lusán stands with you, Bearer of Memories."